Death in

Glenville Falls

DEATH *in*
GLENVILLE FALLS

A Gracie McIntyre Mystery

Carol L. Wright

Best wishes!
Carol L. Wright

Cozy Den Press

Death in Glenville Falls

Published by Cozy Den Press, Center Valley, PA

Cover illustration by Kelley McMorris
Back cover wallpaper design by Teagan White

ISBN: 978-0-9742891-3-7 (Paperback)
ISBN: 978-0-9742891-4-4 (ebook)

Library of Congress Control Number: 2017945571

First edition: September, 2017

TO

Mom, who gave me a love of words
Dad, who was behind me all the way
Mitch, who always makes me laugh
Will, who encouraged me to write
Geoff, who continually inspires me
Emily, who is my best editor and playmate
GG and Teddy, who bring me endless joy
and
Bruce, who has always held my hand . . .
and my heart

CHAPTER ONE

~

Eighteen years ago

As soon as Gracie McIntyre pulled up to the farmhouse, she knew she was too late. The front door hung wide open, and the screen dangled from one hinge. Dave had been there.

Her stomach twisted as she got out of her car and removed her suit jacket. The late-July heat and humidity had abated, leaving the early evening in a soporific haze. A hint of a breeze carried the summer smells of earth and grass. All was quiet except for the cicadas rattling in the hilltop trees on the other side of the corn patch and the lowing of cattle in some distant field. No sirens. No voices.

Her client's rusted Plymouth sat on the gravel drive. Edging alongside, Gracie saw the full ashtray, the cardboard pine tree hanging from the mirror, and the infant car seat—much like the one in Gracie's car.

Caution told her to wait for the police, but concern for her client drew her inside. Gracie believed that, despite her modest height, if Dave were still there, she could summon the authority of her profession, and convince even a big, angry man to back off.

She swept back a few strands of sandy hair that had loosened from her French braid. As she stepped across the driveway, pebbles crunched under the black pumps she had worn to court. She grimaced wishing she had changed into sneakers.

The setting sun reflected off the front windows. Shading her brow with her hand, Gracie tried to peer past the glare for clues of what might wait for her inside, but detected no movement—no sound. Stepping onto the covered porch, past a bench swing that hung from rusted chains, she rapped on the open door. No response.

"Hello?" she croaked. Clearing her throat, she knocked louder, straining to hear a cough, a movement, a breath inside. Still nothing.

Good. Cheryl got out in time. But even as that thought formed, the annoying voice in her head asked, *But where did she go without her car?*

Maybe she ran out into the corn. She knew it was a long shot. Corn fields were good places to hide in the autumn when the stalks reached well over anyone's head, but in New England, corn was only "knee-high by the Fourth of July." Not tall enough to conceal a person's progress through the field. Dave could have followed her. He could easily outrun her. Then another thought surfaced and she choked. Looking over at the field, she tried not to imagine Dave crouching there, watching her.

She stepped over the threshold. Despite the lingering heat of the day, Gracie's skin tingled as if it were electrified. Peering around the doorway into the living room, Gracie saw a shaft of sunlight, alive with dust, slant across the room. A chair lay on its side, and shards of what might once have been a vase lay on the hearth.

A copper-colored spark, lit up by the setting sun, drew her attention to a desk. She shook off a shiver when she realized it was the ragged end of the phone cord, ripped from the wall. As she moved toward the back of the house, a large fly buzzed past her ear. Gracie jumped back as she watched it head for the kitchen. Clearing her throat, she tried to call out for Cheryl, but her voice failed her. Her knees felt about to follow suit, but she drew in a calming breath, squared her shoulders, and pressed on.

There was an odd taste in the air. Something metallic.

Turning the corner into the kitchen, she found Cheryl.

~

"So, you got a call from the deceased telling you that her husband was in the house?" the uniformed officer asked Gracie. Dusk had fallen, and swirling red and blue lights made intersecting patterns on the white clapboard house. They stood outside a taped-off area, awaiting the arrival of the detective and medical examiner.

"Yes." Gracie nodded. "I helped her get a restraining order against him earlier today."

"Yeah, we got a copy," Officer Johnson said. "Sheriff served it this afternoon, confiscated the firearms, escorted him from the premises. He said the guy went quietly, but it looks like it pushed him over the edge."

"A restraining order is supposed to prevent scenes like this, not cause them," Gracie said, a note of accusation in her voice.

Getting the protective order had been routine. Cheryl told the judge how Dave would brood for days, then come home drunk and blame her for everything wrong in his life. Things would have been great, he would say, if she hadn't gotten herself knocked up. He could have taken that track scholarship and gone to college, but because of her he had to stay in Glenville-Freakin'-Falls in the middle of Nowhere, Massachusetts, saddled with a lousy wife and a screaming kid.

Then he would hit her. He would always apologize afterward, but in a few days or weeks the cycle would begin again.

Cheryl's mom had moved to Boston after they eloped, and the old Plymouth wouldn't make it that far, even if Cheryl had money for gas. There was never enough money for anything, except for Dave to get wasted. So Cheryl went to see Gracie who took the case for free.

The officer pointed to the house with his pen. "Seems he used one of the kitchen knives. Looks like one's missing from the set."

Gracie felt her scalp prickle. What would have happened if Dave had still been there when she arrived? Would he have turned on her, too? Would there now be two motherless infants?

"I told her to spend the night somewhere else. This farm is too remote." Gracie's lip trembled, and she turned away from the officer, pretending to be distracted by a passing car. The driver slowed to gaze at the farmhouse before driving on. "She said she would stay in town with a friend."

"Got a name or address?"

"No, sorry." Gracie chastised herself for the oversight. "Anyway, she called me and said she left the baby with her friend and came back to the house for something, and then she heard him coming after her."

"Were those her exact words?" He swatted at a mosquito.

Gracie wrinkled her forehead. "Not quite. She said she heard him on the porch . . . and that he must have followed her."

"She heard him on the porch? Was he knocking on the door, or was he yelling, or what?"

Gracie shook her head. "I'm not sure." Her eyes darted to the damaged door.

"Could you hear anything, any voices or other noises coming over the phone?"

She squinted her eyes, replaying the brief conversation. "No." The air had cooled, but she wiped sweat from her brow and folded her arms across her chest. "I just told her to hang up and call 911 right away. Then I raced over here." Gracie tried to swallow the rock in her throat. "I thought you would be here ahead of me."

"First call we got was from you."

Gracie shook her head at having left her new mobile phone at the office. It had taken all the composure she could muster to drive to a gas station pay phone and notify the police. Then she called Spencer. She needed to hear his voice and know that he and their baby were safe. Every cell in her body told her to go home, but duty sent her back to the farmhouse to wait for the authorities.

"You look a little pale. You okay? You wanna sit down?" The officer nodded toward the cruiser.

"I'm okay. It's just . . . I'm a civil lawyer." She looked down at the grass. "I'm not used to this."

"Me neither," the officer said. His voice was so quiet Gracie wasn't sure he meant for her to hear.

The police radio squawked and the officer picked up the call. Gracie walked back to her car and sat down sideways in the driver's seat. Weary, nauseated, and a little light-headed, she ached for the security of her home, the comfort of her husband, and the innocence of their child. She leaned forward on her elbows, folded her hands, and hung her head.

"That was dispatch," Officer Johnson called to her. "Looks like the husband offed hisself," he said, scratching his ear. "They found his body up at the waterfall. That oughta make this easier to wrap up."

Gracie swallowed, uncertain how the battle with her stomach would end. Hiding her face behind both hands, she had only one thought: *I can't do this anymore.*

CHAPTER TWO

~

Present day

Early September is a time for new beginnings in a college town, and Gracie McIntyre braced for hers. In just one day, the town would transform from a sleepy, New England hamlet of just over 4000 residents into a bustling college town with the arrival of 1600 Glenville College students. And Gracie was ready— or almost so. Having just returned from a trip to Pennsylvania to drop her son Ben off for his freshman year of college, she couldn't wait to start her own adventure.

Armed with her to-do list, she checked off items as she, her husband Spencer Adams, and their fourteen-year-old daughter Carrie, walked the short distance from their century-old home on Elm Street toward the center of the village of Glenville Falls.

"There's only a couple more things to do to before tonight's Grand Opening," Gracie said, checking her list.

"I know. I'm picking up the signs from the Quill Pen," said Carrie, "and placing them in the holders above the book shelves."

"Right," Gracie said. "And Spencer?"

"I'm getting the food trays from the Steaming Kettle," he said with a salute. His eyes sparkled behind his owlish glasses, under a thinning fringe of graying brown hair.

"Okay. And I'm getting the balloons from Posies. Then we'll all meet back at the store. Got it?"

"Got it," Carrie and her dad said in unison.

Turning onto Commonwealth Avenue, Gracie looked down the wide, tree-lined street that wound around the village green to the town hall.

"I'm so glad the shop is here in town instead of that hole in the wall Lois Heller tried to get me to rent at the Pocumtuc Mall."

"She probably would have gotten a bigger commission if you'd rented there," Spencer reminded her.

"Maybe that's why she pushed so hard," Gracie said with a laugh. "But I like being right on the town common. And who but Hal Doyle would have put as much effort into sprucing up the place for a new tenant?"

Spencer shrugged. "I'm off to the Steaming Kettle." He jaywalked toward the café that featured a three-dimensional teapot on the roof, pumping steam into the autumnal sky.

"Okay—it's over to Posies for me." Gracie gave her daughter a hug.

"See you in a few," Carrie said, as she marched on toward the town's art supply and print shop. All those businesses, along with Doyle's Hardware, owned by Gracie's landlord, Hal Doyle, flanked the lower end of the village green known as "the Triangle."

Many townspeople, like Gracie, felt that the three-sided open space was a full-fledged part of the town common, even though it was separated by Chestnut Street from the larger rectangular section. It had the same gas street lamps, the same park benches, and the blue spruce that served as the town Christmas tree. Others insisted that "The Common" was just the rectangle with the war memorial obelisk, Revolutionary War canon, and gazebo-style band stand. The triangle, in their opinion, just didn't count. The nomenclature had become a dispute of some importance over the years.

Gracie crossed to the pink Victorian home that housed Posies, the town's flower shop, stepping over the familiar sidewalk chalk messages, welcoming new students, that had started to blossom on nearby concrete. School-aged children played touch football on the common, while two older men sat on a nearby park bench, arguing about the Red Sox's chances of making the playoffs. A sense of well-being replaced her anxiety. Owning a bookstore was going to be fun.

Potted mums in a riot of colors lined the shop's wide porch, and she took the wooden steps two at a time before entering the cool showroom.

"Hi, I have your order ready." Peggy Kowalski ducked into her back room when she saw Gracie enter. "I really hate these things," she said, trying to force a dozen bouncing, helium-filled balloons back through the doorway all at once.

Gracie laughed. "I want to give them out to the kids who come to tonight's opening." She braced for a loud pop if one got too close to the lit cigarette perpetually dangling from Peggy's lips. *So much for the indoor smoking ban.*

After a bit of juggling, Peggy handed the knotted strings to Gracie. "You already paid, so you're all set."

"Thanks, Peggy. Will I see you this evening?"

"Nope. I hate crowds," she said, shaking her head. "Give me some nice, quiet plants for company anytime."

Gracie tried out her shopkeeper's smile. "Well, maybe sometime soon, then. We have a pretty good gardening section."

Peggy shrugged.

Gracie was the first one back to the shop. She fumbled with her keys and wrangled the balloons through the door, but not without first taking a long, admiring gaze at her bay window display.

As she entered, she took one last look around at the shop she had spent weeks preparing. Coming off the side wall was an L-shaped oak counter near the entry. Built-in oak bookshelves lined the walls, while shorter ones divided the remaining space into small reading areas. Each nook offered books of different genres. Overstuffed chairs—left behind by the building's previous tenant—were strategically located for comfortable browsing, and stood on well-worn oriental rugs. Where the hardwood floor was left uncovered, it was so richly polished that the lights hanging from the high, pressed-tin ceiling reflected in its grain. Set deep into the back wall was the children's section with shorter, built-in shelving. Cut-outs of storybook characters hung against brightly painted panels, and stuffed animal "reading buddies" sat expectantly in beanbag chairs. Past doors to a rest room and to Gracie's office was an open space with upholstered chairs and a table display of items of local interest. It included Glenville College paraphernalia, and some signed books by local authors—most of whom, like Spencer, were professors up at the school.

"I have to admit, it's gorgeous," she said to herself as she tied the balloons to cup hooks she had placed under the back edge of the counter. Then she heard the shop bell over the door ring out. Carrie had returned with the signs.

"There's a note taped to each bookcase, saying what sign it needs," Gracie said, reaching for half the stack. "If we work together, we can finish in no time."

"Okay," Carrie said, getting to work.

Just then, Gracie heard a *thump, thump, thump.* She looked over to see Spencer kicking the door, his hands occupied by two, domed deli trays—one with veggies and dip and the other with finger sandwiches.

Gracie raced over to open up. "I ordered more than two trays," she said as Spencer entered and slid them onto the counter.

"I know." He nodded toward the entry.

A man, dressed all in white, carried four more trays with less effort than Spencer had with two.

"Let's put the fruit and cheese tray here." Gracie took it from the top of the stack. "The others can go in the back until we need them."

The man obliged, following Gracie to the rear of the store.

"It's a good thing there is a kitchenette back here with a full-sized refrigerator," she said, opening the door to her office.

The man put the trays in the fridge and turned toward Gracie who handed him a tip. Then he left without a word.

"Not much of a talker, is he?" Gracie said to Spencer.

"Yeah. He's new over there," Spencer said. "Name's DJ, but I didn't get the impression he was particularly musical." He chuckled at his own joke while Gracie rolled her eyes. "Oh, Kelly sends her best wishes for success tonight. She said if it gets slow at the Kettle, she and Sean will try to pop over."

"Wonderful." Gracie checked the time on the antique regulator clock hanging near the entry. "Twenty minutes to seven. We have to get the signs up."

"I'll just take care of opening up the food trays," Spencer said.

"No, let's leave them closed until the last minute."

"But we haven't had dinner, and I'm hungry."

"Wait until people come."

"Aren't we people?"

"Be good," she scolded.

Spencer grinned, and she turned to the bookshelves to begin placing signs, fairly certain that Spencer would be nibbling behind her back. Carrie was nearly done with her signs and took half of Gracie's share. Within minutes they were finished.

"I'm taking a picture of this," Carrie said, raising her cell phone. Gracie knew it would end up on one of the social media sites Carrie enjoyed, and that was very much okay with her. The free publicity could only help.

The shop bell rang, and Gracie turned to see Del Turner, her best friend and former law partner, enter the store. Her face shone with the exertion of having walked from her law office across the green. A Virginian by birth, Del had come to Boston for law school where she and Gracie met early in their first year. They hit it off immediately, and had remained close friends through the years since. They made quite a study in contrast with Gracie's pale Scottish skin tone and petite build to Del's deep brown complexion and what she called "big bones."

"Hi, all," Del said, her brown eyes sparking.

"Hi, Auntie Del," Carrie said, giving the large woman a quick hug before taking another photo.

"Welcome," Gracie said as she placed paper plates, cups, and napkins near the food trays. "Thanks again for fixing up the front window this afternoon. It looks great."

"I have to protect my investment in this little venture, don't I?" Del said in the slight drawl that charmed juries. "I tell you, I should have been a window dresser.

Then no one would complain when I said I worked with dummies."

Gracie groaned.

"Say, what do you have there, Spence?" Del waggled her eyebrows as she inspected the food trays. Gracie saw Spencer wince at Del's shortening of his name. No one called him "Spence" except for Del, who called him nothing else.

"Hello, Adelaide," Spencer said, using the full name they all knew Del hated almost as much as he despised "Spence." Gracie couldn't understand why two people she loved so well did not appreciate each other more.

Then, apparently sensing a potential ally, Spencer asked, "Have you had dinner yet?"

"Nope," Del said. "I saved my appetite for tonight. Hope you've got plenty."

"We do. Just look," he said, taking the lids off the deli trays. "And there's more in the back."

"It's a losing battle," Gracie said, putting pitchers of drinks on the counter. "Okay, go ahead, but don't let the trays look picked-over."

"We'll be careful," Spencer promised, crossing his heart.

"I think we're ready, with a few minutes to spare," Gracie said. "I only wish Ben could be here."

"Why?" Carrie said, looking a little hurt.

"Because, honey, I want to share special moments in my life with the ones I love, and that includes your big brother."

Carrie looked only slightly appeased. "But his college classes started earlier than they do here," she said.

"I know. And I know he's happy going to school in Pennsylvania, but that doesn't keep me from missing him and wishing he weren't so far away."

Gracie ignored Carrie's grimace. Sometimes she was such a teenager.

Before Del and Spencer could do too much damage to the food trays, the town hall clock struck seven, and the bell over the door jingled. Gracie's stomach did a flip-flop. Her first customer.

She turned to see Wendell Owens, the portly owner, publisher, and editor of the *Glenville Falls Gazette*, push through the door, a camera dangling from his neck.

"Welcome to Gracie's Garret New and Used Books."

"Congratulations, Gracie," Wendell said, handing her a bottle of champagne tied with a red bow. "Am I early?"

"Thanks, Wendell. No, you're right on time. It's the rest of the town that's late." Gracie's nervous laugh escaped before she could stop it.

"I'm happy to see you up and running. It doesn't do the town any good to have an empty store front, you know," Wendell said, eyeing the display of food arranged on the counter.

"Thanks, Wendell," Gracie said. Taking the hint, she added, "Would you like something to eat?" She shifted her glance to the door as more townspeople entered, greeted by Del.

"Don't mind if I do," Wendell rubbed his hands together, looking the array over carefully before heaping food onto a paper plate. "Are you pleased with your ad in this week's *Gazette*?" he asked, picking up a finger sandwich. "It looks great, if I say so myself. I'm glad you decided to put in that coupon. I'm sure it will help bring people in."

"I love it, Wendell. I wouldn't have thought of it without your help."

Their new neighbors, the Antonello family, arrived with their four children. Nick was Spencer's new colleague in the history department at Glenville College, and Sharona worked at the town library.

While Spencer welcomed the parents, Carrie greeted their eldest child, Angela, as if it had been weeks since they had seen each other, despite having spent much of the day together at the town swimming pool. They were making the most of their last few days of freedom before their first day of high school on the day after Labor Day—just four days away.

"You mind if I take a few photos this evening for next Thursday's edition?" Wendell regained Gracie's attention as he brushed a crumb from the top of his camera.

"Please do. I can use all the publicity I can get."

Gracie turned to see to some more arrivals when she felt a tug on her slacks. She looked down to find the youngest Antonello looking up at her. The girl's two older brothers stood nearby with conspiratorial grins on their faces.

"Where's your carrot?" the little girl asked.

Gracie looked at the child. "My carrot?"

"Yeah. Where's 'Gracie's Carrot'?"

"Oh, Maria. Don't be silly," Sharona Antonello said coming up to take the child by the hand. "The store is called 'Gracie's *Garret*,' not 'Gracie's carrot.'" Then Sharona looked at her two sons snickering behind their hands. "Did you two put her up to that?" Their laughter bubbled over.

Gracie knelt down to the child's height. "Well, Maria, when I was about four . . ."

"I'm five," Maria corrected her.

Oh, I beg your pardon. Well, when I was *five*, if I heard somebody say 'garret' I would have thought they said, 'carrot,' too. But this is 'Gracie's Garret', and a garret is . . ." Gracie whispered, and the boys leaned in to hear. "A garret is a sort of attic."

"Then, where's your *garret*?" Maria persisted.

"It's all around you. Many of these books came from bookshelves in my attic . . . and my living room . . . and my kitchen. They came from all over my house, actually." Gracie laughed, a little embarrassed by her book-hoarding gene, inherited from her father, shared by her husband, and passed on to their children. Opening the bookstore seemed a good way to deal not just with an emptying nest, but with a house over-filled with books.

"So, they're all *old*?" Maria wrinkled her nose.

"No. Most of them are new. But, yes, some of them are very old, very dear friends. And I think you might find one of my old friends could be a new friend to you," Gracie said, tapping the girl's nose. "Why don't you go look and see if you can find something interesting over there?" Gracie pointed to the children's section, and Maria bounded over. Her brothers watched, and finally followed.

Sharona shook her head. "Sometimes those boys . . ."

The bell rang again. Hal Doyle, Gracie's landlord and commercial neighbor arrived. His thinning hair was smoothed across his scalp and he'd replaced his usual hardware store attire of a worn plaid shirt and paint-stained pants with a white oxford shirt and grey slacks. He bowed slightly toward Gracie, and looked around as if he had never been in the building before.

"Oh, this is wicked nice, Gracie. It looks real good." He spoke in a near whisper, and appeared about as comfortable as a shy kindergartener on the first day of school.

"Thanks to you, Hal. I could never have done this without the bookshelves you built and the furniture Ollie left behind when he closed his used furniture shop."

"Say, where did those rugs come from? Were they Ollie's, too?"

"Oh, no. They were my grandmother's. We McIntyres never throw anything away."

"They make it feel real nice and homey in here," said Hal, who would never criticize saving things. The whole town knew the back room of his hardware store was full of broken items and miscellaneous parts that, as he said, "I might be glad I have someday."

Gracie realized that town folk and college people might not know each other, so she made a round of introductions as the bell over the door rang again. Soon many more neighbors and college friends came to inspect the new business. The bean bags were a hit with the kids, and Ollie's upholstered chairs soon filled with grown-ups. Gracie felt torn in several directions, having to keep the food trays filled, trying to greet each new visitor, and wanting to help all of her potential customers at once.

"I'll see to the refreshments," Del whispered. "You just see to the customers."

Gracie mouthed a "thank you," and mingled with her guests.

In the middle of the evening, Spencer found her. "It's going well. You forget how many friends we have in this town, don't you."

"We're very fortunate," Gracie said, nodding.

"There are even a few I don't recognize," Spencer said, pointing to a young woman browsing in fiction. "Do you know who that girl is over there?"

"Let's see." Gracie squinted at a girl blowing bubblegum. She felt the blood drain from her face, and shook her head. "No, I don't know who she is," she said, looking away with a shudder.

"No matter. Things are going great," he whispered. "This thing is going to work." He gave her arm a squeeze.

Gracie looked around. Everyone was smiling as they browsed, chatting with friends. She saw Carrie and Angie reading to younger children in the beanbags, Father Andrew and Rabbi Schulman debating in the philosophy section, and Del entertaining neighbors over by the food trays. All the while, Wendell snapped photos for the *Gazette*.

Gracie took a deep breath and looked up at Spencer. "You might be right, sweetheart." She smiled, but stole another look at the unidentified young woman.

"Are these books for sale tonight, or is this just for lookin'?" Hal Doyle stood before her holding an anthology of Wild West stories that had belonged to Gracie's father. Throughout this venture, she had a nagging worry that it would be hard to give up custody of any of *her* books, but since her first sale was to Hal, she found it easier to share. She slipped on her reading glasses, took the book from Hal, and wrote an inscription: *To a great landlord, with gratitude.*

This one's on the house, Hal," she said, handing it back to him.

"Are you sure?" Hal asked.

"Absolutely," Gracie said, squeezing his rough hand. "You've been very good to me, and I want you to know that I appreciate it. Enjoy it with my compliments."

Hal's smile was worth much more than the book. *I just might be in the right business after all,* she thought.

The bell above the door jingled again, and Gracie looked over in time to see the young woman Spencer had noticed exit and walk down the street. Gracie chastised herself when she realized that the thought that sprang to her mind was not a very smart one for a new shopkeeper: *I hope she never returns.*

CHAPTER THREE

Saturday was the first day of Glenville College's freshman orientation, and Gracie's Garret was busy all day. She had announced her bookstore by campus mail, and her coupon in the *Gazette* offered discounts on course books, so parents and students poured in.

"How can you afford to offer discounts?" Del asked as she helped Gracie sort through her orders that evening after closing.

"I learned," Gracie said, lowering her voice even though no one was around who might overhear, "that college bookstores don't discount their trade books. I get a forty-percent discount from my distributor, so I can mark the same books down twenty percent and get some of their business. Textbooks have a lower mark-up, but I can still give a ten percent discount. It's enough to get them down into the village to shop for their books."

"It really brought the customers in today. For a while there, you'd have thought you were giving them away."

"Well, the online stores will still get their share, but," Gracie said as she straightened a thick stack of papers, "all these orders are pre-paid."

"Good thing you had some free help," Del said, arching her brow. "But, hey, you know I have a day job. Tuesday morning, it's back to lawyering for me."

"Yeah, and Spencer and Carrie will be back at school. Next week things should be calmer, but I know I could never have pulled this off today without your help." Gracie felt a twinge of anxiety at the thought of working alone.

Del mimicked Gracie's worried expression. "Well maybe you should take some of your new-found wealth," she said riffling the stack of orders, "and hire some help."

~

Gracie's outlook brightened when she saw Spencer walking toward the shop just as she was locking up.

"Hi, beautiful. How was your day?" he asked as he approached.

"Busy. How was yours?"

"Well, I ran one of the small welcome seminars for freshmen, went to the convocation, organized my handouts for the first day of classes. The usual," he said, putting an arm around her and giving her a kiss.

"And do the students look younger again this year?"

Spencer shook his head. "They look younger *every* year. Anyway, I thought I'd come by and walk you home. I'll even carry your books if you have any." Gracie looked at Spencer's bulging, soft-sided brief case and wondered just how he would have carried her books.

"Such a gentleman. But there *is* something I plan to carry home. I decided to celebrate a successful first day by ordering take-out from the Steaming Kettle."

"Then let's go pick it up."

Fifteen minutes later, they entered their house. "We're home, and have food," Spencer called to Carrie as soon as they came inside. Spencer went upstairs to put his brief case in the spare bedroom he used as his study as Carrie came bounding down. She followed Gracie into the kitchen.

"Would you wash up and set the table, sweetie?" Gracie asked Carrie. She pulled a roasted chicken and three ears of corn wrapped in foil out of a bag.

"Sure," Carrie said, crossing to the sink. "How was your day?"

"Very busy."

"That's good, right?"

"It sure is." Gracie didn't try to hide her ebullience.

"Uh, Mom," Carrie said in a hesitant tone. Gracie met her daughter's eyes. "Do you really have to open the store tomorrow? I mean it's like the last Sunday of the summer and everything."

"It's *like* the last Sunday of the summer, or it *is* the last Sunday of the summer?"

Carrie put a hand on her hip. "Okay, it *is* the last Sunday of the summer."

Gracie pulled out a container of cole slaw and inverted it into a serving bowl. "Yeah, I know, but I really need to be open this weekend. I'll usually be closed on Sunday and Monday, but since this is the first weekend of the school year, students will be buying their books. If I'm not open, I'll lose a semester's worth of sales."

"I know, but it's my last weekend before *high school*." Carrie emphasized the last two words as though high school were a monster about to attack. Glenville Falls was not large enough to have its own high school. After going from kindergarten through eighth grade at the small local schools, the town's high schoolers went to the Billington Area Regional High School. It required a long bus ride, but the larger tax base allowed the school to offer more enrichment than their village could afford. Gracie well remembered Ben's trepidation at going to the high school four years earlier, but she thought Carrie, usually the more confident of the two, would have an easier time with the transition.

"Oh, you'll be great in high school. You've been over there enough times with Ben. You know your way around, probably better than most freshmen."

"I know, but I won't know the other *kids*. There aren't many of us coming from Glenville Falls, and we probably won't be in any of the same classes."

"You'll have that long bus ride with them twice a day. And I'll bet you'll be in classes with some kids you know."

"No, I won't. My schedule arrived in today's mail, and I already called Angie and Emily, and we don't have *any* classes together. I won't know *anyone*."

Ordinarily Gracie would remind Carrie that she could not hear her when she whined, but this was not the moment. She heard a catch in her daughter's throat and saw tears welling at the corners of her eyes.

"Oh, honey," Gracie said, drawing her daughter into a hug. "It's really going to be okay. I know it's scary at first, but before you know it, you'll meet new people, and you'll end up with twice as many friends as you have now. And even if you're not in the same classes, you can probably get together with your old friends at lunch."

Carrie brightened a little. "I didn't think of that. I have to go check and see if we have the same lunch periods." Carrie pulled away and started toward the door.

"Not so fast, Carrie. You can do that after dinner," Gracie said.

"Did I hear someone say dinner?" Spencer said, striding into the kitchen, rubbing his hands together. He went to the sink to wash up and they all settled down at the kitchen table.

The chicken was savory and juicy—the way Gracie wished she could make it. The potato salad was fresh, and the corn, probably from the farmers' market, tasted as if it were just picked. No wonder the Steaming Kettle was a town institution.

Gracie looked over at Carrie. She could tell the good food had not removed the feelings of uncertainty her daughter had about the new venture in her life. And, truth be told, Gracie felt similar qualms about hers.

~

"Do you think I'm being unfair to Carrie?" Gracie asked Spencer as they were going to bed that night. She wanted him to reassure her that she wasn't, but she wasn't sure she would believe him if he did.

"Unfair how?" Spencer asked as he adjusted his pillow, and shooed their ginger cat, Dickens, from his side of the bed.

"I was mostly home for Ben—especially if I wasn't teaching a class up at the college. But now with the bookstore, Carrie will be on her own a lot more." Gracie checked to be sure her alarm clock was set for the correct time. "Of course, she has always been the more independent of the two, but still." She slipped under the covers and picked up her book.

"Where's this coming from? We talked all this out before you decided to open a bookstore." Spencer got into bed and leaned in, lips puckered.

Gracie slid over and gave him a kiss, then nestled into his shoulder. "Well, Carrie asked if I could close the store tomorrow and stay home with her. She's nervous about starting high school."

"Of course she is." Spencer turned off his bedside lamp and put his arm around his wife. "You're nervous about starting a bookstore. That'll dissipate after the first few days, once she—and you—get acclimated. She'll be fine. You know her."

"Yeah, but, I don't know. She's only this age once." Gracie turned off the lamp at her bedside, and turned on her book light. "I just wish I could give her my undivided attention tomorrow when she really needs it."

"She'll probably feel differently tomorrow. And if she doesn't, she can always go to the store with you."

"At least she and Angela have the same lunch period."

"That's right. It will all work out." Spencer kissed Gracie's forehead and rolled over. Dickens curled up behind his knees. In a moment both were snoring lightly.

Unable to concentrate on her book, Gracie turned off her book light and lay in the dark, waiting for the rhythm of Spencer's breathing to lull her to sleep.

~

The next morning, as Gracie was getting ready to go to the store, Carrie came downstairs, still in her pajamas.

"I'll be at the store if you need me," Gracie said.

"Ok, but I think that Emily's mom is going to take a bunch of us to the mall. Do you have any money in case I can find a good outfit for the first day?"

Gracie pursed her lips. She had always enjoyed doing last-minute school shopping. She hated missing out on the fun.

"I think I can help you out." Gracie looked into her wallet and tried to figure out how much she could spare. Between opening the store and Ben starting college, they did not have a lot of extra money, but she pulled a twenty and a ten out and handed them to Carrie.

"Thanks." Carrie looked at the money, and Gracie knew she had hoped for more, but to her credit, Carrie did not complain. "Where's Dad?" she asked.

"Up at the college. He said he'd be back by noon."

"Oh." Carrie looked dejected. "I think Emily's mom is picking me up at eleven." Gracie could tell Carrie had hoped to get more money from Spencer.

Guilt nudged Gracie's elbow, and she pulled out another ten. "That's it. I'm tapped out now," she said, opening her empty wallet for inspection. "Have a good time. And if you find anything, bring it by the store later and show it to me, okay?"

"Okay. Thanks, Mom."

Gracie kissed Carrie on the cheek. She wanted to hold her daughter. She wanted to give her more money. She wanted to help her pick out an outfit for school. But instead, she went to the bookstore.

~

After a busy Sunday, Gracie was exhausted by the time she returned home. As soon as she opened the door she smelled spaghetti sauce. Dropping her things, she went into the kitchen, expecting to see Spencer, but it was Carrie who stood at the stove.

"I didn't know when you'd get home and Dad and I were hungry, so I thought I would cook something." Carrie said, her back to her mother.

"Oh, thank you, sweetie," Gracie said. "What a good kid you are."

"It's just spaghetti with some of those frozen meat-balls."

Gracie smiled and sat in a kitchen chair. "Sounds great. The store was really busy again today. I have so many special orders. It's a lot of paperwork."

"Yeah. I thought you'd be home sooner."

"Sorry I'm late. I wanted to get all the orders processed before I left tonight."

Carrie shrugged.

Gracie stood to wash up and set the table. "How was the mall?" she asked as she grabbed four plates from the cupboard, then, remembering that Ben wasn't home, put one back.

"It was okay."

"Just okay?"

"Yeah. I didn't find anything good in my price range."

Gracie felt a jab of guilt. "Sorry, honey."

"Don't be. I'll just wear my khaki slacks and that blue sweater. It's pretty new."

~

By mid-afternoon of Labor Day, it became apparent that with classes starting, the early semester rush was over. It was now safe for the locals to visit the store. At the end of the day, Gracie counted up her sales and orders, did some quick math, and smiled. Sales for the weekend had exceeded her projections.

Carrie went to a matinee with her friends, and by the time Gracie got home that evening, she was pulling everything out of her closet.

"I'm trying to decide what to wear tomorrow," Carrie explained.

"I thought you were wearing your khakis and the blue sweater."

"Yeah, I was, but then I heard that it's going to be hot tomorrow. No way I'm wearing a sweater to school when it's eighty degrees outside."

Gracie thought about her store's fast start. Perhaps she could afford a little more than she thought for school clothes. "What do you say we run out to the mall and find a new top?"

"Really?"

Gracie nodded, and Carrie ran into her arms.

"Thanks, Mom."

CHAPTER FOUR

When Thursday's *Glenville Falls Gazette* came out, the bookstore opening was rivaled only by the start of the school year for space in the paper. Wendell ran several pictures of the grand opening, including one of Carrie reading to children. The accompanying article made the little shop sound like the best thing that had ever happened in Glenville Falls. He had even edited Gracie's hastily worded classified ad for part-time help so that she sounded more professional. Too bad, she thought, that she had run the unedited version in the campus newspaper.

Gracie put the paper down and began dusting the bookshelves. Her mind went back to the picture of Carrie as she looked at the children's section. She would love to have a regular children's story hour, and Carrie was a natural with the younger kids. *No.* She shook her head. *It's not fair to ask her to give up part of her weekends to work in the store. She should enjoy being a kid as long as she can.*

Then she thought about other activities that could draw people in. She had considered starting a book group, but knew she wouldn't have time to run it herself. She had the space. She'd left a back corner of the shop open for special events. The table she had used for local authors' books during the grand opening still stood against the back wall. She could add a cluster of folding chairs to the upholstered chairs that were already there. It would make a nice setting for a book group. But who could run it?

As she considered this option, the bell above the front door rang. Gracie turned and saw a college-aged woman entering. She didn't need the popping bubblegum to know it was the same person Spencer had pointed out at the party.

Gracie hesitated and scolded herself for it. She put on a smile, and approached her customer.

"Welcome to Gracie's Garret," Gracie said as she moved behind the counter. "I'm Gracie McIntyre. May I help you find something?"

The girl looked at Gracie through narrowed eyes, as Gracie tried to figure out what it was about the girl that bothered her so.

She was a little taller than Gracie, had a ruddy complexion, and a sturdy build. Her straight, light brown hair fell past her shoulders and her overly long bangs fell across her brow. She wore jeans and a Glenville College t-shirt. But it was her eyes that drew Gracie's attention. They were deep brown, but showed no spark.

The girl shook her head, but said nothing. Her focus shifted to her hands. She turned away from Gracie and picked up a book from a table. The more Gracie looked at her, the less she liked having her in the store. There was something disturbing about this girl.

"I'm sorry." Gracie said, breaking the silence. "Do I know you?"

"Oh, uh, I don't know." The girl frowned and put the book down. She grabbed a few strands of hair with one hand and inspected the ends.

"Is there something specific you are looking for?"

"No." The girl raised her eyes. "Well, I think I might be looking for you."

Gracie remembered the job ad. "Of course. How silly of me." She forced a smile. "You've come about the job? Just let me get a little information from you and we can talk about what I am looking for." *Like I'm apt to hire you,* she thought.

"Well, uh, no. I mean, I'm not really here about the job." She pronounced "here" as "he-ah."

Sounds like a Boston accent. How do I know this girl?

"What I am actually . . ." the girl went on, "what I wanted to do was give you a message from my Gram. She said that when I got to town I should look you up because . . . but she said you were a lawyer?" The girl scrunched her face in a questioning stare.

Gracie drew in a breath. "Yes. That is, I used to be. I haven't practiced law for quite a while now. Who is your Gram?"

"Dorothy Walsh?" she said, as if it were a question.

It took a moment for recognition to kick in, but when it did Gracie felt all the blood drain from her face. No wonder the girl looked familiar. "Mrs. Walsh, Cheryl Mercer's mother?"

"Yeah."

"Of course. Oh, and you're um . . . you're Cheryl's daughter? Of course. You actually look a lot like her. You're, um . . ." Gracie tapped a finger on the counter as she struggled to remember.

"Kristen," they said at the same time.

"Kristen Mercer?" Gracie asked, cocking her head and scanning the girl's face again. She now understood her visceral reaction when she first laid eyes on the girl. But this poor child didn't deserve it. It wasn't her fault Gracie had let her mother be murdered.

"Yeah, but I go by Walsh now." Kristen let go of her hair, and turned away.

"Well, welcome, Kristen," Gracie said. "Feel free to look around." Gracie decided if the girl found a book she wanted, she would just give it to her . . . for Cheryl's sake. Then, regaining some of her composure, she added, "Where are my manners? Would you like a cup of tea?" Gracie came around to the front side of the counter and gestured for Kristen to sit down.

Kristen sat in the nearest chair, put one leg over the other, and crossed her arms in front of her. *A defensive posture,* Gracie thought. *I'm not the only one who's uncomfortable.*

"No, thank you." Kristen grabbed her hair again, twirling it between her fingers, and glanced toward the door. "Uh, do you have any tonic?"

Gracie smiled at the word old-time New Englanders used for soda. She had heard it growing up in the Boston area, but didn't realize anyone used it anymore. "No, sorry, I don't." Gracie leaned back against the counter and folded her arms. "I could. I have a refrigerator in back. Next time you come in, I'll have some." Gracie winced. She realized she didn't really want Kristen to come again, and berated herself for being unkind.

The two women looked at each other, both apparently unsure what to say next.

"What brings you back to Glenville Falls?"

"I'm, uh, going to school here. After my parents died, the town created a scholarship for me up at Glenville

College, so it made sense to come here. And, it's a good school."

Gracie nodded. "Do you know what you want to major in?"

The girl shook her head. "Maybe business. Gram says it's good for getting a job."

Gracie tapped a finger on her arm. "You were so young when your Gram took you away."

"Yeah, but she wanted me to look you up and be remembered to you."

Why? It felt like a slap. Gracie never really got to know Cheryl's mother, but felt certain Mrs. Walsh blamed her for Cheryl's death as much as she blamed herself. "Well, that's, uh, very nice. Please give her my best." Another awkward pause.

"So, you run a bookstore now?"

"Yes. Just opened it." Gracie glanced around the store.

Kristen wrinkled her forehead. "But you're a lawyer?"

"I stopped practicing a little after, uh, my son was born. He's about your age, in fact." She didn't want to discuss the real reason for her retirement. "So, do you live in Boston?"

"Yeah . . . Hyde Park?" That certainly explained the accent.

Most people in Gracie's part of New England did not have what outsiders thought of as a New England accent. In fact, natives would tell you they had no accent at all. But many students at Glenville College came from Boston or New York, with a smattering from other states and several countries. It gave their tiny town a bit more cosmopolitan flavor, at least during the school year.

"And how is your grandmother doing?" Gracie asked, not sure what else to say.

"She's doing pretty well, you know?" Kristen looked at the floor.

No, I don't know, Gracie thought, but what she said was, "I'm very glad to hear it. Then you've made a good life for yourselves there?" That sounded lame, even to Gracie's ears.

"Yeah. It was an okay place to grow up, but this scholarship made it pretty cheap to go here, so, you know, here I am." Kristen blew another bubble. Gracie surmised Kristen was not happy about her move to Glenville Falls. *Poor kid.*

"Well, I am sure you will find this is a nice place, too . . . once you get settled in and make some new friends. The semester has barely begun."

"I hope you're right." Gracie could tell that the girl was struggling with a lump in her throat. She found herself wanting to make her feel better.

"Don't feel bad," Gracie said, taking a seat across from her. "Everyone goes through a little homesickness when they go away for the first time. It takes some time to adjust, but before you know it, you'll make some friends and think of this place as home, too." Gracie wanted to put her arm around Kristen, but something stopped her.

"I hope so . . . but sometimes I think I should have maybe gone to UMass Boston."

"Well," Gracie said, leaning forward and patting the girl's knee, "give it time."

"Yeah." Kristen did not sound convinced, but she straightened and looked Gracie in the eye. "So," she said, "tell me more about that job."

~

"I'm home," Gracie called as soon as she entered the house, laden with two cloth bags filled with goods from the IGA market in the village.

"Hi, Mom." Carrie's voice came from upstairs. "Doing homework. Be down in a bit."

"Okay. Where's Dad?"

"In his study."

Gracie and Carrie knew that when Spencer was in his office, he could focus so completely on his work as to be oblivious to anything going on elsewhere in the house.

The phone rang. Gracie dropped the bags on the entryway floor and checked caller ID. It was Ben. She threw herself down against the sofa cushions and answered the phone.

"How's my favorite son?" She beamed.

"Oh, things here are great. I'm really loving college, Mom. So far my classes are all great, except maybe physics. We'll see about that one."

"How about your dorm and your roommate?"

"The room is shaping up. I got a couple of posters at the bookstore, so it looks more lived in. And my roommate's cool. In fact we're going to a movie in a bit, but I thought I'd call—just to check in. It'll be too late to call when we get back."

"Are you sure you can afford the time off on a school night, Ben?" She regretted saying it even before it was out of her mouth.

"Yes, *mother*," Ben said with mock exasperation.

Gracie looked at the ceiling and smiled. "I suppose that you think that just because you're old enough to go off to college that you don't need to take advice from your old mother," she said. "But, I'm here to tell you, that I am definitely not through giving it."

"I know—it's only 'cuz you love me." Ben repeated in sing-song his mother's oft-used phrase.

"Well, would you have it any other way?"

"Not really, but it makes me glad I went to school in Pennsylvania." They both laughed. "Sorry, Mom, but I've gotta go. Talk to you soon. Love you."

"Love you back," Gracie said as she heard a click on the line. The room was suddenly empty. Her son was off enjoying his independence. She missed him more than she was willing to admit. She told herself that he was happy, and that was what mattered most.

Then her thoughts turned to Kristen. There was a girl who was far from enjoying her new life.

"Was that Ben?" Spencer asked, bringing the grocery bags into the room.

Gracie flinched. She had not heard him coming. "What?" she said, following him into the kitchen.

"The phone rang."

"Oh, yeah. Ben called just to . . . to tell us that he won't be calling, I guess. He's going to a movie tonight and just wanted to check in."

"How'd he sound?" Spencer placed the bags on the counter.

"Great. He sounded great." But Gracie's mind was no longer on the call. She reached into a bag and pulled out the eggs and bread.

"Well, that's good," Spencer said, putting the orange juice and milk into the refrigerator. "Where's Carrie?"

"In her room. . . . Um, Spencer?" Gracie said, holding a rutabaga in her hand like a candlepin bowling ball. "Would you say that most incoming freshmen are homesick by this point in the semester?"

"Well, it's a little early," he said, pulling cans from the bottom of a bag and putting them on the table. "They usually get homesick after the novelty wears off, about two or three weeks in. We could get a bout of it in a week or two, I'd expect. Why? Did Ben sound homesick already?"

"Ben? No. He sounded like he was having the time of his life."

"He ought to, with what we're paying for that school." Spencer opened the pantry door and rearranged the cans inside to make room for the new ones. "Why he couldn't have gone to school here where he'd have free tuition, live at home, and cost us very little more than he did in high school . . . ?"

Gracie shook her head. "Well," she countered, tossing the rutabaga in the air and catching it, "he would have missed out on so many things that kids experience by leaving home to go to college."

"Like homesickness?" Spencer faced Gracie, arching his brow.

"Yes, even that." Gracie smirked in response. "We've been through all this before, and we agreed it was better this way."

"Yes." Spencer winked. "But I never agreed not to complain about it from time to time."

They finished putting the groceries away and were folding the cloth bags, when Spencer looked at Gracie sideways.

"So, why do you ask?"

"What?" Gracie's mind had not followed Spencer's train of thought.

"Why do you ask about homesickness, if Ben isn't homesick?"

"Oh, well . . ." Gracie sat at the kitchen table and brushed a stray crumb from a placemat. "A student came into the store this afternoon, and she seemed . . . maybe even more than homesick. She might have been depressed about being away from home." Gracie shook her head. "Well, perhaps I'm just projecting."

"Projecting what?" Spencer took a seat across from her.

Gracie hesitated. "You remember Cheryl Mercer."

Spencer focused his eyes on hers, but his voice had an edge to it. "Of course I do."

"Well, the girl who came into the store today was her daughter, Kristen."

Spencer took a breath before responding, and when he did his voice sounded intentionally casual. "What's she doing back here?"

"The town raised all that money for a scholarship for her to go to Glenville College after . . . everything happened, so she's here to go to school."

"She's in college already? Can it have been that long?" Spencer shook his head and gazed into the distance.

Gracie nodded. "She's Ben's age, you know." She watched as Spencer's focus turned back toward her, but looked out the window before their eyes met. She watched the birds collecting at the birdfeeder they kept filled year around and hoped concentrating on them would help her control the emotion that was rising within her. "I wish I could have prevented the tragedies in her life, but . . . I also kind of wish she had gone to school somewhere else."

Spencer reached across the table for her hand. "Me, too."

"Is that too selfish of me?" she said, turning to Spencer who looked at her, his face filled with sympathy.

"No, just human. That was a hard time for you."

"Yeah. But it was really that poor girl who suffered." Gracie looked down, and put her other hand over Spencer's.

"She was too young to know what happened to her," Spencer said, his voice soothing.

"I must admit, her showing up has brought it all back."

"It wasn't your fault, Gracie."

"I know, I know. But if that's true, why do I keep dreaming about it every time . . ." She pulled her hands away, and pushed her hair back off her face.

"You've had that dream again?"

"Yeah. Same as always. The farmhouse with the door torn open, the phone cord ripped from the wall, me trying to call for help but unable to make a sound." Gracie covered her face and shook her head as if that would push the images out of her mind.

Spencer let out a long sigh and sat back in his chair. "You can't blame yourself for what Dave Mercer did. You did what you could. It wasn't your fault."

"So we've always said."

"It's true. You got her the court order. You told her not to go back to the house that night." Gracie stood and moved toward the sink, looking out the back window, while Spencer continued. "The one to blame is the husband, and he threw himself over the falls rather than face what he'd done." Spencer rose and followed Gracie to the window, wrapping his arms around her.

Gracie turned toward Spencer. How many times had they had this conversation? Spencer, always supportive, just did not understand why Gracie felt responsible for her client's death.

"If only I had called the police before I went over there," Gracie said, a familiar lump forming in her throat and tears stinging her eyes. "I should have known she wouldn't be able to make another call."

"It wouldn't have made any difference. He was already there before Cheryl called you. No one could get there in time."

Gracie shook her head. "I know. But seeing that girl today stirred up a lot of old feelings. I feel like I owe her a chance at a normal life." She felt her throat tighten further.

Spencer put a finger under her chin and tilted her face toward his, but Gracie did not meet his eyes. "It's thanks to that woman's memory and your hard work that there's a women's shelter in the county now."

"Not good enough." Gracie turned away from Spencer and crossed her arms in front of her.

"I just hope that girl will stay away from the bookstore and leave you alone," Spencer said, a hint of anger in his voice.

"I doubt she will," Gracie said, swallowing hard and turning to face Spencer as she regained her composure.

"Why not?" Spencer raised his brows and his hazel eyes locked onto Gracie's.

"Because," Gracie said, evading Spencer's stare, "I hired her as my assistant. She starts next Tuesday."

CHAPTER FIVE

The following week, the days turned cooler. The sky shone a deep blue, vibrant fall colors popped out on branches, and the air carried the crisp scent of autumn. Outside of the village, green corn stalks streaked with tan, and apples and pumpkins appeared at roadside stands.

Gracie left for the shop early on Tuesday morning, carrying a bag with a variety of gourds and a ceramic pumpkin she had purchased from Village Crafts on Chestnut Street. She stopped a moment to watch a flock of Canada geese flying southward in a V, honking at each other as they took turns in the lead. Smiling, she took a deep breath and added a bit of a bounce to her step. It was Kristen's first day of work, and Gracie was determined to make it a good one.

As she approached the shop, she saw Peggy Kowalski sweeping the sidewalk in front of the Gracie's Garret. She picked up her pace to thank her new neighbor for her consideration, but when she got close to her shop, she dropped her bag and heard the pumpkin shatter.

Although Peggy had partially cleared it, there was no question what had been on the sidewalk: a chalking saying "GO HOME!" written in tall, bold, yellow letters.

She looked at Peggy. "Who would write that?" she barked, pointing to the message. "Shopkeepers need the students to stay here and spend money in our stores. We don't want them to go home." What she didn't add was: *Why would someone sabotage my storefront with such a message?*

Peggy stopped her sweeping and squinted at Gracie. "No telling why some people do things," she said, shaking her head and resuming her sweeping.

Remembering herself, Gracie apologized. "Sorry, Peggy. Thank you so much for helping to get rid of it." Then, trying to lift her mood, she joked, "Gee, I sure hope whoever wrote it didn't mean *I* should go home." She gave a half-hearted laugh.

Peggy looked at her sideways, but kept sweeping.

"I have a broom in my office," Gracie said, getting back to business. "I'll go get it."

Hurrying into the shop, Gracie grabbed her broom. Together, they scoured the letters, but while the chalk became less noticeable, they could still read the message.

"Sometimes a little water helps," Peggy offered. "Got a hose?"

"No, but I have a bucket." Gracie retrieved her mop bucket and poured water on the concrete while Peggy used her broom. Soon a trace of color remained, but the message was no longer legible.

"Thanks so much, Peggy," Gracie said, wiping sweat from her brow. "Has this happened to other shop owners?"

Peggy looked skyward. "Nope, never heard of it. I knew when I saw it we had to get rid of it. We merchants help each other out." She picked up her broom, and turned back to her store.

"See you later," Gracie called after her.

Peggy waved a hand, not turning around until she reached the flower shop. Then Gracie saw her look back and wave again. Gracie nodded in response, but by then Peggy had turned to go inside.

"How lucky," Gracie said aloud as she re-entered her store, "that Peggy saw the message and had it partially erased before I got here. I don't think I would have seen it if it had been in front of the flower shop."

But who put it there? the voice in her head nagged at her. *Whoever did it must have wanted to hurt the bookstore. But why?*

It was a question she could not answer.

Salvaging the gourds, she positioned them in the front window and near the register. Then there remained just enough time to turn on the college's classical music station before it was time to open.

Turning the sign in the window and unlocking the door, she decided to let in some of the clean fall air. She propped the front door open and went into the back room to do the same to the door that faced the back alley. Soon a cross-breeze freshened up the place. But it didn't freshen her. She splashed water on her face and smoothed the front of her blouse. Then she looked down. Her grey slacks were speckled with dried droplets of chalk-colored water that splashed up as they swept. She tried to brush them off with her hand, but was only partially successful. *This is the problem of having no one to work with,* she thought. *I can't go home and change without closing the store.*

Even when Kristen arrived at 10:30, Gracie knew she couldn't leave her alone on her first day. She had to introduce her to bookstore operations.

"First, we want to make the customers happy they came in," Gracie began. "For instance, what do you most like about visiting a bookstore?"

"I guess the books," Kristen said, twirling her hair in her fingers. "But I don't go to bookstores much. Mostly I go to the library. I used to go there every day after school until Gram got home from work."

"That sounds nice, but bookstores are a bit different. Let me give you some pointers I learned long, long ago when I was in college and worked at a bookstore."

Kristen nodded. "Should I take notes?"

"If you want." Gracie handed her a legal pad and a pen. "First, greet each customer as they come in and tell them your name," Gracie said, "and try to smile." Gracie worried that this might be the hardest part of the job for Kristen. She continued. "When a customer asks for a book, don't just tell them where to look. Take them to the section, locate the book, and when you find it, hand it to them. They're more apt to buy it if they have it in their hand."

"Okay. What if they don't want to take it?"

"You'd be surprised. When you offer a book to someone, they almost always take it."

"There are so many books here," Kristen said, looking around the store. "How do you know where they all go?"

"They're sorted by subject matter for nonfiction. For fiction we sort by genre, like romance or science fiction and fantasy. Things like that." Kristen nodded and jotted down a few notes as Gracie continued. "You can see the various categories on the signs above each section. Then we shelve the books within their categories, alphabetically by author. Most trade paperbacks—those are the larger, more expensive ones—have the genre printed in the upper left corner of the back cover. The smaller, mass-market paperbacks usually don't. If you ever have any questions about where a book belongs, I've created an inventory. It lists every title in stock and where each should be shelved. And I've drawn a map for you so you can find each section right away."

"Why do some books have the front facing out when the others all you can see is the edge?"

"We do it partly to make the shelves look full, but partly to highlight a particular title. You'll notice that I only put them face out when I have two or more copies of a book. If someone purchases the front one, there is another one behind it and there isn't a big open gap on the shelf. When there is only one left, we turn it spine out." Gracie demonstrated it by moving several books on the self-help shelf.

"I don't know if I'll get the hang of all this," Kristen said, scribbling more notes. Looking at her, Gracie wasn't sure Kristen even wanted to.

"Sure you will. It's not rocket science." Gracie tried to keep her voice encouraging, but not pleading.

"I don't know. I usually only read fiction except for school, and a lot of the store is other stuff."

"Knowing fiction's important. If you're familiar with the work of various authors, you can direct fans of one author to the work of another. For most nonfiction, people already know what general topic they are interested in. Most often they just want to browse their favorite sections or already have a specific title in mind. Your job is to find a book if they ask for it, or to take them to the section they're interested in. Hopefully they'll find something they didn't know they wanted when they came in. As you get more familiar with things, you can start making suggestions there, too."

"I don't know . . ." Kristen looked like she was about to bolt.

"You can shadow me for today, but by next time, you should be able to handle some customers on your own," Gracie said. She knew Kristen had to be a smart to be a student at Glenville College, but she just lacked self-confidence. *Maybe this job will help bring her out of her shell.*

By the end of her first shift, Kristen had learned how to process sales by cash, check, and credit card, and how to handle coupons and special orders. Gracie believed that, if Kristen stuck with it, the heart and soul of book-selling—learning how to match people with the right books—would come in time.

As the day went on, Kristen became less guarded. Gracie was pleased she had left her gum at home, but she dearly wished she would stop playing with her hair.

"You know," Kristen said after a customer left, "You could offer free Wi-Fi in here. Then kids from the college would come to do work on their papers and stuff. You could put in a networked printer, and a coin-operated copy machine, too, so they could copy stuff from all these books and you would make a few cents per page."

Gracie frowned, considering the suggestion. "I'm not sure I want to become a substitute for the library. My books are for sale, not for reference."

Kristen appeared not to hear her. "And maybe sell snacks in that back corner."

Gracie looked at the corner she planned to use for special events, and wondered if it could accommodate a coffee urn, and perhaps a few baked goods. She shook her head. "I don't know about that."

It was Kristen's turn to frown. "Sorry. I just thought you wanted more people in the store," she said, getting up and moving toward the back room.

"I do. I just want them to be book *buyers.*" Gracie paused. "But if you get any more good ideas, let me know."

"Sure." Kristen went into the back and emerged with her backpack. "I gotta go. Bio lab at four."

"Okay. See you Thursday?"

"Yeah, sure." Kristen left, closing the door as the bell tinkled overhead.

Gracie was mad at herself for quashing Kristen's ideas. She realized that most independent bookstores needed more than personal service to compete with the big chains and online book retailers. Some had cafés, others were also gift shops. Many had become boutiques such as cookbook shops that also gave cooking lessons, or craft bookshops that also sold yarn. Gracie knew that the likelihood of succeeding as an independent, books-only shop was not high, and that she would need to be creative to beat the odds. But she wasn't yet sure how best to do that.

That space in back might be large enough to handle a little coffee bar and still allow for small group meetings. *Maybe Wi-Fi for the customers and some refreshments would encourage more people to come in.* She spent the next hour sketching out how she would arrange the back corner into a meeting and refreshment center. Maybe it was not such a bad idea after all.

The bell rang and an older, swarthy man entered.

"May I help you find something?"

The man looked at her with rheumy brown eyes. He had a full head of black hair streaked with grey and a stooped posture, but there was a twinkle in his eye. His brown plaid suit looked old, but well made. Gracie could tell from his expression that he thought he recognized her.

"You don't remember me do you?" he said. His voice was mellifluous; he spoke slowly with perfect diction in an accent that sounded Indian and British at the same time.

"I, uh . . ." Gracie stammered, trying to place him. "You're right," she said at last. "Have we met before?"

"I am Professor Chaudhry from the Economics Department at Glenville College. Or, I should say I am Professor *Emeritus*."

"Oh yes, Professor Chaudhry." Gracie smiled. "I remember now. You gave that great lecture a while back on the economy of global warming. It gave Spencer and me a lot to think about."

"That's right," the professor said, bowing slightly and smiling. "I enjoyed that talk myself. It's not often that one can get the president of the college to sit still and listen for an hour to a professor, but since the talk was funded by one of the college's biggest donors, she had no choice." He chuckled so heartily that his whole body shook.

"I didn't know you had retired, but how nice that they honored you with *emeritus* status."

"Yes it is, isn't it?" His watery eyes sparkled again. "They let me park my car on campus, gave me library and email privileges, and even allow me to use a small office in the economics department, but it is not quite the same as the one I had when I held the endowed chair. I find it a bit confining, and seldom use it."

"That's too bad," Gracie said, extending her hand toward an arm chair. "Would you care to sit?"

"No, thank you. I only look like I could be knocked over by a stiff wind. Actually," he said in a conspiratorial tone, "I am quite wiry." Another chortle rocked his shoulders. "I thought I would come in to see what you have here. This is a charming little bookshop, isn't it? Very inviting."

"I'm glad you think so," Gracie said, warming to the praise. "It's still taking shape, but it's coming along."

"Quite nicely, I think. You have several used books, I see. Where did you acquire them?"

"My father had an extensive library. He was an attorney in Boston. Then Spencer and I have added some of our own. Of course, I have filled out the collection with current titles."

"Very nice. Are any of your older books valuable?" His eyes twinkled with anticipation.

Gracie puckered her lips. "Not very, except for the wisdom they contain."

"Ah-ha. I see we are of the same mind on that, my dear."

"Are you still writing in your retirement, professor?" Gracie knew that at Glenville College, only outstanding teachers who were prolific researchers were given endowed chairs.

"I am mulling over several options. It is nice, you know, to be past the point of writing because it is what I *must* do, and only taking up a project if it is what I *want* to do."

"Are you teaching at all?"

"Not this semester. I have told the department head that if needed I would be willing to teach a course from time to time, but I do not expect to be called. They think me old-fashioned. The theories of John Maynard Keynes are no longer in vogue among my colleagues."

Gracie started to shake her head, but when she saw the gentleman's shoulders bounce with amusement, she smiled.

"I wonder, Mrs. Adams, if I might come just to spend some time here? I know it is late today, but perhaps sometime soon?" Gracie did not bother to correct him about her name. People often assumed she had become Gracie Adams when she and Spencer married, but she had always used her own name of McIntyre, in her law practice and in her private life.

"Of course. You're welcome here anytime. We're open from ten to six, Tuesday through Saturday."

"That's very nice. I will definitely return. I think I would enjoy the ambience here more than in my small office on campus, and I know that Mrs. Chaudhry prefers that I get out of the house more than I currently do." Another chuckle. He moved toward the door, and Gracie followed.

"I look forward to seeing you again," Gracie said as he left. *What a nice man,* she thought. *He would make a pleasant regular customer to have around.*

~

Gracie didn't realize how late it had become until she looked up and saw it was getting dark outside. She called the house to see if anyone had started dinner.

"Nope," said Carrie. "Dad's in his study, and I was about to start my homework, but if you want me to start dinner . . ."

Gracie checked her wallet and sighed. "No, that's okay, honey. I'll stop by College Pizza and bring something home." *But at this rate,* she thought, *we'll go broke eating out before the bookstore clears a profit.*

"Extra mushrooms!" Carrie nearly shrieked with pleasure.

"Okay!" Gracie tried—not very successfully—to match Carrie's tone.

She called her order in to the pizzeria, and locked up the store. She turned north toward the town hall and onto Chestnut Street. As she approached the restaurant, her mouth watered. The smell of baking bread and Italian spices reminded her it had been too long since lunch. Music from a jukebox poured out the open door along with the voices of college kids who filled the shop. Making her way inside, Gracie wove past knots of young people standing and sitting at the many polished, wooden-plank tables. Gracie sighed and wished it were still summer. *But I would never tell them to go home!*

When she stood at the counter, she tried to catch Vito's eye. He was busy shifting pizzas around with a long wooden paddle in his huge bake oven. He looked harried, but when he turned around, a huge smile opened on his face.

"Hey, Miss Gracie," he shouted, raising his arm over the high glass counter filled with various pizzas available by the slice. His accent was New York with a little light Italian thrown in. Gracie smiled and shook the proffered hand. "How's it goin' down at the new bookstore?"

"Great, Vito. Like you, having the students back in town is good for my business."

"It's what we live on," Vito said, looking around his restaurant. "During the summer we go fishing, but once school is back, it's baking, baking, baking, all the time baking. But it's great. Puts food on our table, eh?"

"Well, it puts pizza on mine," Gracie said with a laugh. "I called in an order a bit ago. It probably isn't ready yet."

"Let me see," he said, flipping through a stack of order slips. "You the pepperoni and extra mushroom?"

"Yeah, and the antipasto salad."

"Be about ten more minutes. Here, have a bit of garlic bread while you wait," he said, handing her a warm foil packet.

Gracie held it to her face and inhaled the scent of butter and fresh garlic. "Oh, Vito, you really know how to tempt a person."

"I better." His laugh was robust. Then a young man who had been standing behind Gracie pushed to the counter.

"Dude, where's our pizza?"

Gracie moved out of earshot and opened the foil. Her stomach growled. The packet contained three baked garlic knots. *I really ought to bring these home to share with Spencer and Carrie,* she thought as she lifted one out and took a bite. "Mmmm," she said aloud. Embarrassed, she looked around. No one seemed to have heard her, so she took another bite.

"Pizza's here, Gracie," Vito called a few minutes later. Gracie polished off of the contents of the packet and looked for a place to dispose of the foil. "Here. I'll take that," Vito offered. Then he put the back of his hand next to his mouth and in a stage whisper added, "I put some more in the bag with the salad for you."

"You're a doll, Vito. You've saved the day once again." Gracie left the shop with her hot pizza, salad, garlic knots, and a sense of well-being.

~

When the family gathered around the kitchen table for pizza, Gracie couldn't help glancing in the direction of the empty fourth chair.

"Okay, what's up with you?" Carrie asked. "You haven't even asked me about what's going on at school."

Gracie looked up. *Is Carrie mad at me?* "What do you mean?"

"Apparently, you don't care."

Gracie looked at Spencer who shrugged. "You have been awfully quiet."

"I'm tired. I just worked all day *and* got dinner."

Carrie's look said, "Give us a break."

"Sorry." She thought about telling Spencer about the chalked message outside her shop, but decided it could wait. Instead, she said, "I'm trying to figure out how to arrange things in the back of the store. Kristen, my new employee, said today that she thought we ought to serve food."

"Do you really want to get involved with that?" Spencer frowned. "With that tiny kitchen, you'll never be able to serve anything nearly as good as what they have across the street at the Kettle. Why would you want to try to compete with them?"

"I don't. I just want to make my store as hospitable as possible."

"Then, maybe you should talk to Kelly, and see if she has some ideas about how to make it work. She's the expert, after all."

Gracie wondered how she could broach the subject. *Hi, Kelly. So, tell me how I can set up a competing business across the street.* "Yeah. That oughta work."

Spencer smirked at Gracie's sarcasm. "Just give it a try."

Gracie shook her head. "I'll think about it," she said, not expecting to give it another thought.

Carrie cleared her throat. "Well in addition to all that very important stuff, didn't you get an email from the principal?"

"Why? Was there something important?" Gracie scanned her daughter's face for clues.

"Oh, nothing much. It's just that the high school had a pedophile lurking around today."

"What? Where?" Gracie asked, thinking of the girls' locker room, and wondering if it were one of the staff.

"Outside. I guess some girls saw a man watching them from across the street when they were out on the steps waiting for the doors to open this morning, and then later, some kids said he tried to get them to come over to talk to him. Creepy."

"It certainly is," Spencer said. "Do they have any idea who it was?"

"Nope. But it weirded everybody out. They called the School's Police Resource Officer, but she was over at the junior high building. By the time she got to the high school, the creep was gone. Here's the letter they sent home with us." Carrie pulled a folded sheet of paper from her pocket.

Gracie found her reading glasses while Spencer scanned the one-page letter, then handed it to her. Signed by both the high school principal and the super-intendent, the letter described the incident and said that despite their video surveillance, they could not identify anyone who matched the students' description. None-theless, they said they were taking the reports seriously, and outlined the steps the school district was putting in place to protect students at all age levels.

"Well, I am glad they're taking precautions," Spencer said. "It's good to err on the side of safety."

Gracie finished reading and nodded. "And you be alert to anything or anyone out of place, kiddo," she said. Then she thought about the message scrawled on the sidewalk in front of the store and added, "Even small towns have their share of sickos."

CHAPTER SIX

Thursday arrived—Kristen's second day of work. As Gracie dressed for the day, she had the house to herself. Carrie had to be at the bus stop by six forty-five and Spencer had left for College Hill by eight. Gracie didn't need to leave for the store until nine thirty.

As she brushed her hair, trying to hide the greys, and inspected herself in the bathroom mirror, Dickens jumped up onto the counter.

"Quiet around here, isn't it, boy?" Gracie rubbed his neck. "Sorry, but you're going to be alone again most of the day. Poor baby."

Dickens stood up on his hind legs, pressing his front paws into Gracie's chest and nuzzling her chin.

"Ouch! Your claws need a clipping. Didn't I just clip them last week?" she said, carefully extracting his paw and inspecting her sweater for snags, or worse, blood. She picked him up, took him back to the bedroom, and put him down on the bed next to where she sat. He purred and pushed his nose under her arm to get another stroking while she looked for the claw clippers.

"Poor, attention-starved kitty," she said, petting him and scratching his neck. "But you're the lucky one. I'll be at the bookshop all day with an employee who might wish she were someplace else."

Gracie pressed lightly on each soft toe to extend the claw and clip it, careful to avoid the quick. "After the way she left on Tuesday," Gracie said in a soothing tone to calm her cat, "I don't know if I'll even see her." Gracie paused to consider what she would do if Kristen did not show. Dickens wriggled his paw free of her hold. "Hold on there, boy. One more to clip. There. That's much better," she said when she finished.

As soon as it was over, Dickens jumped down from the bed and left the room, tail held high.

"You're walking out on me, too, eh?" she said to his departing figure. Then, to herself, she added, "Well, if Kristen abandons the job, I'll just find someone else to help out at the store. At least I will have tried."

~

Gracie opened the shop at ten o'clock. It was a quiet morning on the green. The farmers' market on Tuesday and Friday helped the downtown merchants, but this was Thursday.

Gracie did some vacuuming and straightening, and checked on the status of her orders of new stock. Then she made herself a cup of tea and settled down with the new edition of the *Glenville Falls Gazette* while she waited for customers—and for Kristen. She had been so pleased with Wendell Owens' coverage of the bookstore opening in the previous week's edition, but she had little hope of getting more coverage now. She thumbed through the paper looking for the ad she had purchased. There it was, on page eight. Wendell had done a good job with it again, giving her excellent placement at the top of a column of same-sized ads. *That ought to help,* she thought with a smile. Just then, the bell over the door jingled. She looked up expecting to see Kristen, but it was her landlord, Hal Doyle. He looked much more comfortable in his familiar worn flannel shirt, work pants, and battered Red Sox cap.

"Good morning, Hal," Gracie said with a smile, doing a quick mental survey of all the reasons she could think of why her landlord might visit. "What brings you over here?"

"My size twelves," Hal said, his smile a bit sheepish.

Gracie laughed harder than the joke warranted. "So, what's up?"

"Oh, nothin'. I just came over to check on how you're doin'. Everything all right over here?"

"No problems here," she said, looking around the store, then added, "Well nothing that more reliable help couldn't cure."

"You havin' trouble with your help?"

"No, not really. It's just her second day, and she's late for work. She was supposed to be here at ten-thirty."

Hal looked at his watch. "Almost eleven. Not good. No call from her?"

"No. Well, perhaps there is a good explanation," Gracie said, wondering if that explanation was that she had quit.

"You gotta lay down the law with help. Some kids just don't work out. Can't be afraid to fire her if she don't shape up."

Gracie tilted her head. "I'm not at that point yet, but thanks for the advice."

"I know you're new at this. Just want to help if I can." He turned toward the door, then back to Gracie. "Your girl. She from around here?"

"No. She's from Boston." Hal nodded and started toward the door. "Hal, do you know something I should know?"

"Nope" he said, still facing away from Gracie. "Just trying to help."

Gracie did not feel reassured, sensing there was something Hal had left unsaid.

Just then, the bell over the door rang out again and Kristen entered the shop. She walked past Hal without so much as a nod and continued straight toward the back room to deposit her lunch in the refrigerator. Gracie turned her head to watch her go by.

"Good morning, Kristen," she said as the girl passed her.

"Hi."

Gracie looked back at Hal, who had already reached the door. "I better get back. See ya later," he said as he pulled the door open. "But remember what I said." With that he was gone.

Gracie blew out a stream of air, not sure which of them exasperated her more.

Kristen emerged from the back room, pushing back her bangs and pulling her hair into a pony tail.

Oh, good, Gracie thought. She can't play with her hair today.

"Sorry I'm late. There was a campus meeting at ten, and it just ended." A loud popping sound punctuated the end of her sentence, and Gracie felt her anger rising. Her temper was a curse she had tried to control her whole life. She was usually its master, but she wasn't sure who would win the battle today.

"Kristen, are you chewing gum?"

"Yeah." She shrugged.

Gracie took a deep breath and counted to ten. As she did so, she reminded herself that Kristen had grown up without her parents, thanks to her. Her grandmother apparently left her to fend for herself much of the time. No wonder Kristen had missed out on some of the finer points of decorum.

Feeling calmer, Gracie said, "In one way a bookstore is like a library. We don't allow gum chewing at work, okay?"

"I guess." Kristen pulled a tissue from her pocket, wrapped up the gum, and tossed it in the trash. "Sorry. Won't happen again."

"And next time call if you won't be in on time, okay?"

"Yeah, okay." She pulled a strand of hair from her pony tail and twirled it around her index finger. "Anyway, I guess there's a peeping Tom up on College Hill. They wanted to let everyone know."

"Really?" Gracie's aggravation turned to alarm. "There was someone lurking around the high school a couple of days ago, too. Did they catch the guy on campus?"

"Nope, but he must not be very good at it to be seen twice in one week. They just wanted us to be careful about keeping shades closed, that sort of thing. 'If he doesn't see anything, he'll stop looking,' is their theory."

Gracie shook off a shudder. "That's pretty unnerving," she said. Kristen only shrugged.

~

The foot traffic in the shop was a bit slow, but it allowed Kristen to take her time as she waited on the first customers. Gracie relaxed as she saw her assistant handle a variety of questions without having to refer the customers to Gracie. For her part, Gracie quelled the impulse to jump in whenever she saw Kristen pause and search her memory or her notes for the right answer. She had learned long ago that people learn best by doing something that challenges their skills, rather than by watching others. She was surprised, and more than pleased, to see Kristen at work. But she made a mental note to speak to her about playing with her hair.

Gracie picked up the *Gazette* again, and searched through it for estate sales or auctions that might include a large numbers of books. While the store was reasonably well-stocked, and she expected to be able to restock some used books from people selling ones they were finished with, she knew that she would need to bring in a fresh rotation of titles to keep customers coming through the door.

Then she scanned *Publishers Weekly* and several publishers' online catalogues, to decide what new books to order for the upcoming holiday season. Browsing through the catalogues put Gracie in the holiday mood.

"This is so cool," Gracie said calling to Kristen through her office doorway. "They have so many books that ought to sell well here. I feel like I'm Christmas shopping, but for my customers instead of for friends and family." Even without encouragement from Kristen, Gracie stood and let loose her holiday spirit. "Owning a bookstore is such fun!"

Still no response from her employee. Gracie wondered what it would take to put a smile on the girl's face. She started humming "Happy Holidays." Kristen looked at her like she thought she was crazy.

Gracie knew she had to escalate. She did an awkward dance across the shop floor, singing until it echoed off the metal ceiling. Then she grabbed Kristen and twirled her around the store until they almost careened into a bookshelf. They each plopped into an overstuffed chair, and lolled there while Gracie caught her breath.

There it was: a smile from Kristen.

"I know what we can do," Gracie said, trying to keep the smile there. "Your idea for refreshments was great. I'm going over to the market and get some apple cider to serve to our customers. Then, maybe tomorrow I can bring in my slow cooker, and we can have some warm spiced cider. How does that sound?"

"Good." It worked. The smile got bigger. "Maybe we could we have pumpkin muffins, too. I love pumpkin muffins."

"And I know just the place to get them. The Steaming Kettle makes the best pumpkin muffins in New England. We're going to make this the happiest place on the block. Take care of the store for me. I'll be right back." Gracie grabbed her sweater and drew some money from her wallet, and with only a little worry about leaving the store in Kristen's hands, she slipped out the door. *I'll only be gone five minutes,* she thought. *What could happen in five minutes?*

The voice in her head came up with lots of disastrous ideas, but she refused to listen to it.

She stopped at the IGA to get cider, then headed for the Steaming Kettle, hoping they still had muffins.

"You're in luck," Kelly said. "Sean just baked some."

"Great—I'll take a half dozen," she said, secretly hoping that she would have some to take home with her at the end of the day. As Kelly boxed the muffins, Gracie realized she had already been gone from the store more than twice the five minutes she had planned. She looked out the window across the triangle to her bookshop. It looked like all was quiet.

"Here they are," Kelly said, handing Gracie a box tied with string. "Hope you like 'em." Kelly's face was flushed and her huge grin showed her uneven teeth.

"You know I will." Gracie turned to leave, but then thought, *no time like the present.* "Uh, Kelly. Sometime I'd like to talk to you about how I might be able to serve some refreshments at the bookstore on a full-time basis. I know there's a lot involved, and I'm not sure I am going to do it, but I wondered if I could just pick your brain about it."

"Sure, Gracie. Any time." Her smile filled her face. "Just not during the lunch or dinner rush, okay? Other than that, any time—except breakfast."

Gracie laughed. "Thanks, Kelly. See you soon." She raised her plastic jug of cider in a wave as she pushed through the door and walked right into a police officer.

"Oh, excuse me. I wasn't watching where I was going. Are you all right?" she asked him.

The officer was looking down at his shirt, apparently more concerned about whether the cider had spilled on him than with Gracie's apology. "No, I'm okay," he said, looking at her for the first time. "Oh. Ms. McIntyre."

Gracie was surprised to be called by name. She had seen the officer at town functions, but they had never spoken, at least that she could recall.

"Yes. Officer . . . Lowry?" she said, looking at the name pinned over his pocket. The officer looked to be about five foot ten, in his late thirties, with dark hair. He had an athletic build, but his dark sunglasses blocked all view of his eyes, something that Gracie found disconcerting.

"Funny running into you," he said. "I wanted to come and talk to you about being careful about hiring, um, any of the college kids. Or at least be sure to ask for a background check first, and check their references. I can help you with that if you want."

"Oh, that sounds very wise," she said, nodding. "But I have already hired someone."

Gracie wondered if she should have asked for references. What did she really know about Kristen beyond the tragedy of her parents' deaths? Did she even know much about the grandmother who raised her? All she really knew was that she felt she owed Kristen something.

She did not want to admit her rashness in hiring Kristen to the cop. As a civil attorney she hadn't had much contact with the police. In the years since, she'd had even less, and found herself the tiniest bit intimidated by the uniform and badge.

"Well, it's usually okay, but you don't want any trouble. A background check could still be a good thing. Then if she doesn't pass, you could find someone else."

He said "she." Does he assume I'd hire a female, or does he know I did?

"I'll give it some thought," she said, excusing herself and walking across the triangle, wondering if the officer might be right.

When Gracie returned to the store, she tried to mask her misgivings, and raised the jug of cider above her head. "Success!" she said.

"I think I'm going to have to go." Kristen turned away and walked toward the back room. "Sorry, but I just remembered that I, uh, have a paper coming up, and I really have to get to the library to get some research done. That's okay, isn't it? I mean it isn't busy or anything."

"Oh . . . well . . ." Gracie said, trying not to see this as suspicious. She was torn between being upset with a recalcitrant employee and wanting to mother the girl with no parents. Mothering won. "Your school work comes first," she said. "But, uh, will you be here next Tuesday?"

"I think so. I'll let you know, if that's okay."

"Please do. The sooner the better, so I can plan accordingly."

"Sure. Thanks." Kristen started to leave.

"Kristen," Gracie stopped her and handed her a pumpkin muffin. "Is everything all right? I mean, you do want this job, right?"

"Yeah. I mean I need it. And everything's fine, thanks." Kristen turned and walked out the door, calling over her shoulder, "I'll talk to you later."

Gracie watched her go. *Just when I thought we'd turned a corner.*

After putting the cider in the refrigerator, Gracie went to the front counter where Kristen had been working. It was as tidy as if Gracie had been working there all day instead of her new assistant. The cup hooks she had installed to hold the balloons for the grand opening party were still there. Two held a pair scissors; two others held bunches of light-weight, ninety-nine cent cloth bags printed with the store's name, all within easy reach. *What made Kristen leave in such a hurry?*

Gracie opened the register and flipped through the bills in the drawer. It looked like everything was there. Then she noticed the legal pad she had used to list the holiday books she wanted to order. It was lying on a shelf under the countertop. The pages on which she had written were folded over the top, and a sheet of paper had been ripped out, leaving behind a jagged remnant. She pulled the pad out and laid it on the counter, wondering why Kristen moved it in her absence. She took the pad to the window to see if she could detect any impression on the exposed page that might tell her what was written on the missing paper. She couldn't make anything out.

Foolish woman, Gracie chastised herself. *She probably just needed some paper to wrap up more forbidden gum.*

Gracie checked the recycle bin. No crumpled paper. *So what did she need the paper for?* She thought of taking a pencil rubbing of the page under the one that was torn out, but didn't have any pencils in her desk. Then she remembered a gross of Glenville College pencils she had bought for the grand opening.

She grabbed a pencil from the display box. *Blast. They're not sharpened.* She checked her desk, but she knew she had no pencil sharpener. Gracie drummed her fingers on the countertop, deciding what to do next. *Doyle's.*

She dashed next door to Doyle's Hardware. "Hal, do you have any pencil sharpeners?" Gracie said, holding up the new pencil.

"Not for sale," Hal said, "but you can use mine. It's attached to the wall behind the back counter."

"Bless you, Hal," Gracie said, rushing over to the device. After grinding away until she was satisfied with the length of exposed lead, Gracie hurried back to her store. "You're a doll," she shouted over her shoulder as she left.

Gracie rubbed the pencil over the legal pad, and an image slowly appeared. She picked it up to examine it. It was a series of seven numbers with a hyphen between digits three and four. *This looks like a phone number. But whose?*

She wondered if she should call the number to see who answered, but didn't know what she would say if they did. Then she remembered that she could find a reverse telephone directory online. Since her computer was in the back room, she wedged the office door open so she could hear the bell if anyone entered the store.

After a few minutes of playing with search engines, she found several sites. Most of them charged a fee.

"I'm too Scottish to be willing to pay nearly twenty dollars just to satisfy my curiosity," Gracie said aloud. Instead, she spent another twenty minutes before finding a website that would provide the service for free. She plugged in the number, using the local area code.

The screen changed to say, "Your search returned zero matches."

"Hmm," Gracie considered, drumming her fingers on the desk. "I wonder . . ." She tried the area code for Boston followed by one in central Massachusetts, then upstate New York and one in Connecticut. She got two names, but nothing that meant anything to her. She printed out the pages anyway. Then she searched online for more area codes to try, but got similarly disappointing results.

There are so many area codes these days, she thought, I don't know if I am even getting close.

Finally, her frustration and guilt at prying into Kristen's affairs got the better of her curiosity, and she closed down the website. But that did not stop her from turning the puzzle around in her mind.

CHAPTER SEVEN

"**D**oes Dickens look a little skinny to you?" Spencer asked Gracie the next morning. A heavy rain pelted against the windows and thunder rumbled in the distance.

"I hadn't noticed. Is he?" She looked at the cat, lying in his favorite chair, curled up against the cool dampness.

"Well, he's not eating very well. When I go to fill his bowl in the morning, there's still half his meal left from the day before."

"That's not good. He's always been a good eater. Do you suppose he's sick?" She bent down and picked him up, stroking his fur. Then she pinched the skin between his shoulders and let go. It smoothed quickly across his back. "He's not dehydrated, at least. Maybe he just has a hairball. Have you seen him coughing?"

Spencer stroked the cat's head, a look of concern flickering across his face. "Not really. Maybe he's just tired of the kind of food we're giving him. But he's never been picky."

"Do you want to take him to the vet?" Gracie scratched under the cat's chin.

"I don't know. If it's just a hairball, maybe we can just treat him for that and see how it goes."

"Or we can take him to the vet and put your mind at ease. He's nine years old—not a kitten anymore. Better to be safe than sorry."

"I don't have any classes today. I'll try to make an appointment for this morning if I can," Spencer said, taking Dickens from Gracie and walking away, stroking him and speaking to him in soft tones.

Gracie checked the clock. "I've gotta go, Spencer. See you later. Let me know what the vet says."

~

"Thanks for coming in on such a rainy morning," Gracie said as she bagged the first sales of the day. "It was great meeting you. I hope to see you again soon." As the door closed behind the customer, the jingling bell was nearly drowned out by a clap of thunder. Gracie was not surprised when old friends came in to browse, but she had discovered that there were many other people from the college who were glad to have a bookstore in town. And even the rain did not keep them all away.

She let out a breath of satisfaction, and turned to reshelving some books. Looking down at her dark blue sweater, she noticed several strands of golden fur. "Oh, Dickens," she said aloud, picking at the cat hair, then immediately regretted the exasperation in her voice. She hoped Spencer would get good news from the vet. She thought about calling him, but stopped herself. He would call as soon as he knew anything.

The bell rang, and Gracie looked up. Lois Heller, the town's realtor, stepped inside and pumped her umbrella to rid it of some of the rain—and deposit it on Gracie's floor. Her mousy-brown hair was, as always, pulled into a tight bun. She scowled and shook her head as she looked around the shop, her sharp features accentuating her judgment.

"Hello, Lois. Glad to see you. What do you think of what I've done with the place?" Gracie did not need to ask. She smiled inwardly. Somehow, even though Lois and she were about the same height, Lois always managed to look down on her.

"Well, I suppose it is serviceable. I told you this was not as good as the space in the mall."

"I had hoped we would see you at our grand opening party," Gracie said, ignoring the insult. "We had a wonderful time."

"Well, of course I couldn't come," Lois said. "I am far too busy to attend every little gathering to which I am invited."

"What a shame," Gracie said. Lois gave her an arched look. "May I help you find something?"

"Oh, I'm not here to buy anything."

Of course not. What was I thinking? "So what brings you here today?"

"Well, as you know, I'm president of the Village Business Association, and I am visiting all the members to make sure you are prepared for the coming weekend."

"In what way, prepared?" Gracie asked.

Lois tilted her head and arched one brow. "It is only the most important shopping weekend of the autumn season."

Gracie knit her brow. She had thought the weekend before classes started was supposed to be the busiest. Were tourist buses expected that no one had told her about? She did not want to ask, but realized she had to. "Why's that?"

Lois made a slight grunting sound. "Because it's Family Weekend at the college. I should have thought you would be aware of that since your husband works there."

Gracie felt a flash of panic. "Family Weekend?"

"Yes." Lois became patronizing. "It is when the college invites family members of students to campus for special programs and activities."

"I know what it is," Gracie said, trying to keep her voice from rising, "but I thought it was in October. It's only mid-September. How could they be holding Family Weekend now?"

"Something about the Jewish holidays. It was on the VBA calendar I gave you when you rented this . . . place." Lois looked like she had something sour in her mouth.

Gracie remembered a fat manila envelope Lois had given her when she joined the Village Business Association, but she had been so busy getting the store ready to open by the start of school that she had not looked through it. Perhaps she should have.

Lois continued her lecture. "All merchants are expected to have special sales or displays, and, weather permitting, a sidewalk display. "

Easy for her to say. Gracie hoped the rain would continue through the weekend.

"The more uniform the participation, the better for all." Lois said with emphasis on the word "uniform." "I assume you have made some plans for it."

"Of, of course . . ." Gracie stammered. "In fact," she said going in to the back room and bringing out her legal pad, "I have pages of plans." She hoped she was not blushing as she flipped through the pages of prospective orders for the holidays. "I, uh, just didn't realize that it was this weekend. Thanks for reminding me. I am sure it will be no trouble to get this ready by tomorrow."

Lois harrumphed. "I should hope not. As a newcomer to the business association, it is important that you make a good first impression. Everyone will be watching to see what you have to offer." Lois's look told Gracie that she did not expect much from her.

Like I need the extra pressure, Gracie thought. She could feel her face reddening with suppressed rage. "I'm new at this and don't expect my display to be as professional as those designed by others, but I will do my best," she said, hoping that Lois was ready to leave. "Now, perhaps, I should get to work on it." She wondered if Lois would take the hint.

"And I have a lot of other stops to make." Lois exited, extending her umbrella almost before she was out the door. For a moment, Gracie thought it looked more like a broomstick.

Gracie knew that Lois saw through her façade of preparedness for Family Weekend, and she didn't care . . . much. Her glance fell on her legal pad, open to the page with the rubbing of the seven-digit number. She shook her head. There were more important things to deal with. She ripped out the page and tossed it in the trash.

Where to start? Her thoughts were interrupted by the phone ringing.

"Gracie's Garret bookstore," she answered. "This is Gracie. How may I help you?"

"Hi, Sweetie," Spencer said. "How's it going there?" Spencer's voice was subdued, and Gracie immediately imagined the worst.

"What did the vet say?"

"Nothing definitive. Dickens has lost weight. They drew some blood and took an x-ray, but the vet didn't think there was anything clinically wrong."

"Just a hairball, then?"

Spencer paused. "They asked if he might be depressed."

"Depressed? Do cats get depressed?"

"They said they can." There was reluctance in Spencer's voice. "Or he's suddenly become a picky eater. I bought some new flavors of food on my way home, and gave him some right away. He ate it pretty well."

"So, he's not depressed?"

"Well, they asked if there had been any changes in his routine."

There was a long pause.

"Poor kitty has been a little neglected lately with Ben in college and me at the store," Gracie said.

"Yeah, and Carrie's day is longer because of that bus ride. When I am working at home I keep my office door closed to keep him from knocking things over on my bookshelves, but I've always done that. But that means he's alone nearly all day, every day."

"Poor thing. I guess we'll have to make a point of giving him more attention."

"Well, he's happy now, curled up and giving himself a bath."

"Good." Gracie frowned.

"How are things going at the store?"

"Fine, but for some reason the college is holding Family Weekend tomorrow and Sunday."

"Really?"

"Yeah, I think I'm going to have to stay late to get ready for it."

"Do you want me to come down and help?"

Gracie considered the option. "No, I don't think so. Pay attention to Dickens. I think I can manage on my own. Don't wait dinner for me, though."

"You sure?"

"Yeah. Maybe I'll give Del a call and see if she can come over after work."

"Okay, hon. See you later. Call if you need us."

"Love you. And call if you see any change in Dickens, okay?"

Gracie hung up and stared at the phone. She picked it up again and dialed Del's office.

"Steadman, Turner, and Nix, Attorneys at Law. How may I help you?"

"Hi, Shelley. It's Gracie McIntyre. Is Del available?"

"Sorry, Gracie. Del's in Billington. She has a short hearing this morning at the courthouse. Do you want me to have her call you when she gets back?"

"If you would, I'd appreciate it. Thanks, Shelley."

Gracie rang off, rested her elbow on the desk, supported her head in her hand, and drummed her fingers on her cheek. *Now what?*

While she waited to hear from Del, Gracie pulled out her library cart, one of the few furnishings she had actually purchased for the shop. She drove it through the aisles, looking for books for the sidewalk display that would entice customers into the store. By noon the cart was only half-filled, and Gracie despaired of having anything besides a few college items for the Family Weekend sale.

Rather than returning Gracie's call, Del appeared at the bookshop bringing with her two bagged lunches.

"Shelley said you sounded stressed, so I thought I'd come over and see what's what," she told Gracie.

"Thank you, Del." Gracie tried to keep her desperation out of her voice. "I just found out this morning that I need to be ready for an influx of shoppers this weekend. It's Family Weekend at the college."

"Well, there won't be many customers if this rain keeps up."

"Have you seen the forecast?"

"Last I knew, the rain was supposed to taper off tonight, but this storm looks like it's settling in for a while."

Gracie could hardly admit to herself the relief Del's prediction gave her. They sat in a reading nook and talked over how to handle the weekend sales while they ate.

"I really don't think I want to be open on Sunday. I told Carrie that the Labor Day weekend was the only Sunday or Monday I would be open, and I don't want to go back on that promise."

"That's fine. So what are you going to do on Saturday?" Del said.

"I have a gallon of cider in the fridge. I can bring my slow cooker to the store and serve warm spiced cider tomorrow."

"Okay. You might need more than one gallon, though."

Gracie wrote "cider" at the top of a fresh sheet of paper.

"Will your new assistant be working on Saturday?"

"No. She only works on Tuesday and Thursday. I'm not sure how many hours I can afford yet, and I figured I could always offer her more hours if the cash flow is steady enough."

"Okay." Del held her chin and furrowed her brow. The she looked up with an impish grin. "Hey, I know what you can do. . . ."

~

Before long, Del and Gracie had their plans set for the following day. Del tweaked the window display, while Gracie arranged items on the library cart that they could wheel to the sidewalk or display in the store, depending on the weather.

Gracie looked at the clock. "Oh, Del. You've been here all afternoon. I hope I didn't keep you from anything urgent."

"If I'd had anything urgent, I wouldn't have come over. As it happens, I was grateful for the break."

Gracie didn't believe her, and hoped that Del would not have to work through the night to catch up.

"I can't thank you enough for your help. It's only six o'clock," Gracie said, turning the sign in the window to "Closed." "I think I'll be able to get some dinner at home after all. You want to join us?"

Del checked the time on her cell. "Not tonight, thanks. But I'll call tomorrow morning to see if you need any help. You never know, these parents might just beat their own purchasing record."

"Fingers crossed," Gracie said.

~

The next day, the rain had cleared the humidity out of the air, and the blue sky showed the town off to its best advantage. Gracie checked the information sheet Lois had given her. There was a welcome assembly at ten, after which families could choose any of several activities. Lois had made a point of noting that this was the time parents would start to come into town.

The Town and Gown displayed a table of college logo t-shirts, mugs, couch throws, and sweatshirts on the triangle, and the Quill Pen showed off their collection of college postcards, pennants, note cards, and gifts displayed on the sidewalk to attract passersby. Peggy had made up several bouquets and arrangements in crimson and white, Glenville College's colors, and put them on her flower shop's wide front porch. Gracie waved to her as she began work on her own sidewalk sale.

With Spencer's help, Gracie moved the cart outside, and arranged the items she had chosen. She had some books by local authors, some on local or college history, and some college-themed items she still had from the grand opening weekend. To them she had added picture books with fall themes to attract younger siblings, and some titles on the current bestseller lists. As Gracie stood back to admire her work, her daughter came along the sidewalk.

"You don't want kids' stuff on the top shelf," Carrie said after taking one look at the cart. "Little brothers and sisters will want some of the college pencils and key chains and stuff, but they might not see them up top. And where are the photos you have of the college from a long time ago? You can hang them from the sides of the cart. "

"Brilliant," Gracie said, grabbing Carrie for a hug.

"I know," she said. "Now where do you want me to read to the kids who might come by—inside or outside?"

"I thought the kids' section might be best so they can find books to get their parents to buy."

"Cool. What about food?"

"I've already laid out some refreshments."

"And I'll handle the register," Spencer said rubbing his hands together. Gracie smiled.

"That's okay, honey," she said, aware of the history professor's lack of skill with technology. "I'll do the register if you can stay outside and keep an eye out for shoplifters."

Spencer looked a little hurt at the relative unimportance of his assigned task, but agreed to man his post.

Del called a little before eleven, but Gracie was able to assure her that they had things well under control.

"You've already helped enough," Gracie told her, "and we're in good shape. Not half bad for short notice."

"Okay. I have some work to catch up on anyway," Del said.

"Great," Gracie said, looking across the green. The first wave of out-of-towners was already coming into the village.

By eleven-thirty there was a line for lunch at the Steaming Kettle. By noon, Gracie noticed they were nearly out of cider and all the muffins were gone. She looked across the triangle. There was no way they could get more muffins from Kelly while they were jammed with the lunch crowd.

Taking some cash from the register, she asked Carrie to get more cider and oatmeal cookies at the IGA. "Actually," she said, "cookies are pretty easy and economical. Maybe we could do this every weekend."

Carrie gave her a thumbs up, and went on her errand.

Soon the town teemed with people happy to be with their children and happy to part with their money. When there was a brief lull inside the store, Gracie poked her head out to check on Spencer. He was restocking the display in order while recruiting new students to become history majors. He was definitely in his element.

The afternoon flew by. Carrie left at four, and Spencer wheeled the cart back inside at four thirty. By Gracie's closing time of six p.m. the crowds had diminished, but she decided to stay open an extra half hour to be sure to get all the business she could. When she finally closed, Gracie quickly counted the cash, checks, and credit card receipts, and locked them in a small safe in the back office, deciding to leave the final accounting and bank deposit until Monday.

It wasn't until Gracie was home and showered that she thought again of Kristen. She had hoped the girl might stop by, maybe bringing her grandmother. Gracie had only a faint memory of a brief meeting with Cheryl's mother, and hoped that seeing her again would give Gracie a better idea of what made Kristen tick.

As Gracie toweled her hair, Spencer called to her that dinner was ready. When she came into the kitchen, the table was set, and Spencer and Carrie were already dishing out the food. He had grilled some chicken. They had even brewed some tea.

"This is a wonderful ending to a wonderful day," Gracie said. "Thank you both for your help. You made it so much more fun."

"You'll have to replenish your inventory after today." Spencer said with apparent pride.

"I know. Isn't it great?" Gracie stifled a yawn. "And I'll have the money to do it."

"So, are you going to be open again tomorrow?' Carrie asked.

"Nope. We're going to stick to our Sunday closing schedule. This family ought to get some time together. After all, it's Family Weekend."

Carrie smiled. "Cool."

After dinner, Gracie put the food away and did the dishes. "You cooked; I'll clean," she said, giving Spencer a peck on the cheek. When her work was done, she joined Spencer in the living room and picked up a book. Within ten minutes, she was nodding off. Spencer woke her enough to get her to go to bed. She was asleep again before he turned off the light, secure in the knowledge that her store was on a stronger financial footing.

All she had to do was make that deposit at the bank.

CHAPTER EIGHT

The next morning, Gracie awoke at seven forty-five to the sound of church bells and chimes competing for attention. They always rang longer on Family Weekend. She opened her eyes and saw Dickens curled up on the pillow next to her, but Spencer was already out of bed.

Wrapping herself in her robe, she went downstairs, hoping that a pot of tea might already be brewing. Instead, she found Spencer talking on the phone.

"When did it happen?" she heard him ask.

"What happened? Is it Ben?" Gracie did not like the anxious tone in Spencer's voice.

Spencer shook his head and plugged his ear. "Okay. We'll be right over, officer. See you soon." Spencer hung up, but not before Gracie peppered him with questions.

"What's happened? Is someone hurt?"

Spencer waved his hands in front of him. "Calm down. No one is hurt, but . . ."

"But what?"

"It looks like someone broke into your store."

"The store? Why? Did they take anything?"

"They want us down there to check."

"Figures. *Of course* they would break in when I left all that money in the store. Is it all gone?"

"The sooner we get down there, the sooner we'll know. Should we call Adelaide?"

Gracie paused. "No. Let's see how bad it is first."

She dressed in a hurry, and in a few minutes she and Spencer were speed-walking the few blocks to town. The day was overcast, but not too humid. As they rounded the corner of Commonwealth Avenue, Gracie saw a man in civilian clothing and sunglasses pacing in front of the store. As she watched, he stopped, stared in the front window of her shop, shook his head, and paced some more. It was only when they got closer that she could see it was Officer Lowry.

"Hello, officer," Gracie said when they reached the store.

"Ms. McIntyre," he said with a nod. "I'm sorry to have to get you down here like this, but as you can see, you've had a break-in." His voice sounded higher than Gracie remembered.

Gracie looked at her store. The front door stood wide open, and she could see that some chairs were toppled over inside.

"At least the windows are all intact," Spencer noted with some relief in his voice.

"May we go in?" Gracie asked Lowry. "We won't touch anything without checking with you first." She could not read his expression behind the sunglasses, but she supposed that was the point. On the cloudy morning, he certainly wasn't wearing the glasses to protect him from a blaring sun.

"Sure," he said with a casual wave.

Gracie stepped across the threshold, followed by Spencer and Lowry. The gray day provided little light to the store.

"May I turn on the lights?"

"Sure. Go ahead."

Gracie flipped the switches near the door.

"Good Lord," she gasped. "Why would anyone want to do this?" Dozens of books were splayed open on the floor, some with pages creased or ripped out and strewn around the shop. Dust jackets were torn off, and it looked like an arm of one of the upturned chairs was broken.

Spencer whistled. "What a mess." He bent over to pick up some books, but Gracie stopped him.

"Have you finished processing the scene?" she asked the officer. Lowry showed no sign of hearing her. He was looking out the bay window.

"Officer Lowry?" she said, thinking *I'm sorry if my break-in is preventing you from meeting your friends for brunch.* "I asked you a question." Spencer put a calming hand on her arm. Gracie shook it off. If she could not command the officer's undivided attention at the site of a break-in, she did not know who should. And why, she wondered, did he still have his sunglasses on inside the store?

Lowry turned his head toward them. "Yeah. Go ahead and pick things up if you want."

"Were other stores vandalized as well?" Spencer asked as he bent over to sort the books.

"No. Only this one," Lowry replied.

"Why *my* store?" Gracie stood upright with her hands on her hips. "It's like that chalking. Someone wrote 'Go Home' on the sidewalk outside my door soon after the students arrived."

Lowry shrugged. "Probably unrelated." He turned toward the counter. "Did you have money in the cash register?"

"No. I always empty it and leave the drawer open so that anyone who is thinking of breaking in can see that there is no cash there." She snorted. "I guess it didn't work."

"Did you have money stored anywhere else on the premises?"

"Yes. In the safe in back." Gracie went into the back room. The drawers of her filing cabinet stood open and the floor was littered with files.

She checked the safe. It was closed. She held her breath as she punched in the locking code. It opened, and the pouch with the previous day's receipts was still inside. She exhaled with relief. "It's all here," she called as she flipped through the pouch.

"What about these files?" Lowry had come into the back room so quietly that his voice next to her made Gracie jump. He picked up some files, and looked at their labels. Gracie took them from the officer and placed them on her desk.

"Don't worry about these. I will straighten them out myself later on." Even she heard the edginess in her voice.

"Where are your personnel files?"

"They're secure," she said, closing the pouch in the safe. She was glad she had stored Kristen's private information there, too.

"What about your computer? Do you keep any confidential files there?"

"It's password protected," Gracie answered. "I keep track of inventory, sales figures, tax reports, payroll, that sort of thing. Nothing that would be particularly interesting to a burglar."

"What about customer information? Credit card numbers, addresses, telephone numbers?"

"I don't keep customers' credit card numbers. I have a mailing list, but why would anyone care about that?"

"To be on the safe side, we should have our computer experts take a look at it. They should be able to figure out whether someone breached its security." Lowry rubbed his nose and pushed up his sunglasses.

"When will they come? I need to be able to use the computer." Gracie wondered if it was the request or the person who made it that made her feel uneasy.

"Oh, I'll take it to them. They have all their equipment set up at the crime lab in Billington."

"Should I back up my files first?"

"Um, better not to." Lowry looked out the window, then turned back to her. "You don't know what evidence you might disturb. Fingerprints and such. And they might have planted a virus or a worm or something that you could activate. I'll have it back to you in a day or two. You're not opening the store today, are you?"

"No, but I thought I'd get some work done."

"Well, I should have it back to you late Monday or early Tuesday. That will do just as well, won't it?"

Gracie looked at her computer and wondered how she would run her business without having access to it. "Not really."

"Here," Lowry said, handing Gracie a pocket-sized notepad. "Why don't you give me a list of your passwords so that we can open the files and check them for any problems."

Gracie squinted at Officer Lowry. "Really?" Even Spencer did not know the codes she used to encrypt her files. And if the police computer people were so smart, why would they need her codes?

Lowry's glance appeared focused on the pad of paper he was holding, but behind those glasses, Gracie could not tell for sure. "Yeah. Here you go," he said, encouraging her to take it.

Gracie took the pad, found a pen, and prepared to jot down the information Lowry requested. She surmised it was the pad he used to take notes at crime scenes and wondered what he had recorded at her shop. Spencer was talking to Lowry, so Gracie turned her back to them, and flipped through a few pages. There were some unfamiliar names listed with telephone numbers, and some notes in a type of shorthand Gracie could not decipher. None of it appeared to have anything to do with her break-in.

Her emotions that morning had vacillated between relief that the damage was no worse, and anger that anyone would vandalize her store. Now she was infuriated that Lowry did not consider the break-in important enough to make any notes about it.

Gracie turned off her computer, closed the notepad and walked over to where Lowry and Spencer were talking. Handing the pad back to Lowry, she said, "On second thought, I'll just keep the computer and ask that your expert come over here to check it out. I'll be happy to refrain from using it until they come. Then I can input any passwords myself without having to write them down and . . ." she thought about saying *perhaps letting them fall into the wrong hands,* but, instead, finished with, ". . . have to change them all later."

Lowry looked like he was about to object, but instead, he took the pad and put it in his shirt pocket. "Okay. I'll check with them for you."

Spencer asked, "Is there anything more we need to do today?"

Lowry hesitated. "Well . . ." He scanned the store, then looked at the computer. "I guess not. I'll file a report." Then, he added almost as an afterthought, "Oh, and, um, let me know if you find anything missing."

"We will. Thank you, officer," Spencer said as he walked him to the door. "Thank you for your assistance."

"Sure," Lowry said, already out the door. "Be in touch."

"So, how did the thugs get in here?" Gracie asked after Lowry left.

"He said there were no signs of forced entry."

"What does that mean?"

"That the door was unlocked, or the burglars had a key. A lock usually shows some telltale signs if it has been jimmied, and he said yours didn't look like it had been tampered with."

"Unlocked?" Gracie's outrage rattled the ceiling. "Does he think I am foolish enough to leave my store unlocked?"

"Well, I guess he knows that most people around here don't bother to lock their houses."

"Well, still, you'd have to be an idiot to leave a store unlocked. Is that what he thinks? That I am some kind of moron who brought this on myself?" Gracie's face was hot, but no hotter than her temper.

"C'mon, Gracie. He didn't say it *was* unlocked. Only that in cases such as this, where there is no sign of forced entry, that is one of the possibilities. It was probably jimmied."

Gracie wasn't mollified. "I don't like him accusing me of . . ."

"He didn't accuse you of anything. He was just saying. . ."

"I know, I know. But, still, how dare he?" Gracie paused. "And, why would anybody break in here just to damage a few books? I mean," she lowered her voice. "I had a lot of cash in the back room. Granted, I didn't have a neon sign saying 'cash stored here' or anything, but still." Gracie looked around. "And what's the purpose of this vandalism? What did anyone gain from it?"

"I don't think they know why it happened." Spencer said, pushing his fingers through his hair.

"And why just *this* store? Why not any of the others? Is it books or just *me* they don't like? It's not the closest shop to campus, assuming it was college kids. It's not the most obvious target for juveniles. There's no liquor here, no drugs, no cigarettes, they didn't take the money. I don't carry rare books. There's nothing else here to tempt anyone." Gracie looked at Spencer sideways. "You know, you don't very often hear of roving bands of bibliophiles striking bookstores to steal a copy of *A Catcher in the Rye*. It just doesn't make sense."

Spencer chuckled. "Not unless you count that notorious Gilkey fellow, but I don't think he'd bother with Glenville Falls."

"And if the door was locked, *which it was*," Gracie continued as if Spencer hadn't spoken, "is there anyone out there who has a key besides you, me, and Del?"

"And Hal. Doesn't he have a key?" Spencer asked.

"I don't know. I guess he would. I'll ask him. But, he wouldn't do anything like this. I'm his tenant. There's no benefit to him from scaring off a rent-paying tenant."

"Lowry asked if your assistant had a key. I told him she didn't, but he said he wanted to talk to her anyway. Is there anyone else who might have a key?"

Gracie furrowed her brow. "I guess it's possible that Ollie has a key. He had his used furniture store here for years before he moved to Florida. It's possible he never turned his key back in to Hal. But I think Hal changed the locks. Besides, that makes no sense. What possible motive would Ollie have for rampaging through the store?"

"Well, that leaves someone with burglar's tools who knows how to pick a lock."

"But, again, why bother?" Gracie shook her head.

"That is a question for which I have no good answer," Spencer said, shaking his head.

Gracie's stomach grumbled, reminding her that she had not yet eaten.

"Why don't we go home and get some breakfast," Spencer offered. "Then, we can get this place back in shape to open on Tuesday."

Gracie grimaced, but took his hand, and let him lead her out of the store.

~

When they returned after breakfast, Carrie came with them. Together it took them less than an hour to get everything back in order. Spencer set the broken chair aside with a sign saying, "Hal, please mend me!" on it. Gracie repaired and replaced dust jackets, and stacked the irreparably damaged books on her desk. She found that most of the books survived without lasting damage.

"Maybe it was a pyro and they were piling the books up to start a fire and were interrupted," Carrie said.

Gracie wished she had taken a picture of the scene before she had cleaned it up. It might give her a clue as to whether Carrie was right.

Gracie called Officer Lowry. "The books that are ruined aren't valuable, and nothing seems to be missing, but I'll need access to my computer inventory to be certain."

"No need to make an insurance claim, then?" He did not sound surprised.

"Not with my deductible. I'll talk to my landlord about getting a better lock."

"Sounds like a good idea," Lowry answered. "You sure you don't want me to bring in your computer, just to take a little look?"

"No, thanks. Let me know when your computer expert wants to come here."

There was a pause on the line, and Gracie wondered what distracted Lowry this time.

"Oh, and another thing," Gracie said. "Could I have copies of the crime scene photos?"

Lowry still didn't speak.

"Officer Lowry?"

"Not my decision," he said, and hung up.

Gracie wondered about Lowry's interest in the computer. If the cash was safe, it seemed unlikely the computer had been invaded. If the burglars had wanted the information she stored on the computer, wouldn't they simply have taken it with them?

"So, why didn't they take the computer?"

"What?" Spencer asked.

"It's portable, relatively new, and probably worth something on resale. Why is the computer still here?"

Spencer frowned at the ceiling and shook his head. "I can't imagine."

"Nothing about this whole mess makes sense."

"Ready to go?" Carrie asked. Spencer nodded and moved toward the door.

"You guys go ahead. I still have some stuff I want to do here," Gracie said.

Carrie groaned. "What are you going to do without your computer?"

"I want to give the place a good cleaning. I can't stand the feeling that someone was in here just to make a mess of things. I won't feel right until I have cleaned them out of here. It won't take me too long. I'll be home in an hour or so."

"Okay, but be sure to lock up after us," Spencer said, giving her a hug.

Gracie followed them to the front and locked the door.

She glanced across the triangle and saw students strolling through town with their families. *This was supposed to be such a happy weekend.* She sighed, then turned to her work.

When at last she had cleaned the place to her satisfaction, and was winding the cord to the vacuum cleaner, she glanced outside again. The triangle was mostly clear. Families needed to head for home early, she guessed, and looked down. Then she looked up again.

There was a young woman standing across the triangle in front of Peggy's flower shop, staring at the bookstore. *Is that Kristen?* she wondered.

Gracie almost choked on her next thought: "Was this the culprit returning to the scene of the crime?" She remembered the seeds of doubt Officer Lowry had planted. She had never done a background check. She chided herself for the thought when she had no reason to suspect Kristen of anything. After putting the vacuum cleaner away, she looked again. The girl was still there, so Gracie went to the door and waved. She was pleased when Kristen waved back.

"Come on in," Gracie called to her.

Kristen shrugged, and after checking for traffic jogged over to where Gracie stood.

"I didn't know you were coming in today," Kristen said.

"I hadn't planned to, but circumstances demanded my presence."

"Oh, Family Weekend business?"

"We were busy yesterday, but I still planned to be closed today." Gracie watched Kristen's face for her reaction. "We got a call early this morning that the store was vandalized sometime overnight."

Kristen's face remained placid. No surprise. No guilt. "Who would want to vandalize your store?"

"I have been wondering the same thing," Gracie said. "The police said that there was no forced entry. They say that means that either the door was unlocked, or the person had a key." Gracie wondered if Kristen would have had time to copy her key when she left her alone in the store on Thursday. Why hadn't she thought to take her keys with her?

"Did they take anything?" Kristen looked around the store.

"They ripped pages out of a few books, and turned over a couple of chairs, but didn't do too much damage. I've spent the past couple of hours getting things back in order. It doesn't look like they took anything, except maybe my sense of security."

"Huh, funny." Kristen said it matter-of-factly.

"Not to me." Gracie pursed her lips as she tried to keep the flash of anger from her voice. "I think the police officer who called us thought I left the door unlocked, and that some kids came in and tossed the place as a prank."

Gracie cringed. She had watched her father, once an accomplished lawyer, fall victim to dementia. She knew it could be inherited, and did not want to think she might have had such a lapse. She thought she had locked the door, but could she be sure? "Perhaps I'm getting a little absent-minded. All those years with Professor Adams rubbing off at last," Gracie added with a smile.

"I don't think you'd forget that."

Gracie felt some relief at that. "Well, I hardly ever lock my house door, so I suppose it is possible. If it is, as Professor Adams says, just a random act of violence, we might never know for sure. I don't get the feeling it's high on the police's list of cases to crack."

Kristen shrugged and looked away. Gracie turned to look her in the eye.

"Did your grandmother come to Family Weekend?"

"Nah. She said it was too far, and she couldn't stay overnight, so it wasn't worth it."

"Oh, that's too bad." It seemed rather harsh for Mrs. Walsh to tell Kristen that visiting her "wasn't worth it."

"Oh, well, I really didn't expect her to come."

"Perhaps some other time." Gracie couldn't tell whether Kristen was disappointed or relieved that her grandmother hadn't come.

Kristen shifted from one foot to the other and looked toward the door. "I'd better get back up to school. See you on Tuesday."

"See you then."

The bell over the door jingled as if nothing out of the ordinary had happened that day. Gracie put away the rest of her cleaning supplies and left through the front door, locking it and checking it twice.

She started toward home when a thought struck her. She turned back and examined the front door. The lock was clean—not a scratch on the lock, not a nick in the paint, and not a bit of dust on it anywhere.

CHAPTER NINE

Gracie spent the rest of Sunday and all day Monday trying to put the break-in out of her mind. She did her banking early Monday morning and heaved a sigh of relief when she no longer had to worry about cash lying around. She went home at midday, and found Dickens lying in a patch of sun on the living room carpet.

"How you doing, sweetie?" Gracie said, bending over to stroke his fur. He lifted his head and closed his eyes. Then he put his head down again and rolled on his back. She ruffled the fur on his tummy. He did feel a little thinner. She went into the kitchen to check his food dish. His breakfast was still in his dish—dry and untouched.

She looked at the clock, drumming her fingers on the kitchen countertop. Spencer was in class. Starting the tea kettle, she looked up the vet's number and punched it into her ancient flip phone.

"Village Animal Hospital," a young woman said.

"Hi. This is Gracie McIntyre. My husband, Spencer Adams, brought our cat, Dickens, in last week because he hasn't been eating well, and I wondered if you had the results of the blood tests you took then."

C a r o l   L.   W r i g h t

"Can you hold please?"

Gracie was about to answer when she heard music come over the line. In a moment, a voice said, "Hello."

"Hi . . ." Gracie began, then realized it was a recorded ad for heartworm treatments. The music returned when the ad was over.

Gracie hung on for what seemed to be several minutes while the ad/music/ad/music pattern repeated itself. The teakettle boiled, and she poured the hot water into her waiting mug.

"Okay, I have the heartworm commercial memorized," she said into the phone. "May I please speak to a real person now?" As if she had heard her, the young woman came back on the line.

"What did you say your name was?"

Gracie knew that Dickens' vet records were under Spencer's last name. "It's under Adams," she said.

"Okay, Mrs. Adams." Gracie heard the flipping of papers. "It looks like the lab work is back and everything is within normal ranges."

"So why isn't he eating?"

"It doesn't appear to be organic. From what it says here, the doctor thinks he might be depressed."

"How do you treat that? Send him to a shrink? Give him Prozac?" Gracie was trying to be funny, but the person at the other end displayed no sense of humor.

"The best thing is to pay him extra attention. Spoil him a little. Maybe give him some new kinds of foods, play with him more, buy some new toys, that sort of thing. We have high-calorie foods here, too, if you see him losing more weight. His weight is just on the light side of normal, but if it gets worse, we also have some appetite stimulants we can prescribe. "

Gracie looked at her pet. "What can cause depression in a cat?"

"Lots of things. Being too confined, vitamin deficiency, lack of companionship, illness can all contribute. It says here that he's alone all day?"

"Yes, and that's a change for him."

"Well, you might think about getting another cat to keep him company, or hiring a cat sitter to come in when the family can't be around. If he has someone to play with, he'll get more exercise, and that can help him feel better."

"Anything else?" Gracie carried her mug into the living room and sank into a chair. Neither option the vet's assistant had mentioned sounded good to her. The notion of bringing a kitten into a house where no one was home to train it sounded like a sure way to end up with clawed furniture and shredded drapes. Gracie's natural thrift and current financial pinch made hiring someone to keep her cat company an extravagance.

"Watch him, and see if his appetite returns, and if you have any more problems with him, you can call for an appointment. . . . Oh, and you can bring him in any time to check his weight. It would be a good idea to keep an eye on that."

Gracie rubbed her forehead. "Okay. Thank you."

"Call anytime."

"Thanks." Gracie hung up the phone and looked at her cat. "Depressed? Seriously, Dickens?" She walked over, lowered herself down, sat on the floor next to him and stroked his fur. He raised his head, looked at her, and started to purr. "Maybe you do just need a little more companionship."

~

Humidity had returned by Tuesday when she walked to the store. She attracted more than the usual attention, but could only return her friends' waves with a nod. She felt like she had packed for a long trip with her backpack, a bag from the Furry Friends pet shop in her left hand, and a cat carrier in her right.

"You might have lost some weight, Dickens," she said, putting the carrier down when she arrived at her shop door, "but ten pounds of cat plus a carrier is still a lot of dead weight to carry." She bent her elbow and rubbed her arm. "If I do this every day, I'll be ready to arm wrestle with the best of them by Christmas."

Dickens peered out the front of the carrier and watched as she checked to make sure her lock was secure before inserting her key. All was as it should be—just as she was sure it had been every other day when she came to work.

She brought Dickens and his paraphernalia into the back room, closed the door, and opened his pen. The cat stayed inside for a few moments before stepping out, one paw at a time.

"What do you think of this place, boy?" Gracie said as she pulled a small litter box out of the pet store bag and a plastic jug of kitty litter from her backpack. She set it up near the back door, and let Dickens inspect it. In a moment he was digging in the litter, marking it as his own.

Gracie emptied the rest of the contents of her bags. She had brought three saucers, some canned and dry cat food, a few new toys, and some cat treats.

"Okay, buddy. We're going to get you eating again." The cat was hunched up, creeping around the perimeter of the back room, sticking his whiskers into every corner and investigating each item within reach. He scratched at Gracie's desk chair in a behavior she knew was intended to mark his new territory. From there, he investigated her desktop, jumping up onto the filing cabinet adjacent to it, and down onto the table that held a combination copier/fax machine/printer.

"Careful there, kitty," Gracie said, lifting him off the printer top and placing him on the floor. I don't want you to break anything. She went to the small sink in her kitchen unit and poured some water into one of the saucers. Dickens followed her and jumped up onto the kitchenette counter. Then he studied the distance to the top of the refrigerator before scaling it as well. From there he could see out the window to the back alley. He played with the cord on the window blind while Gracie filled a dish with dry food. She thought she would wait to put out some canned food until the cat felt more at home.

"Sorry, fella. There is no birdfeeder out there for you to watch."

She heard the bell jingle over the front door, and peeked into the shop to see who had entered. It was Hal Doyle. She slipped out of the back room and closed the door behind her.

"Hal, how did you know you are just the person I wanted to see? I was going to come over to your store as soon as I dropped my, uh, stuff off here." She glanced toward the back room and saw a golden paw reach under the door.

"I beat you to it," Hal said with a grin. "I have some help over there, so I thought I'd come over and see how things were."

"Things are fine now, but we got a call early Sunday morning about a break-in."

"You're kidding—you shoulda called me. Did they break anything?" He looked around as if he expected the ceiling to fall in on him.

"One chair needs some repair, but I don't think anything's missing. They made a mess and left, but it's all cleared up now."

"Let me see the broken chair."

Gracie showed him to the damaged wing-back. "That sign is Spencer's idea of a joke," she said, a little embarrassed.

"I can fix this for you, no problem," Hal said, laying the chair on its side. "Just some glue and maybe a couple screws." He held the leg in its proper position. "It'll be good as new. No charge."

"Great. Thanks, Hal."

Hal righted the chair, stood, and brushed his hands together. "You're insured, aren't you Gracie? Things like this happen to people when they aren't insured, and it can ruin them."

"I'm insured."

"I wouldn't have a store without it. One slippery floor could cost you your business if the wrong person takes a spill."

"I know. I didn't lose anything of great monetary value, so there's no need to make an insurance claim."

"Oh, that's good. Once you make a claim, your rates can skyrocket. It can go up so high that a new business can't afford it and they drop the insurance. Then next rainstorm, Pow!" He clapped his hands together. "It can ruin you."

Gracie wondered how many other ways Hal knew to ruin a business. "Well, I'm okay in that department. Thanks for your concern, though." Gracie hesitated, trying to figure out the best way of raising the next topic. "Hal, there's something else I wanted to talk to you about."

"Shoot."

"Apparently whoever came into the store might have had a key. Do you know if anybody has one besides me?"

"Nah. Well I got one. In my back office."

"What about Ollie? Might he still have a key to the front door?"

"Old Ollie?" Hal looked at the ceiling, picking up his baseball cap and scratching his balding head. "Yeah. He probably still does have a key. But it doesn't matter if he does." He put his cap back in place.

"Doesn't matter?" Gracie said, placing her palms on her hips, trying to remain calm.

"Nah. I changed the lock when you took over the lease. No problem with old Ollie."

"Oh." Gracie let out a breath. "That's good to know."

"Now me, I have a security system in my store. Too much inventory not to. And, I get a nice discount on my insurance for having one, too. You might think about it."

"I'm thinking more about getting a second lock added to the front door."

"You want one? I can put one in for you. I have some in stock next door. I'll get it installed for you, if you want. No charge."

"That would make me feel more secure. Thanks, Hal."

When Hal left, Gracie hurried back to check on the cat. He had found an empty box under the table and had curled up there. Gracie tucked a towel she had brought from home around him, hoping it would make him feel more comfortable. His food dish looked undisturbed. She brought out a rubber ball with a jingle bell inside, and bounced it across the floor. Dickens barely opened his eyes.

"Exercise is supposed to be good for you, boy. Come and play." She went after the ball and bounced it again. Next she opened a bag of kitty treats, and stooped under the table to put a couple in the box with him. Dickens ignored them as well. "C'mon, boy. You're not alone now. You have to snap out of this," she said, stroking his side.

The phone rang, and Gracie nearly bumped her head on the underside of the table, trying to get to it before it went to voice mail.

"Gracie's Garret," she answered, a bit breathless.

"Hey, girl, you never called to tell me how wonderfully Family Weekend went." It was Del. "Did you sell everything in sight? 'Cuz if so, I would be happy to help you spend all the profits."

"Hi, Del." Gracie smiled so that her voice would sound upbeat. "We did very well on Saturday."

"But?" Del could hear the hesitation in her voice. Gracie decided to tell her at once, like ripping a bandage off.

"Someone broke in on Saturday night. They didn't take anything; they just threw some books around and did minimal damage. I just can't use my computer until the police have done whatever they're going to do with it, but otherwise, things are fine."

"Fine? That doesn't sound fine. And I'll tell you what else isn't fine. When my best friend has her—no our— new business broken into and she doesn't even call when it happens. That is not fine."

"Everything's okay. There's nothing to tell."

Del sniffed. "You know, it's not as if I'm not involved, too. I'm your silent partner, remember?"

Gracie grimaced. There was nothing silent about Del.

~

After hanging up with Del, Gracie checked her phone messages. There was one from Del and one from Hal, but since she had talked to them both since the messages were left, she deleted them. The third message was from Kristen. Tuesday was her regular day to work, but she called in sick. Gracie wondered if the coughs that interrupted Kristen's message were genuine or the product of the kind of acting skills kids perfected to use on days with math tests. It didn't matter. Gracie was in no mood for company. Fortunately, it looked like it was going to be a quiet day.

Still it bothered her that there was no message from Officer Lowry.

"I can't get much paperwork done without my computer," she said aloud. Dickens raised his head and blinked.

Gracie tapped her index finger on her desk and scowled at her computer. She was tempted to just turn it on. What was the worst that could happen?

She let her fingers float over the keyboard. *I could just check my email. Surely they wouldn't break in to send me some damaging email.*

She overcame the temptation when her glance shifted to the stack of damaged books on her desk. She opened one that appeared to have the most damage. Flipping to the remnants of the missing pages, she realized that the pages were cut out—not torn. *This guy used a knife on my books,* she thought. *That implies more anger than just pulling pages out. And premeditation. What was he so mad about?*

The bell rang over the door and Gracie jumped. She went into the shop and saw Officer Lowry in jeans, a light-blue, button-down shirt, and his omnipresent sunglasses.

"Hello," he said, leaning against the counter. "I just wanted to tell you that, uh, we have decided that you can use your computer."

"Oh?"

"Yeah. The computer experts said there is no, uh, probable cause to check it out."

Probable cause? Gracie knew from her days practicing law that "probable cause" referred to a sufficient reason to believe that a crime had been committed. Authorities needed probable cause to get a search or arrest warrant, but not to search places, or in this case a computer, when the owner granted them permission.

"I don't understand, Officer." Gracie narrowed her eyes, trying to see past the tinted plastic and read the policeman's face.

"Nothin' to understand. You can use your computer is all. But I want you to know that I, uh, we're not taking this lightly. I need to know everything you know about your clerk. Looks like we're gonna run that background check after all." He took the notebook from his shirt pocket. "What did you say her name was?"

"I don't think I mentioned it." Gracie could not account for her sudden urge to shield Kristen. She rested her arms on the back of a tall chair.

"I'll need her permanent address, social, and date of birth from your records," Lowry continued as if Gracie had not spoken.

"Well, I uh . . ."

"I told you. You can't be too careful. An average employee can steal you blind, and a really clever one can ruin you." His tone was businesslike, but Gracie detected a note of paternalism, even though the man was probably ten years younger than Gracie.

So Hal has company in his "Ways to Ruin a Business" club, Gracie thought. "Do you have any particular reason to suspect my employee? If she had wanted to steal from me, wouldn't she have done it when I left her in charge of the store?"

Gracie thought she saw a flinch on the officer's part, and his face flushed. "Just checking all the angles." He slapped his notebook shut.

"If you want to talk to her, she should be here on Thursday. You could stop by then."

Lowry's brows came together and he looked out the window. "Look, Ms. McIntyre," he said, turning toward her again. His voice had lost its paternalistic tone. "We don't want any trouble in town. You've already had more than most places see in a year and you've been open what? Two weeks?"

"Three," Gracie mumbled to herself.

"I think you should cooperate."

"I *am* cooperating, Officer. I haven't used my computer for three days, I have told you how to contact my employee, and," she said, her voice getting louder, "I didn't leave my store unlocked. Beyond that I really don't know what more I can do."

"You will see me here on Thursday," he said, nostrils flaring. With that he turned and left. The banging of the door behind him drowned out the bell.

Gracie went into the back room, shaking a little from the unexpected confrontation. *I'm the victim. Why does he treat me like the enemy?* She slumped into her chair, then looked at the box under the table. Dickens was gone. He had not touched his food as far as she could see. She looked around the back room, but could not find so much as a strand of yellow fur.

I left the door open when I went out to answer the bell, she thought. He could be anywhere in the store.

She spent the next several minutes searching every shelf, chair and perching point for her cat, but had no luck. Where was he?

She heard a tapping on her front window, and looked up to see Wendell Owens waving at something in the display. She went over to see what he was looking at and found Dickens, curled up in front of an array of picture books, his paw covering his nose.

Wendell came into the store. "Nice window dressing you have there," the newspaperman said. "How do you get him to do that?"

"He's a cat. He does what he wants." Gracie laughed. "I had lost track of him. I'm so relieved you found him there."

"Are you interested in having his picture in the paper? I have a nice spot for it in this week's edition."

"Sure. Free publicity is always welcome."

Wendell took out his camera and took two pictures through the glass and one from inside the store. Dickens barely noticed the fuss. "That ought to do it," Wendell said, snapping one more. "You want one of you with the cat?"

Gracie looked over at her sleeping pet. "No. Let him rest."

"Okay," Wendell said, taking out his notebook. "What's his name?"

"Dickens," Gracie said.

"Like the author? That's great." Wendell chortled and wrote it down.

"Yes, like the author, but also because he can be a bit of a handful from time to time. He likes to climb. When he was younger he would sometimes perch on top of the dresser and pounce on your back when you were making the bed." Gracie laughed at the memory. "Spencer just hated that." Gracie shook her head and hoped her cat might show that kind of energy again one day.

CHAPTER TEN

The next day, Gracie left early for the store. After dropping Dickens off, she locked up and went next door to Doyle's Hardware.

"Mornin' Gracie," Hal said when he saw her walk in.

"Good morning, Hal." The air inside the hardware store smelled as old as the worn floor boards and ancient shelves. The floor squeaked under Gracie's slight frame. After the refurbishing Hal had done on her shop, she wondered that he never repaired his own. *A case of the shoemaker's children going barefoot,* she thought.

"What can I do for ya?"

"After yesterday, I got to thinking about what you said about your security system. Can you recommend a good company?"

"Sure. Got their card right here," he said, looking through a stack of cards on the counter near his telephone. "Here it is. L&S Security." He handed the card to Gracie.

"May I keep this?"

"Sure. I got others. Besides, I have a sticker on my phone with their number, and it's on the keypad in the back that's hooked up to the alarm. All state of the art."

Gracie smiled at the incongruity of a modern security system in an antique-looking shop.

"Thanks, Hal," she said, turning to leave. She stopped when she got to the door and turned back. "Say, I wonder if you can help me with something else."

"If I can, I will."

"Do you know anything about a town police officer named Lowry?"

"Richie Lowry? Funny you'd ask. Yeah, I've known him pretty much his whole life."

"What kind of person is he?"

Hal swiped off his baseball hat, scratched his head, and replaced the cap in one motion. "Y'know, I remember Rich when he was a kid. He was, well, let me put it this way. He was just about the last guy you'd expect to be a cop."

"Really?" Gracie tried to make her expression appear interested, not judgmental.

"Yeah. He straightened up okay, y'know. Decided to catch the bad guys 'stead of bein' one of 'em."

Gracie moved closer. "What did he do as a kid?"

"Oh, him and his friends would go around town. Too much time on their hands. Nobody at home. They'd knock over trash cans, throw rocks at street lights, some minor shopliftin'."

"Not too serious, I guess."

"Yeah, but by high school, they got into drinkin', joyridin', drag racin', stuff like that. Heard stories about drugs, thefts. Never knew for sure. Then, all of a sudden it just stopped. Richie straightened out. Grew out of it, I guess. Next thing I knew, he was workin' on gettin' to be a cop."

"A victory for the juvenile justice system?" Gracie smirked, crossing her arms and leaning against a shelf. It wobbled, so she straightened up again.

"Could be." Hal scratched his stubble. "Or maybe just scared straight."

Gracie's gaze moved toward Hal's back room. "Do you keep the key to my store handy?" she said nodding toward the doorway.

Hal turned and followed her nod. "Yeah, sure do," he said reaching inside and pulling out a ring that held a dozen or more keys. "All my property keys are right here." He tossed it to Gracie. "Here. See if you can find yours."

All the keys were similar in shape, but most of them were tarnished. Only one was a bright new brass. And it looked familiar.

"Is this the one?" Gracie asked, holding up the new key.

"Sure is. Told you I put a new lock on when you took over the lease."

Gracie tilted her head. "Did you tell anyone else about the new lock?"

"Don't think so." He frowned. "Well, I mighta told old Ollie. Least I think I told him he didn't need to send back his old key."

Gracie pursed her lips. "Have you heard anything from Ollie lately?"

"Can't say I have. Why?"

"Oh, I'm not sure. I'm just trying to puzzle this out. There are just too many missing pieces."

"Maybe that's 'cause there's not much there." Hal gave Gracie a knowing look.

"Maybe you're right." Gracie shook her head. "Um, how long have you known Ollie, Hal?"

"Well, went to high school together, him and me. He was a year ahead, but we played ball on the same team. I guess we've known each other most our lives. His kid worked for me some years back."

"His kid?"

"Sure. He has two—a boy and a girl. Kenny, the boy, worked for me when he first got outta high school. Dated my daughter, but it didn't go nowhere. That was a long time back. She's married now. Lives in West Springfield with two little kids. Married a computer guy."

"Does Kenny still live around here?"

"Kenny? Sure." Hal's eyes rolled to the ceiling. "Seems to me, him and Lowry was friends." He wagged his head and laughed. "Small world, ain't it?"

"Well, small town, anyway." Gracie was not laughing.

~

Thursday arrived, and with it, Dickens' third day in the store. By then he recognized the place, and when Gracie opened his pet carrier, he came out and went right over to her desk chair to scratch it. Gracie scowled, but she did not have the heart to scold him.

She checked for phone messages, but there were none. Gracie wondered if that meant she would see Kristen. She was virtually certain she would see Officer Lowry.

After putting change in the cash register and turning the "Closed" sign to "Open," Gracie picked up the new edition of the *Glenville Falls Gazette*. Flipping through the pages, she found the photo of Dickens. The caption read, "Dickens the cat curls up with a good book in the window of Gracie's Garret Bookshop on Commonwealth Avenue." She smiled and showed the paper to the cat.

"See this, boy? You're famous."

Dickens did not even glance her way. He made a stop by his dry food dish, ate a bit, and lapped up some water before leaving the back room to cruise the store. Gracie was happier with that than she was with the photo in the paper.

Next Gracie checked the police blotter. One thing about a small town was that everybody knew everyone else's business, and the local paper was one reason why. The report mentioned a call to campus, an underage drinking violation, an auto accident near the highway, but nothing more.

"Where's the story about my break-in?" she said aloud. "Now that I think of it, Wendell didn't even ask me about it. It's not like him to miss a story like that."

The bell rang and Gracie checked the clock. *Kristen's early today,* she thought. She left the back room, and instead saw Professor Chaudhry enter, carrying a brief case.

"Hello again, Mrs. Adams," he said, nodding at her.

"Welcome back. I hoped I would see you here again."

"As I said, Mrs. Chaudhry likes me to get out of the house. I believe she would prefer that I had not retired. There is just too much husband around for her, I fear." His shoulders rocked in amusement.

Gracie grinned. "I see you have brought some work with you?"

"Yes. I wonder if it would be too inconvenient if I were to occupy one of your very commodious-looking chairs for an hour or so."

"Not at all. Would you like some tea?"

"Tea would be lovely."

"I hope to have other refreshments on Saturdays, if you're interested in coming then."

"I will bear that in mind, thank you."

Gracie went into the back room and heated a cup of water in the microwave. "Is Earl Grey okay?" she called out to the professor.

"Who?"

"No, would you like Earl Grey tea? I have other varieties as well."

"Any good black tea as long as it is from the *camellia sinensis* plant. Those flowery herbal concoctions are not tea."

"A connoisseur. How nice."

Gracie went into the back room and rethought her options. Instead of using the microwave, she filled the coffee urn with water and plugged it in. When the water was hot, she drew a cup of water into her ceramic teapot, swirled it around, and poured it out.

"Why do you always throw the first cup of water out?" she remembered Ben asking when he was about Carrie's age.

Gracie had thought a moment. Was it to warm the pot? Was it to rinse it out? Finally, she gave him the only answer she was sure was correct. "Because my mother always did." New Englanders love their traditions, whether they know why they follow them or not.

After putting tea in the pot, she poured in the steaming water. She had chosen a tea she enjoyed but rarely served since most of her friends could not tell one from another. She had a suspicion that the professor could.

She placed the teapot on a tray, then opened a cupboard and brought out an opened package of tea biscuits. She took a bite of one to be certain they were not stale, and placed three more on a plate. She frowned at using a paper plate, but it was all she had. Then she washed and dried the single bone china tea cup and saucer she had dared bring to the store. She added a paper napkin to the tray, wishing it could have been linen. When she was satisfied, she brought the tray to the front of the store, but she did not see the professor. *Did he leave?*

"Professor?" she called.

"Over here." His voice came from behind a grouping of bookshelves. He had found the most secluded corner in the store. It held two chairs with a small table between them. The shelves surrounding them held philosophy, history, and biography, but no economics. Gracie wondered why he chose to sit there.

"How lovely," he said, admiring the tray when she set it on the table.

"I hope you enjoy it. May I pour?"

"Please do."

He took a sip of the tea, closed his eyes, and savored it. "Darjeeling . . . First Flush. Delightful."

"Would you like milk or sugar?" Gracie wished she had lemon, but knew she did not.

Professor Chaudhry only smiled. "My dear, tea such as this is meant to be enjoyed for itself, not buried by other flavors."

Gracie grinned. "I couldn't agree more."

The bell over the door rang again.

"Excuse me, please, professor," Gracie said, sorry to leave such an enjoyable respite. Walking around the bookshelves, she saw Officer Lowry leaning against the front counter in full uniform, including his sunglasses.

"Any progress with the case, officer?" Gracie asked, hoping not too loudly. She did not want to disturb her customer. The sight of Officer Lowry spurred annoyance in her, but she tried to appear cordial.

"No." His answer was blunt. "I still want to talk to your employee." *Was that a sneer?*

"She is not here. I don't expect her quite yet," Gracie said, checking the clock and realizing Kristen could arrive at any moment.

"I'll come back later then." He turned to go.

"If you don't mind my asking, what other leads are you pursuing?" she said stepping toward him, hoping he would not leave until she had some answers.

"There aren't any. Chances are this one won't be solved." Even though he wore sunglasses, Gracie could tell he was not looking at her.

Gracie drew in a breath. She was not going to let it go at that. "It wasn't in the police blotter in today's paper. I wondered why."

"Just an oversight. It happens."

He's not the least surprised. "Might I, at least, have a copy of the police report?"

"What do you need that for? You're not filing an insurance claim are you? Because you said yourself you didn't lose anything of value, and that would be fraud." He put his hand on his sidearm. "Just a friendly warning."

Gracie detected nothing friendly in his tone. "It's a public record, isn't it? Don't I have a right to know what's on the record about a break-in at my store?"

He hesitated. "I suppose."

"Is there some reason you don't want me to see the report?" She assumed he had written that she had left the door unlocked, and did not want her to know it. "Are you hiding something from me?"

Lowry stuck out his jaw. "I'll bring a copy of it over for you." He turned toward the door.

"Thank you. I would appreciate it."

"I'll come back when your clerk is here." He left and walked toward the town hall at the other end of the green.

Gracie peered around the bookshelf to where Professor Chaudhry sat. He appeared to be concentrating on reading a book. Dickens lay in the chair next to him.

She turned back and sighed. The soothing effect of spending a moment with the professor was lost because of Officer Lowry. When she was a lawyer, Gracie dealt with confrontations with contentious people on a daily basis. It was one thing she definitely did not miss when she left her practice. But in the intervening years, she had become less inured to conflict, and knew she was more affected by it.

By the time Kristen arrived for her shift, Gracie was once again sorting through her holiday orders and deep into her paperwork, and Professor Chaudhry appeared content to sit and read, surrounded by books and a yellow tiger cat.

"Sorry I couldn't come on Tuesday," Kristen said as she entered the back room and dropped off a sweater. She was a little hunched over, her nose was red, and there was a rasp in her voice that told Gracie she had indeed been fighting a cold.

"That's okay. I hope you're feeling better."

"Some. What do you want me to do today?"

"It would be nice if you could do some dusting, and then reshelve that stack of books I left on the counter. Oh, and a police officer will come by to see you sometime later today. He just wants to ask you if you have any ideas about the break-in." Gracie watched for Kristen's reaction, looking for some sign that she was trustworthy.

Kristen straightened up. "Why should I know anything? I wasn't even here. I don't know anything about it. I hardly even know anyone in town." She pulled a tissue from her pocket and dabbed at her sore-looking nose.

Gracie held out her hands. "Shhh. We have a customer. I think the officer just wants to cover all the bases."

"Well, you can tell him that I don't know anything," Kristen hissed. "Tell him to leave me alone, okay? Besides, I have to leave early today anyway. That's okay isn't it?"

Gracie squirmed a bit. Was Kristen hiding something? If so, Gracie wanted to know what it was. But Kristen's expression was so pathetic that Gracie agreed to let her leave at one o'clock.

Kristen got to work, and when the clock in the town hall tower struck noon, Professor Chaudhry gathered his things. Gracie heard him greet Kristen as he left. She came out of the back room to say good-bye, but he was already out the door. Kristen looked back toward Gracie and saw Dickens, apparently for the first time.

"Wait, mister," she called as she ran to the door and opened it. "You forgot your cat."

~

Officer Lowry arrived just before four. He looked around the store. "Where's your clerk?" he said with his lips drawn into a frown.

"She left early, but I asked her if she knew anything that might be helpful and she said she didn't."

The officer scoffed. "Well that's hardly worth anything."

"Perhaps, but it's all I know. Did you bring the report?"

Lowry handed her a piece of paper.

"Thank you," she said without a smile.

"No problem." Lowry turned to go, and then stopped halfway to the door. "You know, ma'am, I am only trying to help you." With that he left.

"Help, my eye," Gracie said after the door closed. She took the report to the back room and laid it on the desk to look at after the shop closed.

When six o'clock arrived, Gracie locked the front door, and went into the back room to examine the report. As soon as she sat at her desk, her cat leaped into her lap.

"Well, Dickens, you look happier," she said scratching his neck. "Did you have a good time today?"

He responded by purring and rubbing against her chin. "Oh good," she said with some relief in her voice. "Now let's see what we can figure out from this police report, shall we?"

The paper was a photocopy of an incident report form. "Glenville Falls Police Department" was printed on the top under which was a row of small boxes. Lowry had filled one with the date, and another with the time: 8:00 a.m. Below that were several sections set off in large blocks, a few of which had been filled in by hand. The top block was for a description of the incident, which Lowry had listed as "malicious mischief."

"Hmm," Gracie grumbled. "You're mischievous, Dickens. Whoever broke in here was a vandal."

Next was a block for "Victim name and address." Lowry had written the store's name and location. The next two blocks, for vehicle information and witness names and addresses, Lowry had filled with hash marks.

"They're not applicable," she said as if explaining it to her cat.

Next was a section filled with short questions followed by check boxes in columns headed by "Yes" and "No." They included whether a weapon was used, a suspect named or located, property damaged, property lost, significant evidence present, or an arrest made. All the "no" boxes were checked except for "property damaged" and "crime scene processed." They were checked as "yes." Gracie thought about the clean lock on her door. Not even fingerprinted. *Great job of scene processing, Lowry.* She wondered if she should show him that a weapon was used: a knife cut pages from her books.

The last section consisted of a block with horizontal lines for a narrative of the officer's observations. It was blank except for a scribbled note saying "loss less than $100." Lowry had signed the form in the appropriate block at the bottom.

"At least there is nothing here about me having left the door unlocked." Gracie said as she folded the paper and stuffed it into her bag. She urged Dickens into his carrier, and headed for home.

As she walked along, she tried to remember the details of the incident report. There was something about it that felt odd to her, but she could not quite put her finger on it. She would have to study it more when she got home.

CHAPTER ELEVEN

After dinner, Gracie moved to the sofa and took the police report from her bag. She hadn't seen a police report in years, but something about this one did not seem right.

"What's that?" Spencer asked, looking over from behind the *Boston Globe*.

"Police report on the break-in," Gracie said, tapping an index finger against the temple of her reading glasses.

"What's wrong with it?"

Gracie looked up. "What do you mean?"

"You clearly don't like what you see. What's wrong with it? Does he say the doddering old fool who owned the place just forgot she left her shop door open and the wind blew her books around?"

Gracie smiled. "Nooo, it doesn't say that. It doesn't say much at all, in fact," she said looking back at the paper. "I just wonder . . ."

Carrie bounced into the room and placed a sheet of paper on top of the report in Gracie's lap. "Hey, Mom, I need you to sign this permission slip."

"What's it for?" she said, reading the form. Carrie had already filled it in with her name and student number, and checked "yes" in the permission box. All it needed was Gracie's or Spencer's signature.

Carrie sat down next to her. "It's a field trip to go to Springfield to the Science Museum. It's really neat. They've got this live animal section with things from different eco-systems, and an African section, and a dinosaur hall, and best of all, a planetarium." Carrie's eyes were wide with anticipation. "The whole ninth grade is going and we're going to spend the whole day. It sounds really cool. And it's really cheap." Carrie's face turned to concern. "I can go, can't I?"

Gracie hesitated when she looked at the cost.

"If you don't want to pay for it I'll use my babysitting money," Carrie said, but her tone clearly said she didn't want to pay the fee herself.

"I see it's next Wednesday."

"Yeah. That's not a problem is it?"

"No, I don't think so. Do we have anything going on next Wednesday, Spencer?"

"I'm teaching," he said without looking over.

"And I'll be back by six o'clock. You're not even home then, so what could be the problem?" There was an edge in Carrie's voice.

It stung Gracie to hear it, but her daughter was correct. Even if Carrie went on the field trip, she would likely be home ahead of Gracie. *No,* she thought. *I will make a point of getting home early that day, to hear about her trip as soon as she gets in.* It was one of the things she missed about being around when her kids got home from school.

"What about lunch?"

"The school is giving us box lunches. It's all part of the fee."

Gracie looked over toward Spencer who was still hiding behind the newspaper. "I don't see a problem with it, do you honey?"

No answer.

"Honey?"

"What? No, I don't see a problem with it, do you?" he said, lowering the paper.

"Okay then," Gracie said, looking on the table next to the sofa for a pen. Carrie handed her one she'd been holding and Gracie signed the form.

"Thanks, Mom," Carrie said, taking back the paper and managing a meek smile. "But, uh, they want the money turned in with the permissions slip."

Gracie grabbed her bag and pulled out her checkbook. "Hope you have fun," Gracie said, handing her the check.

"I will. Thanks." Carrie gave her a quick hug and bounded up the stairs to her room. They heard her door close behind her.

"She's probably going to go onto her phone and online chat with everyone she knows that she got her permission slip signed," Spencer said, folding the paper.

"I think they call it texting when they do it on their phones," Gracie said.

"Well whatever, for tonight at least, Carrie does not have the meanest parents on the planet."

Gracie laughed. "Don't worry. It won't last."

She turned back to the police report, still puzzled by the sense that something was not quite right.

"Why is this handwritten?" Gracie asked out loud.

"What?"

"*Something* about this feels a little hinky to me. See what you think." She handed Spencer the paper.

"Hmmm, odd." Spencer said with a grimace.

"Yes, isn't it? In the computer age, why would there be a handwritten police report?"

"No. That's not it."

"It's not?"

"Nope."

Gracie knew he was teasing her, but she was in no mood for it.

"Then what exactly is odd about it?"

"Look at the time."

"It says that he found the door open at eight o'clock on Sunday. Isn't that about right?" She thought back to the morning of the break-in. "No it isn't. I was awakened by the church bells playing hymns *before* the eight o'clock service, and you were already on the phone with him by then."

"Of course, it could be just an approximation. It's not like it makes a lot of difference if it was eight o'clock or seven-forty-five."

Gracie sighed. "I guess." She tucked her legs under her and stared at the paper. She almost had it. Looking at Carrie's permission slip had jogged something in her mind. What was it?

"I've got it," she said after a moment more.

"What is it?"

"There is no incident report number on this form. There's a space for it, but it isn't filled in. *Every* form gets a number when it is filed. This one's blank."

"So he made that copy before he filed it and never bothered to copy the number down."

"Possibly. Or perhaps he just didn't want me to see the official report."

"Why would he bother writing up a fake report when you can just go down to the police station and get a copy of the original?"

"That, my dear Watson, is an excellent question."

~

On Friday, Gracie left early for work, dropped Dickens at the shop and released him from his carrier, then locked up and went to the police station in the basement of the town hall. She hoped that Officer Lowry would not be on duty, or if he were that he would be out on patrol. She wanted to speak only to the desk clerk.

Gracie pulled the report Lowry had given her from her book bag, and approached the desk. A woman sat there, focused on some papers. After a few moments, Gracie cleared her throat. The clerk looked up.

"Can I help you with something?" she said. She looked to be in her early thirties, with pallid, pockmarked skin and brown hair pulled back tightly. Her manner was efficient, if not abrupt.

"Thank you, yes. I wonder if you could help me understand this report." She smoothed the paper out on the desk in front of the officer.

"Looks like an incident report."

"Yes, it is."

"No it's not. It just looks like one. This isn't one because it hasn't been filed. The computer gives them an incident number when they're filed, and they're not official until then."

"I thought something like that might be the case," Gracie said. "I wonder if I could get a copy of the official report on a break-in that occurred at my store last Sunday morning."

"You have the incident number?"

"No. All I have is this draft."

The dispatcher looked at the paper. She turned to her computer and typed several commands. Gracie sighed, wondering why it took so long. Then the printer on the desk started to hum, and Gracie looked at it, waiting for her report to print. As the paper emerged, a young officer came over, grabbed it, and walked away.

"Was that my report?" she asked the dispatcher.

"Nope."

"What's taking so long?" She didn't intend to sound impatient, but realized she did. "Sorry. It's just that I need to get back to my store to open on time."

"No problem." She clicked a few more keys. "There you are."

"Where?"

"Well, not really. There's nothing I can print for you. No report has been filed on that incident."

Gracie felt her face grow pale. "What do you mean?"

"I mean that there is no report that's been filed on that incident. Maybe you ought to talk to the officer. It shoulda been filed by now."

"There's nothing at all?"

"Nope."

Gracie almost asked her to check again, but instead grabbed the form Lowry had given her and started toward the door.

"Thanks," she called out behind her.

"Don't mention it."

"Can you answer another question for me?" Gracie said, turning when she reached the door.

"I'll try."

"Do your officers hand-write reports, or are they usually typed?"

"Officers fill out the forms right on the computer."

"Would there ever be a reason for a report to be handwritten, like if an officer was busy, or not near a computer?"

"I don't even know how they would file a report that was handwritten. They enter the reports right on the computer. Then if they need a copy, like for court or something, or like for your insurance company, we print one out."

"Thanks." She turned to go but stopped again. "I'm sorry. One more question. How long have you had the computer system for filing reports?"

"As long as I've been here, and that's over five years."

Gracie grabbed the door frame and looked at the paper in her hand. "I don't understand."

"Me neither. I'd say ask the officer."

"Thank you. You can bet I will."

~

Gracie drummed her fingers on her desk, trying to make sense of what she had learned. Unless there was some glitch in the system, Lowry had never filed the report on her break-in. Why would he fail to do something that was in the normal course of his work, and then try to convince her otherwise?

She picked up the phone to call Spencer. Without any classes to teach, Fridays were his day to work at home.

"Spencer?" she said as soon as he answered the phone.

"Yeah. What's up?"

"You're not busy are you?"

"I am in the middle of the Revolutionary War, babe. Things look grim. Why?"

"Spoiler alert: the colonists win." She giggled, but could tell Spencer was not amused. "Oh, sorry. I didn't mean to interrupt." She heard the creaking of his desk chair and could envision him leaning back, removing his glasses, and rubbing his eyes.

"What's done is done. What is it?"

Gracie thought about discussing her experience at the police station over the phone, but decided it could wait. "It's quiet here, and I just wanted to hear your voice. You go back to your work, and I'll talk to you later."

"Okay. I'll see you later." His chair squeaked again, and Gracie knew he was back at work before he even hung up the phone.

She did not have long to consider her puzzle before the bell rang. The customer who entered was a delivery driver. Gracie greeted him and asked if she could help him find anything. She was surprised by a sudden inspiration that she should stock audio books for people to listen to as they drive.

"Do you have any local maps?"

"Yes. We have free copies of the village businesses from our Village Business Association, and some road atlases of New England and New York."

"I need to find a local road, and my GPS doesn't recognize it."

"The maps are over here," Gracie said taking him to the correct section and picking up the VBA map. "What's the road you're looking for?"

"Tadpole Road. Do you know where that is?"

"Sounds like it might be in one of the new housing developments on the east side of town." She put the VBA map down and opened the road atlas that included Glenville Falls. She scanned the list of roads, and found Tadpole. "Here it is," she said opening it to the correct page. She handed him the map with her finger planted on the correct spot.

"Thanks. Do you have a copy machine so I can make a copy?" He had a very winning smile, and at first Gracie wanted to accommodate him, but she knew she should not.

"No, I'm sorry. This is copyrighted material, but I'd be happy to sell you the book." She tried to make her smile as disarming as his.

"Gee, that's not very neighborly."

"Perhaps, but I really can't make a copy for you."

"Oh, I get it." His smile turned into a snarl. "The almighty dollar is all anyone cares about. Okay, take your pound of flesh. How much is the map book?"

"Nine ninety-five plus tax. The total is ten dollars and fifty-seven cents."

He pulled out cash and Gracie made change. "Quite a racket you've got going here, lady. I'll warn my friends." With that, he left.

Gracie tilted her head back. "Arrrrghhhh!" she said, shaking her fists in the air.

The outburst spooked Dickens who scaled a bookshelf and stood atop it, fur standing on end.

"Sorry boy," Gracie said, going over to coax him down, but he would have none of it.

Kristen opened the door, and the bell startled them both.

"Hi, Gracie."

"Hi. I didn't expect to see you here today."

"I know. I had a class canceled, and I thought I'd come by and see if there was anything I could do. Kind of make up for the day I missed, if that's okay."

Gracie shrugged. "I guess so." Then, remembering why Kristen left early the previous day, she added, "I don't expect the police to come by today."

Her assistant gave Gracie a sidelong look. "Thanks." She took her lunch and sweater into the back room.

Gracie found it hard to concentrate on anything, so she decided that she and Kristen should make a scan of every shelf in the store to make sure that no books were missing, in the wrong section, or out of alphabetical order. It was just the kind of work that she needed to keep her mind off of her troubles.

She had collected a short stack of misshelved books when the bell rang again.

"Hello there. I'll bet you thought I forgot about that chair and the extra lock, but I didn't."

Gracie looked around the shelf where she was working to see Hal Doyle wearing his tool belt. He held up a drill in one hand and rattled a box over his head with the other, a big smile on his face.

Before long all three of them were hard at work at their various tasks. Hal fixed the chair with some glue and a couple of strategically placed screws. Then he went to work on the door. The sound of the drill drowned out the classical background music, and set Gracie's teeth rattling. It was only when Hal's drill had stopped that she realized that the door had been wide open and she had no idea where Dickens was.

"Hal, did you see my cat?"

Hal was focused on installing the deadbolt, but he looked up and adjusted his Red Sox cap.

"Nope. Didn't notice."

Gracie stood and searched the tops of the book-shelves. No cat. She went to the front window, hoping he had found refuge from the noise there, but he had not. Then she reasoned he might have escaped into the back room to get as far from the drilling as he could.

"Kristen, could you check around for Dickens? I'm going to look in the back room."

Kristen nodded and straightened up from her crouch by the shelves in the biography/memoir section to search for the cat while Gracie headed to the back.

The door to the office was ajar, certainly wide enough for a cat to walk through it. She opened it further and entered, and found Dickens in his box. Gracie let out a breath.

"Here you are. Thank goodness. All I would need to make this day complete would be to have you escape and not know where you were." She called to Kristen to let her know she had found him, then bent down and scratched his neck. Dickens leaned into it and purred.

By the time she returned to the front of the store, Hal was testing the lock.

"You're all set here," he said. "Here are your new keys." He handed Gracie two keys on a thin metal ring.

"Thanks, Hal." Gracie took the keys and inspected the door. "Looks great. I'll feel a little more secure now."

"Good. We aim to please. You ladies have a good day." He touched the bill of his cap, picked up his tools and left.

"Do you think that will make any difference?" Kristen asked.

"I hope it will be a deterrent if anyone gets the idea of breaking in here again. But I must admit, I don't feel as safe here as I used to." She put one of the new keys on her key ring, and put the other in her coin purse to take home for safekeeping.

When she looked up, she noticed a man in jeans, a light blue, long-sleeved shirt, and sunglasses standing in front of the Steaming Kettle looking her way. She went to the front window for a better look, but as soon as she neared the glass, the man turned and walked toward Chestnut Street. Gracie squinted, trying to identify him, but he kept his face turned away from her. His size and gait looked familiar.

"Was that . . . ." Gracie turned to Kristen. "Did that look like Officer Lowry to you?"

"Who?"

Gracie turned back. The man was out of sight.

"Just stay here a minute, okay, Kristen?"

She opened the door and hurried to the corner. Looking up the street, she saw light traffic moving in either direction, two women coming out of the Quill Pen, a young mother pushing a stroller on the other side of the street, and students milling around near the pizza shop. But the man had disappeared.

There were several cars parallel parked on her side of the street. Gracie walked past them, looking into windshields, inspecting the cars for occupants. When she was half way down the block, she heard a car engine start with a roar somewhere ahead of her. She looked toward the sound, but the sun blinded her. She could only sense the movement of a dark vehicle into traffic heading in her direction about a block away, followed by the sound of screeching tires and a quick honk of a horn.

Gracie maneuvered between two parked cars to stand near the edge of the travel lane, hoping she could catch a glimpse of the driver as the car came past. She shielded her eyes with her hand and realized that the car was accelerating—right toward her, aiming directly at the back of the car next to her. She knew she would be crushed by the impact. In a panic, she turned in the narrow space to scramble to the sidewalk, but tripped over her feet, and smashed onto the gravel-strewn pavement. She threw her hands over her head and braced for the crash, but the sound never came. The tires spat gravel at her as the car roared off toward the green.

Gracie picked herself up off the pavement, and tried to get the license number of the car, but by the time she was upright, the car had disappeared down the street.

A passerby came up to Gracie.

"Are you okay?" he said, helping her to the sidewalk.

"Yes, yes, thank you," she said, brushing small bits of gravel from her arm, realizing that she was bleeding. Looking up at her Good Samaritan, she could not conceal her surprise. He was in uniform and wore dark sunglasses.

"Oh, uh." She straightened up and stepped back. "Thank you, Officer Lowry. I'm fine."

~

"Are you okay, Gracie?" Kristen rushed up to her as soon as she entered the store. "You're bleeding. Come sit down." Kristen led Gracie to a chair, and went to the bathroom to get a towel to clean Gracie's wounds. "Do you want me to call Professor Adams?"

"No, thank you, Kristen. I'm okay. There are some bandages in the first aid kit in the back room, and some antibiotic ointment. Then, I'll just stay here for a bit and collect myself. It's getting late anyway. You can go back to campus. I think I'll just close a little early today."

Kristen finally left, after a little more coaxing and lots of assurances that Gracie would be fine. *Now, if I could just convince myself.*

When Gracie left for the day, she had two locks to secure. *It might at least slow the bad guys down a bit.* Gracie hoped that would be enough; she hated the thought of giving in to fear by getting a security system.

~

Carrie and Angela had plans to get pizza and go to a movie that evening, and while Gracie felt guilty for thinking it, she was glad she would have a little time alone with Spencer. As soon as she got home she let Dickens out of his carrier and headed for the shower. She let the warm water pour over her and lathered up with lavender-scented soap. When she got out, she bandaged her arm, put on a sweat suit, and felt better than she had all day.

After throwing together a tuna casserole—a dish Spencer merely tolerated, but was easy to cook—Gracie was disappointed when Spencer hardly spoke at dinner, preoccupied by his research. As she cleared the dishes and Spencer put the leftovers away, Gracie looked for a chance to draw Spencer out of his reverie. It came unexpectedly when Spencer bumped her arm as he opened the refrigerator door.

"Ow!" Gracie jumped back.

"What's the matter?"

"My arm. I hurt it today."

"What happened?"

Gracie told him about the close call with an oncoming car.

"What are you doing chasing after strange men anyway?" he asked as she sponged off the counter top. She gave him a look that she intended to be withering. He wrapped an arm around her and pulled her toward him, kissing her temple.

"I've had kind of a bad day all around," she said, leaning into his shoulder. They moved into the living room and took their accustomed seats as Gracie recounted her visit to the police station.

"It doesn't add up," she concluded. "First, I have someone writing 'Go Home' on the walk in front of my store, then a cop intent on discrediting my employee. Then, there is supposedly a break-in at the store."

"Well *something* happened there."

"Yes, but did you notice that only one officer was on the scene? There was no dusting for prints. If there had been, my front door would have had powder on it, and it was clean as a whistle. Then he claims I left my door unlocked and tries to get me to relinquish my computer to him."

"True, but that was because he worried about what the vandals had done to it."

"But whoever broke into the store didn't steal anything. They just wrecked some books and made a mess. Why would he suspect them of something that required finesse like planting a virus on my computer? Later he said I could use it without investigating further, offering the lame excuse that there was no 'probable cause.'" Gracie's voice got louder and she pronounced each word more crisply as she spoke.

"I guess he was trying to be thorough." Spencer's voice was calming.

Gracie pulled her feet under her and leaned forward. "If the burglars wanted to do something to the computer, wouldn't they just steal it?" She shook her head. "And what would motivate anyone to cut pages out of books?"

Spencer looked like he was searching for an answer, but Gracie didn't wait.

"The break-in doesn't make it onto the police blotter, and when I asked Lowry for a copy of his report, he gave me a handwritten one. When I tried to get an official copy of the report, I was told it didn't exist."

"That part is strange, I'll grant you."

"Then I saw a man standing across the street, seemingly spying on my store, but when I followed him I was nearly run down by a car. And then, who was there to pick me up, but the very same officer." Her voice hit a crescendo. "I have so many pieces, but I have no idea what the puzzle is supposed to look like."

Spencer wrinkled his brow and leaned forward on his elbows. "So, you're saying that you don't think the police report you got from Lowry was legitimate? Why would he do that? It could risk his career."

"I'm not only saying the report was illegitimate; I'm saying that I don't think the break-in at the store was legitimate." Gracie surprised herself a little. She had not realized that was what had been rattling around in the back of her mind.

"How do you reach that result?"

Now that she'd said it, she went into full advocacy mode to support her possibly unfounded conclusion.

"It's the only reason I can come up for the mix-up on the police reports. The police clerk told me that they never have handwritten reports, and that all reports are filed electronically. If there were a report of the break-in, she would have been able to find it."

"Okay, so there was no report. How does that get you to no break-in?"

"Well, think about the way things were when we got to the store Sunday morning."

"Yeah."

"The door was standing open, and books were scattered all over the floor."

"And Officer Lowry was standing outside assessing it all."

"Yes. But except for a few inexpensive books, nothing was damaged. Nothing else was disturbed. But, my computer was turned on."

"It was?"

"Yes. He kept asking me about passwords and such, but I was so upset about the books, and worrying about the cash, that I didn't think to ask why the computer was turned on."

"You didn't tell me that the computer was on. Lowry kept implying that you had left the door unlocked, but you wouldn't have left your computer on, too." Spencer gave her a wink. "You wouldn't want to waste all that electricity for two full days when the store was closed."

Gracie gave him an exasperated look. "What are you saying, that I'm absent-minded enough to leave the store open to burglars, but that I'm such a skinflint I wouldn't forget to turn out the lights?"

Spencer shrugged his shoulders and gave her a playful grin. "Something like that."

"Well," Gracie had to admit, "You're partly right. I wouldn't risk either the cash or the waste of electricity. I am certain I locked the door, *and* turned off the computer."

"So, who turned it on?"

"Maybe Lowry. He was awfully eager to get my computer passwords." Gracie paused. "I wonder if he could have a key to the store. Hal's key was right where it was supposed to be, and he said no one else had a copy, but . . ."

"Of course, there's a key-making machine at Doyle's." Spencer tossed the remark off, but it reminded Gracie of how easy it had been for her to find her key on the ring. *If someone were looking for the newest key, to copy or to borrow, they wouldn't have any trouble finding it. Had Hal said Lowry used to work for him, or was that Ollie's kid?* Gracie tapped her fingers on the arm of the sofa.

"He might think I have something on the computer that he wants. Maybe something about Kristen. He suspects she could be involved, but I can't trust anything he says anymore." Gracie closed her eyes and rubbed her temples. "And let's not forget that none of this was a problem until I hired Kristen. It's possible she's hiding something."

"Any idea what?"

Gracie shook her head. "Even if the break-in was Kristen or Lowry, neither one was driving that car this afternoon. I don't know. Perhaps I'm wrong, but it sure felt as if the driver was heading right for me."

"Maybe it was just someone on a cell phone who lost track of where they were going."

"Perhaps, but what about all the rest?"

Spencer stood. "You're missing the bigger question."

"What's that?"

"It's not just 'who,' but 'why'." Spencer extended his arms to his sides. "Why would a police officer risk his career over information in your computer? And why would anyone want to run you over with their car in front of witnesses? Nope." Spencer paused and looked at her over the top of his glasses. "It seems to me that if someone is doing all this on purpose, it would have to be someone with . . ." counting on his fingers, "something against you or the store, something to hide, or something to lose. Otherwise, why bother?" He lifted his hands into the air. "I can't think of anyone who would have it in for you."

Gracie thought a moment, and shook off the notion that Kristen might want revenge against her for the death of her mother. "Me neither," she said. "But, I have a feeling if we can answer that question, we'll have the answers to the others."

CHAPTER TWELVE

B efore opening the shop on Saturday, Gracie went into her office and dialed the police non-emergency number. *I'm going to get to the bottom of this.*

"Glenville Falls Police Department." Gracie heard a beep on the line and knew the conversation was being recorded.

"I wonder if I could speak with Chief Johnson?" she asked.

"Could I have your name, ma'am?" The beeping continued.

Gracie knew that with caller ID, they must already know where she was calling from, but gave the officer her name.

"And what is this concerning, Ms. McIntyre?"

"Um." Gracie paused, then heard the recorder beep again. She felt a wave of unease. *What if it's not just Lowry? What if he has friends in the department?* She shook her head.

"Ms. McIntyre?" the officer said again. The beeping continued.

"Oh, um, it's okay. I just had a question. I'll try again another time." Gracie almost hung up, but stopped. "But

I wonder, could you possibly check and see if Officer Lowry was on duty on Sunday morning—last Sunday?"

"Let me check the duty roster. One moment."

Gracie bit her lip and drummed her fingers. The clerk came back on the line and gave Gracie the answer to her question.

"Really? You're sure? Thank you so much." Gracie hung up the receiver without even saying good-bye. She regretted her rudeness, but wanted to get off the phone as fast as she could. *Why would a real break-in be handled solely by an off-duty patrolman?*

The sound of the bell brought Gracie back to the moment. Lois Heller was her first customer of the day.

"Hi, Lois." Gracie felt her shoulders tense.

"Hello, Grace. I thought I would come by and see how you are."

"I'm well, thank you. We survived Family Weekend rather well, I think. And how have you been?"

"I'm fine, but I didn't have a car try to run me down yesterday."

Gracie's breath caught in her throat. "You were there?"

"Yes. I was just coming around the corner when I heard the car gun its engine and tear down the street. It was shocking." Lois shuddered, but Gracie thought it was more for effect.

Her sore back stiffened. "It was just an accident."

"Hmmm. I hardly think it *could* have been accidental. I think whoever it was sat there waiting for you. Why else would they come out so suddenly?" She looked at Gracie, wide-eyed. "What in the world could you have done to cause someone to do such a thing?"

Gracie was not interested in adding fodder to the town rumor mill, but wanted to keep Lois talking in case she had noticed anything that might be helpful.

"Could you see the driver? Was it a man or a woman?"

"I'm not . . . let me think. Oh, I don't know. I was watching you as you tripped over your own feet trying to get away." The smirk on Lois's face was fleeting, but unmistakable.

Gracie placed her fingers against her lips. *Shaden-freude,* she thought. Some people just enjoy the pain of others. She wasn't going to get any information from Lois, and she was determined that Lois would get none from her. She had to think of the fastest way to get Lois to leave.

"Lois, I'm so glad you stopped by. I have a new shipment of books, including some lovely hardcovers I know you'll just love. Expensive coffee table books to use when you're staging houses."

"Oh, I don't have a minute more today. It's Saturday. I'm so busy showing properties. My office is constantly humming." She exaggerated a glance at her watch.

"I'm surprised you were able to get away at all." It was Gracie's turn to smirk.

Lois's eyes narrowed. "Well, I'm glad to see that you're all right."

"Thank you, Lois. And thanks for dropping by." The bell over the door rang as Lois turned her back and left. "And don't hurry back," Gracie muttered through clenched teeth.

After Lois left, Gracie's concern returned. "So someone *is* out to get me, and I don't know if I can rely on the police to help," she said to herself. "What am I supposed to do now?"

She wished she could call her dad. He always knew what to do, before dementia took his wisdom from her. She brushed a tear from her eye.

Looking across the street, she saw Peggy standing just off the sidewalk in front of her flower shop, smoking with a man dressed in white. Although they were standing side-by-side, there was no sign that they were engaged in conversation.

I wonder if Peggy knows anything about the break-in, or the guy who was loitering around yesterday afternoon, she thought. She put on a sweater, and started out the door.

As she crossed the street, she shielded her eyes and recognized the man standing with her as the one from the Steaming Kettle who had helped Spencer with the party trays. *What was his name? Just initials . . . something musical. DJ!*

Neither of them took notice of her until she had made it nearly to the curb. She prepared a cordial greeting to them both, but as she approached, DJ looked up, dropped his cigarette, and ground it into the sidewalk under his foot. Before Gracie could say anything, he had turned and walked back toward the Kettle.

"Hi, Peggy," Gracie said. An autumn breeze shot down the street, forcing her to pull her sweater tightly around her.

"Gracie," Peggy said with a nod. She took a long drag on her cigarette, and held the smoke in her lungs.

"How're things?" Gracie tried to appear casual, but knew she didn't sound that way.

"Fine," Peggy said, letting the smoke out through her nose.

What was I thinking, trying small talk with Peggy? Gracie thought. She decided to get right to the point. "Did you know that I had a break-in at my store last weekend?"

"Yeah, I heard. Everything okay?"

"Only some minor losses. Did you happen to see anything?"

Peggy blew out another puff of smoke before answering. "Nope. Sorry."

Gracie shook her head and looked at her shoes. "I'm afraid the police are not taking it very seriously. I worry that other downtown merchants might be at risk." She looked at Peggy hoping that, at least, might engage her interest.

"Hope not." Peggy shook her head.

Gracie saw that half of Peggy's cigarette had turned to ash. If she didn't hurry, Peggy would be done with her smoke and back in her shop before Gracie could find out anything.

"Did you see the man who was standing around outside your store yesterday afternoon?"

Peggy looked at Gracie through half-closed eyes, took another drag, and blew it out. "Don't think so." Her voice took on a less conversational tone.

Gracie fought the urge to yell, *Don't you understand this is important?* Instead, she tried to make strong eye contact through the smoke as it blew past them both.

"I think whoever it was tried to run me down yesterday. If you can think of anything that might help us find out who he was, I would really appreciate it."

Peggy stubbed out her cigarette, and brushed her hands together. "Gracie, I don't think anyone was trying to hurt you. Just leave well enough alone and everything will be all right." With that, she turned and took the stairs to her porch two at a time, passing multi-colored baskets of mums and small pumpkins painted with cutesy faces.

Gracie massaged her hand as she watched Peggy disappear into the flower shop, then turned and walked back across the street. She stood outside her door and looked across at Posies and the Steaming Kettle. Except for the darkening clouds and chilling autumn breeze, the triangle looked as peaceful as it ever did. Why didn't it feel that way?

She went inside. "That was a waste of time," she said to herself.

"What was?" a man's voice called from behind the bookshelves and Gracie jumped.

"Who's there?"

"Oh, my dear," Professor Chaudhry said coming around a bookcase. "I did not mean to startle you."

"Oh," Gracie let out a breath. "I just didn't see you come in."

"You were across the street when I arrived. I hope it was appropriate for me to enter. The door was unlocked." He nearly bowed as he spoke.

Gracie shook her head and smiled. "Of course it was appropriate. I'm sorry I wasn't here to welcome you."

"Oh, your lovely books did that quite well, along with your very accommodating greeter," he said, stroking Dickens' back.

Gracie smiled as Dickens rubbed up against Professor Chaudhry's leg. He left a furry yellow swath on the dark trousers "Oh, I'm sorry about his shedding."

"Not a problem at all, I assure you. He and I have become good friends. Who could turn down the affection of a *felis catus,* so willingly bestowed?"

Gracie laughed. "Would you like a cup of tea, professor?" she asked, moving toward the back room, wishing she had more to offer him.

"Not today, thank you. I cannot stay long, but I wanted to spend a bit of time in my favorite bookshop before going off to run the errands Mrs. Chaudhry has assigned to me."

"Well, let me know if you need anything."

Gracie went into her office and sank into her desk chair. She took a deep breath and drummed her fingers on her desk.

Lowry wasn't on duty last Sunday. What does that even mean?

She shook her head and pulled out some paperwork. She needed to get Kristen's paycheck ready for her, but she lacked focus on the task. After only a moment, she caught herself staring at a thumbtack on the cork board above her desk. It was no use. This puzzle would not solve itself.

Putting her lawyerly skills to work, she got out a piece of paper and her Glenville College pencil to write down what she knew. In the upper left corner, she drew a circle, in which she wrote the name "Lowry–cop–false report, checkered past, wants info from my computer, doesn't trust Kristen." In the bottom left corner she formed another circle labeled "Ollie–in Florida, knew about new lock," and in the center at the bottom, another circle in which she wrote "Hal –has copy of key." Then, at the top of the page, in the center, she put a box that she labeled "Me." Then she drew an arrow from Hal to Ollie. There was a connection there. They had known each other in high school, and Ollie had been Hal's tenant. Then she looked at the space labeled "Lowry." *What is his connection?* She tapped the eraser end of her pencil on the desk and frowned. Then she wrote "Kristen" in the upper right. She circled it and considered what else she might write there. After some thought, she realized there was more to write than she wished there were. "All started after she came, has avoided police, a little secretive, not always reliable, chews gum and plays with her hair too much." Gracie knew the last were just her pet peeves, so she turned the pencil over and erased them.

"Well, Dickens," she said when he jumped up onto her desk to inspect what she was doing, "Does this make any sense to you?"

The phone rang and Dickens jumped down.

"Hi, Gracie. It's Kristen."

"Oh, hi." After chronicling all the reasons she might be suspicious of Kristen, Gracie found it hard to be cordial.

"Um, I just wanted to tell you something about last night."

Gracie could picture her clerk twirling her hair.

"Oh, thanks for your help last night," Gracie said, making herself smile.

"You're welcome." Kristen paused long enough that Gracie wondered for a moment whether they had been disconnected.

"Was there something else you wanted to talk about?" Gracie asked.

"Well, yeah. You see, after I left the store—well you know, it's getting dark earlier than it used to, and the footpath up College Hill is kind of overgrown."

Gracie couldn't be sure where this was leading, but she did not like the sound of it. "Did something happen last night, Kristen?"

"Yes. Well, no. Not really. It's just that I had the feeling all the way up the path that I was being followed."

"Did you see anyone?"

"No. It was dinner hour by the time I got back up here, so there really weren't many other students around. I just got really creeped out. I ended up running the last stretch to the dorm."

Gracie wasn't sure how to respond.

"Maybe I was just letting my imagination run away with me after what happened to you and all," Kristen continued. "But I definitely wished I had taken the long way around on College Street."

Gracie caressed her injured arm. "I'm glad you weren't hurt. Please be careful in the future, and keep to the street where there's better lighting and people around in case you need help. And I guess we'll have to be sure you're home before dusk from now on."

Despite the very low crime rate in Glenville Falls, there were occasional incidents, including sexual assault, on the college campus. Although most such cases were among acquaintances instead of stranger assaults, Kristen's story unnerved Gracie almost as much as it intimidated her young assistant.

"And report this to the campus police, Kristen," she said, hoping that they would be more responsive than the town's police had been for her. "If it's that peeping Tom, they'd want to know."

"You're right, I guess." Kristen sounded reluctant. "I just wanted to tell you." Was she turning to Gracie for comfort?

"I'm glad you called. We'll keep an eye on what time the sun sets, and have you out of here well in advance of it."

"Okay, good. Thanks, Gracie." As Gracie started to hang up, she heard the girl's voice. "Sorry about that."

"That's okay," Gracie said after returning the receiver to her ear, but all she heard was a dial tone. With a long sigh, Gracie remembered that it wouldn't be long before they changed their clocks to standard time, making the sunset an hour earlier than it was at present. She hated the weeks when it was dark by 4:30 and wondered how much time Kristen would lose at work by going home before dusk. *But, I'll save some money on payroll,* she thought, trying to look at the bright side.

When Gracie returned to the front of the store, she spotted Dickens sprawled in the bay window. Peering into the area where Professor Chaudhry had been sitting she saw a stack of books on the table, but no professor. Had she missed the sound of the bell when the gentleman left?

Retrieving the books Chaudhry had left behind, she turned them to read their spines. The subjects were varied, but they had two things in common. All were old, and all were bound in leather.

"I guess he likes leather-bound books," Gracie said to her cat. As she replaced the books in the bookcase reserved for her older editions, she noticed there was an empty space on the shelf. It had been full. "Did we sell one?" she asked aloud, but shook her head knowing they had not. One was missing.

Gracie counted the volumes, and checked her inventory. Sure enough, one book was missing. It was an old dictionary her father had kept in his law office for all the years Gracie could remember. She had put the ridiculous price of four hundred dollars on the book, harboring the hope that it would never sell. Searching her memory, she could not be sure whether she had seen it since the break-in. But surely it had only sentimental value. Why would anyone want to break in to steal it? Professor Chaudhry wouldn't be the kind of person who would make off with one of her books, would he?

Perhaps it is just on the wrong shelf somewhere. She wanted to search for it, but decided it could wait until later. Her arm throbbed, and she had the beginnings of a sinus headache. What she needed then was a nice hot cup of tea.

CHAPTER THIRTEEN

Walking home at dusk, Gracie was pondering where the missing book might be hiding when she had the sensation that she was being followed. *This is nonsense,* she thought. *I'm only feeling this way because of what Kristen said.* But try as she might, she could not shake the feeling.

Dickens' cat carrier was heavy, slowing her down. She quickened her pace, but her injured arm ached from the strain of keeping the carrier steady at a jog.

As she approached her yard, it was dark. No one had turned on the porch light for her. Even the front windows were dark. As she turned up the walk, she looked back. Was that someone's shadow by the neighbor's hedge?

She hustled to the porch, pushed the door open, and shut it quickly after her. She put Dickens' carrier down on the hall rug, then did something she could not remember doing except when they went out of town. She bolted the lock.

~

After dinner and a phone call from Ben, Gracie decided to turn in early. The rains forecast by her earlier headache had arrived. The soft sounds of droplets against the window pane lulled her to sleep. When Spencer joined her, she awoke and found it hard to resume her slumber. Her mind was too alert; dreams didn't stand a chance. At first, she thought about the latest call from Ben, and how much his life had changed in only a few weeks. That led to thoughts of Kristen, and how she had started to come out of her shell. Her life, too, had changed dramatically, shifting out of childhood and becoming more independent. That made her think of the person who might have followed Kristen, and then her. Was it her imagination, or was someone there? Then there was the unfinished paperwork for Kristen's paycheck. It was enough to bring her fully awake.

She rolled over and fluffed her pillow, trying to push these thoughts from her head. As soon as she did, however, she saw in her mind's eye the man standing across the street from the store, looking in. *Who was that?* Reliving her pursuit of him, almost being crushed between cars and Lowry helping her up, made her heart beat speed up. Her arm throbbed.

I'll never get any sleep this way, Gracie thought as she slipped from bed. Spencer's snoring continued uninterrupted. She put on her slippers and robe, and went to the kitchen to start the tea kettle boiling. Dickens followed her and rubbed against her ankles.

"Oh, kitty," Gracie said as she picked up the cat. "Do you do need a little something to calm your nerves, too?"

Gracie got some cat treats from the cupboard, but changed her mind about the tea. The best remedy for her, she decided, was hot chocolate.

She settled down in her favorite spot on the sofa with her mug of cocoa and a granny afghan. As she pulled her feet up, Dickens hopped up beside her, purring loudly. Gracie petted his soft fur, as the warm cocoa calmed her. Before long, Gracie and Dickens were asleep. The light coming through the window, the sound of church bells, and the smell of Spencer's coffee wakened them hours later.

"I'm getting old," Gracie complained when she joined Spencer in the kitchen.

"Nonsense. You're a year younger than I am." Spencer missed the point.

"Okay—how about, I am feeling my age today. My neck is stiff. I can't turn it to the right."

"You don't get to be closing in on half a century without picking up a few aches and pains along the way."

"That was a rotten thing to say."

"And sleeping on the couch doesn't help," he said, turning and giving her a kiss.

"I woke up and couldn't get back to sleep."

"I wondered where you were when I woke up."

"Sorry." Gracie scratched her head and put her cocoa mug in the sink.

"So what happened last night?"

"I just couldn't turn my mind off." Gracie thought about listing the reasons, but Spencer had stopped listening. "Writing today?"

"Umhmm. Gotta send in some chapters by the end of the month."

"I know. You'll make it."

Spencer nodded as he put an English muffin in the toaster, while Gracie checked her bandaged arm, and tried to stretch her stiff neck. "I'm a wreck today."

Spencer came over and rubbed her neck.

"Better?" he said after only a moment. The muffin popped up, and he went to butter it.

Gracie wanted to say *don't stop now*. It wasn't much better, but that wasn't Spencer's fault.

~

After breakfast, Gracie grabbed the kitchen phone from its wall cradle and dialed the police station.

"Will Chief Johnson be in today at all?" she asked the young-sounding male who answered.

"He's not making appointments today, ma'am. Would you like to make an appointment to meet with him some other time?"

An appointment. Why hadn't she thought of that before?

"Yes, please, if I could."

"And what is this concerning?"

Again that question.

"Well, I'd rather keep that between me and the chief." Gracie sat down and propped her elbows on the kitchen table.

"Is it concerning an open case?"

"Umm. Well, in a way, but in a way not."

"Okay, ma'am. How's tomorrow morning for you? He has an opening at 10:45."

"Thank you. That sounds fine." She gave him her name. "See you then"

"Yes, ma'am."

Gracie drummed her fingers on the table. In twenty-four hours she would be talking to the Chief of Police to register a complaint about one of his officers. How would he react?

Gracie did not know the chief well. She remembered he was the responding officer the night she called in

Cheryl's murder, but that was many years ago. Since then she had seen him around town, at school functions, and town meetings when he was acting in his official capacity, but they weren't even on a first-name basis. Perhaps if she had continued to practice law she would know him better.

She picked up the phone and dialed again.

"Hi, Gracie," Del answered on the first ring. "What's up? Not another break-in, I hope." There was an edge to her voice.

"No, nothing like that. I just wanted to ask you something."

"What?"

"What kind of a cop is Chief Johnson?"

"Divorced."

Gracie rubbed her eyes with one hand. "That's not what I meant, Del." Her exhaustion had made her impatient.

"Well you weren't very specific."

Gracie sighed. Perhaps calling Del wasn't such a good idea after all.

"Fair enough. I just wanted to know how he might react to a complaint about someone in the department."

"Who do you want to complain about?"

"This is just hypothetical."

"Then hypothetically, he is apt to jump out his office window." Del paused. "Good thing his office is in the basement, isn't it?"

Gracie wasn't laughing; neither was Del.

"Look," Gracie said, trying to control her frustration, "I know you're mad at me for not telling you sooner about the break-in, but right now, I really need a friend, not an angry business partner."

There was a pause. Gracie planted her feet on the floor, bracing for a lecture.

Del sighed. When she spoke, her voice had a more sympathetic tone. "Okay. What's the problem?"

After Gracie related her doubts about Officer Lowry, Del clicked her tongue.

"I can't tell you too much about Johnson. I can only tell you that you really have to talk to him about this, and if he doesn't give you satisfaction, you should go to the state police. It sounds like something fishy is going on, and at the very least there ought to be an investigation."

"Thanks, Del. I have an appointment for tomorrow morning."

"Good. Let me know how it turns out. I'm going out of town in the morning for a federal case. I'll be gone all week, but you can always reach me by cell."

"I'll call you after the meeting."

After clicking off, Gracie sat at the kitchen table, the receiver still in her hand. How would she approach Chief Johnson? What if he didn't listen?

Spencer entered, took the phone from her hand, and put it back in its cradle.

"I think you need a break. Let's take a drive."

Gracie looked up at Spencer. His eyes were determined, and his mouth turned down. Although Spencer loved driving, today it was clearly not what he most wanted to do.

"What about your book deadline?"

"I can spare a few hours. It's nearly October, the rain has cleared out, and the sun is shining," he said. "If we head north I'm sure we'll see some great colors."

It was their autumnal tradition—tracking the changing of the leaves from Vermont to the Berkshires. Going on a Sunday meant competing for space on the roads with other leaf peepers, but how could they begrudge others a chance to appreciate what nature gave them for free?

Gracie gave Spencer her hand and stood.

"You have a deal," she said, and realized that just the thought of it helped to chase some of her demons away. "I'll go get dressed—and ask Carrie if she'd like to join us."

Carrie declined. She had a project to work on for school, and hoped to get together with Angela later in the day. Gracie was disappointed that Carrie did not want to spend the time with her. They had so little time together.

"We'll be home before dark," Gracie called upstairs to Carrie as they left the house.

"Okay, Mom. See ya."

Spencer grabbed the front door handle to pull it open, but it was still locked.

"Who locked this?"

Gracie looked down. "I was kind of spooked last night, and for no good reason was convinced I was being followed." She forced a laugh. "Too much happening at once, I guess."

Spencer looked at her. She hated seeing the worry in his eyes.

"It was nothing. It was just so dark last night, and all the lights were out when I got here."

His expression softened. "Oh, sorry. I meant to turn the porch light on, but didn't realize how quickly it got dark."

"No problem." Gracie thought back to the night before. "Maybe we ought to get one of those motion-activated lights."

Spencer shrugged, unlocked the door, then paused. He called up to Carrie. "Hey, kid. You're coming with us. Make it snappy."

After the inevitable moans and complaints, and a call to Angela to cancel their plans, Carrie established herself in the back seat with her books and a laptop so she could work as they drove along. Gracie sat in the front and watched as Spencer locked the front door and slid into the driver's seat.

"And we're off," he said, starting the engine.

They took the local roads out to the highway, then followed it east and north. They avoided the faster route of the interstate. The trees along it would be turning, too, but the back roads took slower twists and turns past ponds and streams and around hills. As they drove they saw the early flaming crimson of the Red Maples offset against the brilliant yellow poplars and yellow-green of birches and beeches. Crossing into Vermont, they noticed White Ash adding a deep purple to the palette. Soon, the russet Chestnuts and Sugar Maples with red, yellow, orange, and green on a single tree, delighted Gracie's eye, while other trees still held their summer hues.

"It's still early," Spencer said.

"But it's already beautiful," Gracie said without taking her eyes from the side of the road. "I think I like it best when there are still some green trees."

"You say that every year, until the green trees turn, too."

Gracie thought about that. It was true that the brownish-orange of the late-turning oaks and the dark yellow aspen added depth to nature's glory.

"What a gift to live here," Gracie said. "Carrie, are you seeing this?"

"Yeah. Hey are we going to stop somewhere? I'm getting hungry."

"Want some apples?" Spencer asked as he turned off at a roadside stand.

Bushels of apples and bins filled with pumpkins sorted by size stood outside the large, garage-style building. Dried corn stalks decorated posts that held up an overhanging roof from which hung baskets of mums in various colors.

"Oh good," said Carrie, already unbuckling her seat belt, and opening the door as soon as the car came to a stop.

Gracie and Spencer followed her into the open, car-sized doorway. As soon as they entered, the scents of autumn enveloped them. Baskets of apples of many varieties were arranged on and under tables. Shelves along the back wall displayed jams, jellies, apple butter, and of course, maple syrup. In front of them stood a table filled with boxes of maple sugar candies in a variety of shapes. On one side, shoppers debated their choices among clusters of Indian corn, the reds, oranges, yellows, blues, and browns making festive autumn decorations. Gracie thought about getting some for her shop window, but Spencer distracted her, pointing to several diamond-shaped, plastic warning signs displayed against one wall. There were replicas of actual road signs, such as deer, moose, or bear crossings, but they also had a few with more whimsy.

"I should get that for my office," Spencer said, pulling down a sign that read "Genyuss at Werk."

Gracie giggled. "No points off for spelling." Then she noticed one that appealed to her. "I should get this for the store," she said, pointing to one that said, "Premises Guarded by an Attack Cat."

Spencer took one off its hook and handed it to her. "Sold," he said, grinning. Gracie laughed, but when she saw the cost, she put it back on its hook.

They spied Carrie on the other side of the building near a tall refrigerator case that held soft drinks. A case next to it held wedges of Vermont cheeses and processed meats. Breads and crackers filled shelves standing by its side. They joined Carrie and made a few selections.

Together they pick out a pumpkin for the front porch, pecks of two varieties of apples—sweet Jonathan and tart McIntosh—and enough cheese and crackers to hold them until they got home. At the checkout counter, Carrie suggested they get one of the plastic containers of chocolate, maple, or peanut butter fudge, but Gracie shook her head.

"Where're you folks from?" the high-school aged boy at the register asked Carrie as they stacked their purchases on the counter. When she told him, he looked a little disappointed. "We've got a lot of folks here from more away than that today. Good weather helps. I have a bet with the boss that I can find someone from farther away than he can."

"Sorry we can't help much," Gracie said counting out her money. "It must be nice to be able to keep your wares outside and not have to worry about anyone stealing them," she said. She didn't mean to sound wistful, but that was how she felt.

"No, the boss has security cameras and alarms. If anyone tries anything, they'll get caught."

"Really? I didn't notice any security measures."

The boy winked. "There are cameras there and there," he said pointing, "and a couple more outside."

Gracie followed his gestures. She sighed. Even there, they couldn't afford to be too trustful. But at least their security wasn't intrusive.

They loaded their purchases into the back seat, and Carrie broke out the cheese and crackers.

"We'll wait until we get home to have the apples," Gracie said. "We'll want to wash them well first."

"I know," Carrie replied, around a mouthful.

Spencer turned the car southward, and they returned the way they had come. As the sun angled lower in the sky, the yellow trees at the hilltops looked like they were ablaze.

Gracie mused about the rustic, roadside farm stand with an up-to-date security system. If they could do it, she could, too.

She put her hands behind her head and sighed. This day was just what the doctor ordered, even if that doctor was a Ph.D. in history.

When they arrived home, it was nearly dark. Gracie looked at the dark porch and the wave of fear she had felt the night before returned. Unable to brush it away, she waited for Spencer to unlock the house and turn on the lights before she got out of the car. She put the pumpkin on the porch, then scanned the neighborhood before going inside. She cleaned the apples and placed some in the refrigerator, and others in a wooden bowl on the kitchen table. Then she started dinner.

All the while, she wondered whether someone was out in the darkness, watching her every move.

CHAPTER FOURTEEN

On her way to the town hall on Monday morning, Gracie placed a call to L&S Security and made an appointment for a consultant to give her a free estimate on a security system the next morning. *One thing checked off my to-do list,* she thought, glad to be doing something to take control of her situation.

Arriving at the town hall, she went into a side entrance and down several steps before reaching the police station reception area. As she waited in a wooden chair to see Chief Johnson, Gracie wasn't sure whether it was hunger from skipping breakfast or nerves that had her stomach upset. She crossed her legs and bounced her foot in an even rhythm as she looked at the clock again. Ten forty-eight. One minute later than the last time she looked. She had arrived early, and had been waiting about fifteen minutes, getting more agitated every second she sat there. What if Officer Lowry should see her?

Just think about the fall leaves, she told herself. She closed her eyes, breathed deeply, and envisioned the scenes of the day before. She could feel her pulse slow.

"Grace McIntyre?" Gracie jumped when the chief's voice boomed out her name.

"Yes," she said stumbling to her feet.

"This way," he said, extending an arm toward the door of his glass-enclosed office. Gracie felt she was in a fishbowl, but at least the seat available to her faced the chief's desk and, behind it, a high half window at ground level. If Officer Lowry came by, all he would see was her back.

The chief closed the door and went around the desk, sitting in a squeaky rolling chair. He leaned forward and put his elbows on his desk, making a tent with his fingers.

"So, what can I do you for?"

Gracie cleared her throat. She had rehearsed what she would say, trying to express herself clearly and concisely. She saw anger flicker in the chief's eyes when she mentioned the non-existent incident report, and hoped it was not directed at her. When she pulled out the handwritten report, he took it, and looked it over while Gracie remained silent.

"Well, this could just be some notes he was taking, couldn't it Ms. McIntyre?" His tone was not dismissive; he was just making an observation. It made Gracie wonder for a second if she could have misconstrued. No. She was certain of all she had said.

"Perhaps, but that's not what he told me. And it would not explain all the other issues with Officer Lowry's supposed investigation," Gracie said, trying to sound logical, reasonable, and calm.

"Well, I'll look into this and see what I can find out for you. I'll keep this here if you don't mind."

Del's words from the previous day about going to the state police if she could not get satisfaction from the chief, echoed in her mind. "Might I keep a copy also?"

"Sure." The chief pressed a button, and when a young staff person came to the door, he said, "Make a copy of this for Ms. McIntyre before she goes."

"Thank you, Chief Johnson." Gracie reached over to shake his hand.

The chief reciprocated, then looked her straight in the eye. "Don't I know you from somewhere?" he asked.

"I used to practice law here, but that was a lot of years ago."

"Oh, yeah," he said, leaning back in his chair and knitting his fingers together behind his head. "I remember. Over with Mack Reynolds, right? You and Del were the only gal lawyers in town then." He laughed at some private joke.

"Yes, that's right." Gracie couldn't help but ask. "What's so funny?"

"Oh nothin'. It's just that we used to call you two Mack's little harem. No offense of course."

Gracie felt her ears turn red. The chief apparently saw her discomfort.

"Oh, c'mon. That was years ago. You can't be offended by that now," he said, chuckling harder.

"Mack Reynolds was the only lawyer in the area who was open-minded enough to hire women back then, but he hired us for our brains and nothing else." She felt perspiration break out on her upper lip.

"You sure about that?" He leaned forward and slapped his knee as he became nearly overcome with mirth.

Gracie stood. "Yes, I am. And now he's a respected county court judge."

"Woohoo!" More laughter.

Gracie's jaw tensed and she clenched her fists. "Thank you for looking into this issue. I look forward to hearing from you," she said and turned to leave. She fumbled with the door handle, much to the chief's amusement, grabbed the copy of the report the clerk handed to her, and stormed from the station.

Crossing the green from the town hall, Gracie went directly to Del's law office.

"Hi, Shelley. I've got to talk to Del."

"Oh, sorry, Gracie. She's out of the office. Big federal case over in Boston. She won't be back until next week."

"Oh drat. She told me that. Never mind. Thanks, Shelley."

As she left the office, she pulled out her cell and hit Del's speed dial number. It went straight to voicemail. She thought of calling Spencer, but knew he was in class. Then she thought of her son Ben. He would understand her. *No, I shouldn't bother him in the middle of a school day.* She let out a cry of aggravation, snapped the phone shut and jammed it in her pocket.

Stomping down the street, she was oblivious as to how she might appear until she came to the Steaming Kettle. Kelly Dowling was posting the list of lunch specials on a blackboard outside the door.

"Whoa, there, Gracie. Let me get out of your way. You look like you're loaded for bear."

Gracie stopped so fast she nearly lost her balance. "Oh, Kelly. Sorry. I didn't see you there."

"Nor anything else," she said, wiping her hands on her apron. "Something wrong?"

"I'm just, uh, a little preoccupied, I guess." She drew a deep breath, trying to calm herself.

"Have time for a cup of tea and a pumpkin muffin? You can tell me all about it."

Gracie shook her head. "No thanks. Maybe a rain check?"

"We're always here." Kelly opened the door to her restaurant.

Gracie turned to go, but then had another thought.

"Kelly, did you happen to see anyone standing around outside the Kettle on Friday?"

Kelly raised her eyebrows. "Friday? Don't remember anyone" She scanned the sidewalk and lowered her voice to a whisper. "Is that who you're so mad at?"

"Among others," Gracie said in a low voice.

"Sometimes DJ comes out for a smoke. You wanna ask him about it? He's in back, changing into his work clothes."

Gracie looked down. "He's the guy who buses for you?"

"That's right."

"I've seen him working at other jobs around town, haven't I? Maybe at the IGA?"

Kelly nodded. "People think he's slow, but he's smart enough. He's working out just fine for us so far." She opened the door. "Come on in. I'll get him. We still have about twenty minutes before the lunch crowd starts to come in."

Gracie shrugged and went inside. Kelly followed, and disappeared into the back.

All the tables were empty, so Gracie chose one by the front window. She touched her injured arm as she looked over at her darkened shop. All looked well. She rubbed her temples, then looked up when Kelly returned.

"What's the matter?" Gracie said, seeing that Kelly's face was a bit flushed.

"Nothing." She shook her head and gave Gracie a half-hearted smile. "I just talked to DJ, and he says he didn't see anything." She cast a furtive glance toward the back room.

Gracie curled her lip. "He didn't want to talk to me, did he." It was not a question.

Kelly giggled and crossed her arms. "Oh, it's not that, Gracie. He's just a bit shy. And he's changing into his work whites, so he's not ready to come out front yet."

Gracie nodded, her mouth drawn into a thin line. "That's okay. It was worth a try, I guess."

"Well, would you like some tea anyway? I'll give you the downtown merchant discount." Kelly looked so hopeful, Gracie could not help but laugh.

"Sure. Why not?" she said. "And how about that pumpkin muffin?"

Kelly's broad-toothed smile returned. "Comin' right up."

~

After her belated breakfast, Gracie felt better able to deal with her day. As she left the Kettle, the lunch crowd had started to filter in, and Kelly was doing several things at once. DJ had not yet made an appearance. Gracie shrugged. That was more Kelly's problem than hers.

"Well," she said, standing on the sidewalk, hands on hips. "I guess I might as well check another item off of my to-do list. She strode across the green and entered Doyle's Hardware.

"Hi, Hal," Gracie said as she entered the store. She enjoyed the interesting mix of aromas in Hal's store: paint mixed with rubber mixed with a hint of sawdust.

"Hello there, Gracie. What can I do for you?"

"Actually, Hal, I am looking to pick your brain."

"You got a problem at the store?"

Gracie shook her head.

"At the house, then?"

"Actually, yes." Gracie scanned the store. Did he carry lighting fixtures? "We're thinking of putting up a yard light. You know, it would be nice if we're coming home after dark to have a little light near our walkway."

"Good idea. Everyone ought to have 'em. They're good for security, too. You never know."

"So I have heard." Gracie tried to smile.

"Well, we got a few different models here. Some operate on a switch, then there are the motion-activated ones."

"Yeah, I think I want one that is motion-sensitive." More than once, Spencer had forgotten to turn on the porch light, but the idea of leaving a light on all day just to have a little illumination when she got home at night bothered Gracie.

"Okay." Hal pulled a fixture from a shelf. "Now, here's a good model. It would go nice with your house." He was right. It looked similar to their existing porch light.

"Yeah, that looks good. How does it work?"

Hal described each option: solar versus wired, with or without an outlet, post or wall mounted.

Gracie considered. "How do the prices compare?"

"The lights are about the same, but a post is extra. You can get 'em in bronze and a bunch of different finishes, but all I stock is aluminum with a black finish."

Gracie wondered if it would be worth paying more to illuminate part of her lawn, or if she could get by with just adding a motion sensor to her porch light. "Can we put one up ourselves, or do we need an electrician?"

"Well . . ." Hal stroked his chin. "You and Spencer might want to call an electrician. I can give you the name of a good one."

"Let me think about it," Gracie said. She left shaking her head. She still had no idea how much it might cost to add security to the store. The person who broke in might not have taken anything tangible, but he certainly stole Gracie's peace of mind.

As she reached the sidewalk, her cell phone rang. She drew it from her pocket and checked the screen. It was Del.

"We're in a lunch recess," Del said, speaking quickly, "I don't have a lot of time, Gracie. I have to use lunch to do some prep for this afternoon, but Shelley said you looked like Hurricane Gracie blowing into town and I should call you." Gracie laughed. "Are you okay?"

"I wasn't, but I am now," Gracie said. "I had a bit of a run-in with the Chief of Police. Did you know they used to call us 'Mack's Harem' back in the old days?"

"Sure. Didn't you ever hear that?"

"No, I didn't." Suddenly it did not feel like such a big deal.

"Well, I heard it from time to time. Mack knew it, too. I think he kind of liked it."

Gracie looked down and shook her head.

Del cleared her throat, and Gracie could picture her in the courthouse hallway, shifting her weight impatiently on her four-inch heels. "So what was so important you needed to talk to me about?"

CHAPTER FIFTEEN

C huck Salerno from L&S Security Company arrived at the store promptly at nine the next morning. Gracie hoped they could complete their work before the store opened at ten.

"We can get you set up with video surveillance on the register, and some in other parts of the store, even give you remote access. You won't need more than six or eight zones here," Chuck said, as if rattling off today's specials. "Then get motion detectors, perimeter sensor, and intrusion protection on your doors and windows." He pointed with his pen. "Then we assign different pass codes to each of your employees. Get you a panic button at the register. A siren with battery back-up for on-site to scare 'em away, and alarms at our office and maybe at the police station. Anything else you want covered?"

Gracie winced and looked around. "I'm not sure. Can you price it out in segments?"

Salerno put his clipboard under an arm and scratched his temple, looking confused.

"All this is new to me," Gracie continued. "I'm not sure what I need, or what I can afford."

"What did you have mind, then?" His tone was impatient.

Gracie pursed her lips and shook her head. "We had a break-in here and I guess I wanted something on the doors to alert someone if a burglar broke in again."

"We can do that, but you might want to think about these other options, too. You will increase your security when you're in the store with the video and panic button. Robbers don't just come at night, you know."

Gracie shuddered.

"And by the way, you could really improve your security if you moved some of these bookcases around," he said, waving an arm toward the middle of the store. "Get better sight lines."

Gracie frowned. When she designed the store, she was thinking more about how cozy reading corners would help her customers feel comfortable. She had not considered the possibility of shoplifting. Aside from the law dictionary, she was not aware of any books that might have gone astray, but she realized that she did not have any real means of tracking the books that were still supposed to be on her shelves.

"Is there any way to protect inventory?"

"What? You mean like tags with a checkpoint gate at the door?"

"I guess." Gracie rolled her shoulders. She didn't really like the idea of a gate at her front door. It would crowd the entry and make her store less hospitable.

"Sure. We can do that, too. They use 'em in libraries and such." He bent over his clipboard and made some notes. "I'll work up some figures and fax 'em over to you. Then you sign the estimate and we can get you set up for installation."

"How soon could it all be installed?"

"The video and alarms can go in—I'm thinkin' end of next week." He scratched above his left ear. "The other, for the door, we'll have to order, so I can't give you a definite date on that yet. I'll check into it and include it on the estimate."

"Okay. Thanks for coming by."

"Sure thing. I'll be in touch," he said, handing her his card and shaking her hand with a little too much enthusiasm.

The doorbell rang as he left, and Gracie sank back into one of her overstuffed chairs. She had thought the bell over the door was all the security she would ever need. *How naïve.*

~

Gracie had just enough time before opening to get Kristen's paycheck written. Then she flipped the sign on the door to "Open" and propped it wide. The fresh fall air was dry and cool, and she did not want to miss out on it. Then, realizing that Dickens might escape, and she would have no bell warning her if someone came into the store when her back was turned, she started to close the door again.

As she did, she heard a man's voice saying the word "bookstore," carry across the green. She held the door open and cocked an ear to see if she could catch anything more. She was sorry she did. The next words she heard were "rip-off" and "be sorry," followed by an unpleasant laugh. She pulled the door open and stepped onto the sidewalk to try to see where the words were coming from.

There were two men, one sitting on a bench, the other standing over him with one foot on the seat. Each held a paper coffee cup. The one standing wore some type of uniform. *Could it be from a delivery company?* Gracie tried to see their faces, but they were too far away. She thought if she could just get a little closer, she might be able to overhear a bit more.

She closed her door as quietly as the bell above it would allow, and stepped carefully down the sidewalk, staying close to the building. She watched as they continued talking, intermittently taking sips from their cups. A car drove past, drowning out for a moment any chance she had of overhearing them. Then, as she reached the door of Doyle's, Hal stepped out.

"Hey, Gracie. Coming back in to get that post lamp? I set it aside for you."

Gracie jumped back, and raised her hand to her chest.

"Hal, you startled me." She stole a look across at the green. The man who was standing looked at his wrist, and the one sitting down stood up. It looked like their coffee break was over.

"Oh, weren't you headin' in here?"

Gracie forced a smile, and patted Hal's big hand. "No. I haven't decided yet, Hal, but when I do, you'll be the first to know." She looked again toward the green. The men had walked away, each to a different vehicle parked near the Steaming Kettle. The one in uniform entered a dark, late model car; the other a vehicle that looked like a Jeep.

"Okay. I'll just keep 'em behind the counter 'til you tell me otherwise," Hal said, his head tilted to one side.

"Thanks, Hal. I appreciate it." But Gracie's attention was still elsewhere.

As she walked back to her shop, she struggled to remember her dealings with the lost delivery man. *Was he one of those men?*

~

When Kristen arrived for her shift, Gracie was glad to hand her the paycheck.

"Thanks, Gracie. How's the arm?"

"It's a lot better, see?" Gracie rolled up her sleeve. The swelling was gone and the wounds had scabbed over.

Kristen wrinkled her nose. "It still looks painful to me."

"It isn't really, unless I lean on it."

Kristen shook her head and looked away.

"Could you reshelve that stack of books on the counter, please?" Gracie asked. "And while you're at it, keep an eye out for an old, tan, leather-bound law dictionary, would you? I seem to have misplaced it."

Kristen nodded. "Sure."

Gracie turned to go into the back room, but halfway there, looked back toward Kristen.

"Did you have any more problems like the one you called me about the other day?"

Kristen looked up from the books she was sorting and started playing with her hair. "Um, not really."

Gracie focused on her eyes. She had heard such half-hearted denials from clients when she was practicing law, and from her children in the years since. "Is that a 'no,' or an 'I'm-not-sure?'" she asked.

Kristen averted her eyes and shook her head. "I'm not sure there was anything."

"What happened that made you not sure?"

Kristen placed her hand on her cheek and closed her eyes. "Nothing really."

"But . . . ?"

"But I got the feeling a man was hanging around outside my dorm building on Sunday. It was a nice day, and the dorm is on a quad. Maybe he just liked the weather."

"What did he look like?"

Kristen looked up and to the left. "Nothing special. Sort of average, I guess. Dark hair, blue jeans, I think. He was reading a paper." Kristen looked back to Gracie. "I saw him from my window, and when I went to lunch, I thought I caught him watching me go by."

Some might consider that a compliment, Gracie thought. "How old was he?"

Kristen shook her head. "I'm not good at guessing ages. Thirties? Maybe forty?"

"Had you ever seen him around before?"

The girl drew her mouth into a straight line. "He sort of looked familiar, but I can't say why. Maybe he works at the college somewhere. That would explain why he would be on campus."

Gracie grimaced. "Well, we'll still be sure you get back up College Hill before dusk from now on."

"It wasn't anything." Kristen shook her head and went back to sorting books. "Maybe I'm just still spooked from the other night."

Gracie had to agree. A man reading a newspaper in public was hardly a reason to notify the campus police. But if it were someone keeping an eye on Kristen, then perhaps whoever was causing trouble for Gracie and the bookstore, had it in for Kristen as well, just because she worked there. *How unfair,* Gracie thought. *Haven't I caused the poor girl enough grief?*

Gracie went into the back room and sat at her desk. Clouds gathered outside making it dark in the back office. She closed her eyes and leaned back in her chair. There was a rumble of thunder in the distance.

The next moment she was back in the farmhouse, stepping around broken glass in the sunlit front room. She did not want to go into the kitchen, but moved slowly, inexorably, toward the back of the house. She tried to turn back, but was suddenly at the kitchen doorway. Beyond there, it was dark. She fumbled for a light switch. When she flipped it on, Dave was standing there, a bloody knife in his hand, ready to plunge it into her chest.

Gracie awoke with a start, and nearly tipped her desk chair onto its back. Her heart pounded. Drawing a deep breath, she took a quick look around the office. There was no one there except Dickens who was curled up in his cat bed.

A heavy rain bombarded the back of the building, and Gracie got up to make sure the window was tightly closed. Then she scooped up her sleeping cat. He stretched out, pushing himself away from her, but she held him and kissed his head.

"I just need a hug, sweetie."

The cat relented, and nestled into her arms. She stroked his back.

"Hmmm. You don't feel quite so bony these days. Are you happier keeping shop with me than being alone at home?"

Dickens jumped down, and walked away, curling up in his bed once again.

"Now if we can just see some of your energy return." Gracie stretched her back and shook her head, trying to dislodge the vestiges of her dream. "Back to my paperwork," she said aloud as she moved back to her desk. She closed the opened check ledger and put it away. Then she straightened up the other papers on her desk. As she did so, one paper slid from her grasp and fell, face down, onto the floor. She bent to pick it up and turned it over. It was the diagram she had drawn several days before.

She laid the paper on her desk and looked at it again. Circles in three different corners for Lowry, Ollie, and Kristen. Then a box centered at the top for her and a circle at the bottom for Hal. There was still an empty corner. She picked up a pen and drew another circle in the empty corner. Inside it, she wrote, "stalker," followed by a question mark, and drew a line to Kristen.

Then she looked at the two-sided arrow she had drawn between Ollie and Hal and shook her head. *That's not much of a connection,* she thought. Then she remembered something Hal had said. She wrote the word "Kenny" above the line between Hal and Ollie. He was Ollie's son and had worked for Hal, and he would have known where Hal kept his keys. *Did Hal say Kenny knew Lowry?* She wondered what he looked like . . . and what kind of car he drove.

What about Chief Johnson? Gracie wasn't sure she could trust him. She knew so little about him. Still, he was the current chief of police and obviously knew Lowry. Would he defend him? She became angry all over again at how he had treated her when she came to him for help. She wrote his name along the left margin and connected him with a line to Lowry.

As she was about to slip the diagram into her desk drawer when another connection caught her eye. She drew another two-sided arrow, this one linking her to Kristen. And while this arrow was short on the page, Gracie knew that the connection between them was strong. It was not just that Kristen worked for her. They also shared a link to a long-ago tragedy.

CHAPTER SIXTEEN

The clock said 2:42 a.m. Gracie cursed her sleep-lessness, rolled over, and adjusted her pillow. Closing her eyes, she willed herself to sleep. A moment later, she realized her eyes were wide open again. *I wish my mind had an off switch,* she thought.

Spencer snored next to her. She tried to match her breathing to his, and consciously relaxed her limbs, her shoulders, her neck. Her eyes closed again. She listened to her own breathing, hoping to sleep until morning. It didn't work. No matter how long she forced her eyes closed, sleep evaded her. Questions about Kristen and Lowry and Ollie and Hal swirled in her brain. She felt the answers she sought were close enough to touch, but still they eluded her.

The chime of the grandfather clock reminded her every quarter hour that she was losing prime sleeping time with nothing to show for it. Her stomach grumbled. Finally, she slipped out of bed, found her slippers, and put on her robe. She walked toward the steps, but hesitated. She had planned to go downstairs and make a cup of chamomile tea, but she changed her mind as she stood in the dark hallway. Reversing course, she went up the winding stairs to the attic.

The glow of the moon coming past the lace curtains of the windows centered in dormers on each of the four attic walls told her when she reached the top. She felt for the light switch and flicked it up, turning on a lamp that stood on a desk across the finished room.

The previous owners of the house had turned the attic into a library; it was one of the reasons Spencer and Gracie had bought the place. But now, with so many of Gracie's books moved over to the bookshop, all she could see as she scanned the room was empty shelves lining the walls, already gathering dust. On the floor were some empty boxes, and a stack of books that Gracie had decided not to take to the store. Spencer was planning to use the attic as his study, but with his publisher's deadline looming, he decided to wait until he had finished his current writing project before making the move.

The floor squeaked under the worn braided rug as Gracie crossed the room to three short filing cabinets built in under the eaves toward the back of the house. She pulled on the top drawer of the left-most cabinet. Inside were several hanging files. Opening the first, she discovered that it held a stack of drawings Ben had created as a youngster. Gracie bit her lip and smiled. Looking at the long-stored treasures, she considered taking the file over to the desk to peruse it further, but instead, put it back and closed the drawer.

The bottom drawer held old tax files and insurance policies. She slammed that drawer shut, then shushed it, as if it were its fault that it had made so much noise. She held her breath and glanced down the stairs listening to see if she had disturbed Spencer or Carrie. Hearing Spencer's snoring resume, she turned back to her work.

She moved to the next cabinet. Spencer stored his class notes and speeches in the top drawer. His research notes, she knew, were still stored in his office downstairs. The bottom drawer held class notes for courses Gracie had taught at Glenville College over the years as an adjunct professor. Behind the hanging files was a stack of old newspapers, turning yellow. Gracie knew they were from important dates in her life: their wedding announcement, reviews of Spencer's books, the kids' birth announcements, honor roll listings, and other achievements. She reached to pick up the pile and felt the bottom paper flake a bit at her touch. A pang of regret washed over her for never having taken the time to mount those articles to preserve them better. But, she knew newsprint was not made to last through the ages. She made a mental note to photograph these articles before they were lost forever. She put the stack down and closed the drawer.

She knew the next cabinet should hold what she sought. She pulled it open and peered in. It was full of manila file folders, each with a typed label. The paper smelled old and dry, and the file folders had yellowed. They were pressed so closely together that it was hard to know how many there were. She had not looked at her files from her days as a practicing attorney for many years.

She stooped down, but could not read the labels. *Darn it,* she thought. *Why didn't I bring up my reading glasses?*

Deciding more light would help, she went to the desk and picked up the lamp. She brought it as close to the filing cabinet as the cord would permit, and sat cross-legged in front of the drawer. Her knees cracked, and she landed more heavily than she wanted to. *Getting old.*

She could not remember how she had stored the files. *Was it alphabetical or by date?*

It had been so long since Gracie had practiced law that the copies of files she took with her when she left the firm seemed like the record of someone else's life. She could hardly recall being the person who represented those seeking a prenuptial agreement or a divorce, disputing child custody, or needing protection from abuse.

She flipped the tabs on the folders and read them from arm's length. Names that were no longer familiar flew past. She wondered if they remembered her any better than she remembered them. Probably not, she decided.

The files appeared to be alphabetical. She was in luck. Mercer would be about halfway back, rather than all the way to the rear of the drawer as it would have been if filed by date.

She grabbed a couple of files from the middle, pulled up the one behind them to mark the place, and held them by the lamp. "Landry, Charlotte" and "Lewis, Stephen." Not far enough back. She replaced them, and reached a few files further back: "Messer, Janet," Too far. She took the one in front of it. "Mercer, Cheryl."

There it was.

Her reaction was a mixture of excitement and dread. Did she really want to open this file, or was it better to leave it in her past?

With Kristen here, it's not really in my past, anymore, is it? She stood up. Last chance to put it back without looking at it.

She shook her head. The demons that haunted her might be exorcised if she were to look at the file again. There was only one way to find out.

Each side of the open file folder had two-pronged metal clasps that held neat stacks of photocopies in place. The originals stayed with the firm in case the client needed any future assistance. This client would not. On the left side, Gracie knew, were copies of the pleadings, proofs of service, correspondence, receipts for filing fees, and records of hours worked for the client. The most recent papers were on top. She glanced at the first page. It was a notation that the file was closed because the client was deceased.

On the other side of the file was a cover sheet with information in a format Gracie had honed over her few years of dealing with domestic relations issues, starting with: Client's name and address, spouse's name and address, each of their dates of birth, how long each had lived at the current address, date of marriage, place of marriage, children's names, birthdates, birthplaces, et cetera. It was all the basic information she would need when filing court documents.

Under that lay copies of Gracie's notes, written by hand on a legal pad. She looked at her handwriting. It was neat, more skilled than what she produced today. She wondered if her increased use of a keyboard was the reason her penmanship had degraded in recent years. Or maybe she was just getting careless.

Gracie's stomach growled. She got up, file in hand, and checked the desk drawers to see if Spencer had brought any snacks up to his new office. Finding nothing, she brought the lamp to the desk, half wondering if she should go downstairs and make a cup of tea. Her curiosity trumped her hunger, and she sat down.

In her notes was the story of Cheryl and Dave Mercer, Kristen's parents. They were high school sweethearts; Cheryl found out she was pregnant close to the end of their senior year. Gracie swallowed, thinking about who Carrie might be meeting at the same high school.

While Cheryl was happy about the baby, Dave never was. He repeatedly pushed her to get an abortion, but she refused. In the end, they got married against the wishes of all their parents. Cheryl had hoped that once the baby was born, they could be a happy family.

Gracie sighed.

Cheryl was raised by her divorced mother, Dorothy Walsh. Her father was not in the picture. When Cheryl decided to get married, Mrs. Walsh abandoned her and "the bastard," as she referred to Kristen, and moved to Boston, "so they couldn't sponge off of her anymore." Gracie winced at the record of the woman's cruelty. She couldn't help but wonder whether Mrs. Walsh had been as unkind to Kristen as she had been to her mother.

As soon as Dave gave up his plans for college in favor of marrying Cheryl, his working-class parents also disowned him. Dave got a minimum wage job at a business in Billington, but soon afterward, he was laid off. At least that's what he told Cheryl. She told Gracie they probably fired him for showing up drunk.

Neither of them had a steady income, and by the time the baby came, they lived on food stamps, WIC coupons, and whatever they could scrounge up from odd jobs. Dave drank most of their money away. That's when he started hitting her.

Letting out a long breath, Gracie read on.

Next came a list of the times Cheryl could remember Dave threatening or beating her. There were copies of Polaroids of Cheryl with bruises on her face and finger marks on her neck from his latest rage. Gracie closed her eyes and turned away. Her old professional distance had eroded over the years.

She flipped through more pages of handwriting, stopping at a page that was typed. She tucked the top pages over the back of the file, brought it up to the light, and leaned back to focus on it. It was a list of a half dozen names and addresses—places where the sheriff might find Dave to serve him with papers, should he not be at home when the sheriff tried there.

At the top of the list was his parents' home in Billington. Gracie tapped her finger on the file. The rest of the list included the homes of his friends or his favorite hangouts. Gracie recognized one of the latter as being a business that was finally closed some years later for serving alcohol to minors. She clicked her tongue, remembering what a problem that place had been with too many college students coming into town for binge drinking and then causing trouble or leaving trails of vomit along the town's sidewalks. She shook her head. *Why did it take so long to close that place down?*

She ran her finger down the page until a familiar address caught her eye. Her finger stopped and she pulled the file closer. When it became blurrier, she pushed it back to arm's length. *What is that doing on this list?* One twenty-eight Commonwealth Avenue. It was the address of her bookshop. At the time, the storefront was occupied by "Glenville Falls Furniture," known to townspeople as "Ollie's." *Why would Dave Mercer be there?*

Dave was unemployed, so he did not work there. She lifted page after page of notes, trying to find some indication of why he might be at a furniture store, but found nothing.

Letting the papers fall, she rubbed her eyes. Perhaps she should have retrieved her reading glasses.

She was overtaken by a yawn and wondered how long she had been there. At least it was still dark, but it would be a terrible day at the bookstore if she didn't get some sleep. Closing the file, she stood and stretched. She thought about returning the folder to the filing cabinet, but decided to leave it on the desk. She would come back to it when she was more alert. Turning toward the door, she hesitated. She opened the file and ripped out the page of names and addresses. Perhaps, she thought, this was what they called in crime novels a "lead."

CHAPTER SEVENTEEN

Spencer's good-bye kiss woke her the next morning. "I'm off to the college. Just thought I'd let you know it's eight-thirty."

The fog of sleep cleared, and Gracie opened her eyes. "How did it get so late?"

"I knew you were up part of the night. Carrie and I tried to be quiet this morning to let you catch up a little on your sleep. It's the day of her field trip, remember, so she won't be home until dinner time."

Gracie propped herself up on her elbows and shook her head. "Oh, yeah. I almost forgot. I'm going to make sure to be here before she gets back. I don't want her to think that the store is more important to me than she is."

"She doesn't," Spencer said, wrinkling his forehead.

"Well, if she doesn't, she is doing a good job of convincing me otherwise." Gracie sat up and put her feet on the floor. "Did she ask you for money?"

Spencer just smirked. Carrie had a way of wrapping her father around her proverbial little finger.

"Way to go, Dad," Gracie said. "I hope you didn't give her too much."

"Just enough," he said with a wink.

"Have a good day, sweetie."

"You, too," Spencer said turning to go. He stopped at the door and looked back. "Oh, and it's chilly out. You'll need a coat."

Gracie closed her eyes to make a face, but when she opened them again Spencer was gone.

Once downstairs, Gracie found Dickens perched in the kitchen window watching activity at the backyard birdfeeder.

"Be nice to me today. I slept late and I'm still tired," she said to the cat while putting the kettle on to boil.

Dickens looked at her through nearly-closed lids.

"I see I am not getting any sympathy from you."

Dickens hopped down and rubbed against her ankles.

"Don't try to convince me you haven't had breakfast. There is still some wet food in your dish." Gracie looked at the dish again. He had done a good job with his breakfast. His appetite was returning. And truth be told, she was happy for his company at the bookstore. She reached down and scratched his head.

An hour later, Gracie unlocked the shop door just as the town hall clock struck ten. "Made it!" she said as she opened the cat carrier and let Dickens walk ahead of her. He went directly toward the back room, then hesitated and looked back over his shoulder, checking to see if Gracie was following him.

"I'm coming, I'm coming. Keep your fur on." Gracie flipped the sign to open and turned on the lights. The store held a chill, and Gracie wondered if it was time to turn on the heat. She decided it could wait a while longer. "Shoppers will have jackets on, and we don't want them getting overheated," she said out loud. It sounded like a good justification to her.

In the back room, she took off her jacket and hung it on a hall tree—another item Ollie had left behind. Sitting down, she pulled a sweater across her shoulders and flipped through the mail. Most of the envelopes looked like bills. She blew out a long breath. Running a business was expensive.

She started her computer and grabbed her reading glasses to look at her sales records. With the exception of two wonderful weekends, the opening and Family Weekend, the store was just holding its own. At this rate, she could probably still keep Kristen, but she wouldn't be able to take any draw for herself. She was working for free. She had known that the business would start out that way, but for a moment she wondered if this was worth doing just for the "fun" of it.

Dickens jumped onto the desk and flopped down across the keyboard. He nuzzled her hand and started to purr. She leaned over and put her forehead against his. He rubbed down her face, and she kissed him. Then she pulled back to wipe fur from her nose.

"How am I supposed to keep you in catnip if I don't get a paycheck, little buddy?" she said, scratching Dickens' neck. The cat looked up at her and then closed his eyes and leaned into her moving fingers.

When the bell over the door rang, Gracie slipped away from her cat. "I'll be back, sweetie. Wish me luck." Then she added in a stage whisper, "If I make a sale, there's that much more for cat toys."

The sale did not take long, and in a few minutes, she was back at her desk, grabbing her reading glasses, preparing to delve into a stack of bills. Dickens had moved to his cat bed.

It looked like one of the bills was from the *Gazette* for her advertisements. Good old Wendell. He had been so helpful designing her ads when she was getting things going. She wondered how many more she would be able to purchase.

The holiday season ought to liven sales up around here. She opened her filing cabinet and thumbed through files, drawing out one labeled "Marketing Ideas."

Opening the folder, she found a page with a bullet list of ideas to stimulate interest in her bookstore. "Food" was listed first. She picked up a pencil and drew a line through that. While she had no intention of competing with the Steaming Kettle, she had decided to keep a pot of hot water for tea or coffee during the week. And she had arranged with Kelly to get a discount on a tray of muffins every Saturday as long as she had a small sign directing people to the Steaming Kettle. If things didn't get better, though, she might have to stop even that.

Next on the list was "Diversify—Gifts?" *Nope,* she thought. *I don't have time to become an expert at stocking and selling gifts. I can barely handle books.*

The next bullet was "Reader's Group." *That one has possibilities—especially if I can find someone else to run it.* It would probably have to be on Saturday, unless she could stay open in the evening. She tapped the eraser end of the pencil against her forehead. She would have to think more about that.

"Children's Story Time" was next on the list. She liked that idea. Perhaps Kristen could handle it. She put a check next to that one, and made a note to ask Kristen if she would like to give it a try.

Her fax number rang, and lights lit up on her all-in-one printer. After making the requisite responding high-pitched beeps, the machine rolled a piece of paper through the system, laying it face-down on the tray. Gracie had to stand to reach it. She turned the paper over and found it was the estimate from the security company.

"Good grief," she said when she saw the bottom line. "It's more than the whole store is worth."

Dickens got out of his bed and moved into the shop, apparently to find a quieter place to sleep.

Gracie put the estimate down on her desk top, and scrutinized the itemized list. Taking out her pencil, she began crossing off the items she could live without—or simply could not afford. In a moment, she stood, balled the paper up, and threw it into the trash. "I can't afford this store," she shrieked, stomping one foot, her hands clenched at her sides.

The sound of the doorbell told her she could no longer indulge her tantrum. She took a deep breath, unclenched her fists, and tried to put on a smile as she went into the front of the store.

"I don't know what your game is here, lady, but I'm warning you, you'd better just give it up." Officer Lowry's voice was loud and angry, and Gracie wondered if he would finally remove those sunglasses to stare her down. He didn't.

She felt herself calm down in response to his outburst. It was a technique that had served her well with opposing attorneys. The angrier they got, the calmer she would try to seem. Meeting anger with anger only escalated things.

"I am not playing a game, officer," she said with a well-modulated voice.

"Then what do you call filing a complaint against me?"

"I am only trying to find out what happened at my store. Since you have not been forthcoming, I have sought help from your superior." Gracie was glad to see that her visit had provoked some action on the chief's part.

"Well, I'm not playing, either, and unless you want things to get a whole lot worse around here, you will keep your meddling nose out of police business. Understand?"

"No." Her voice was flat, but she knew her expression was defiant. "In fact, there are many things about my supposed break-in that I do not understand. And unless I'm mistaken, 'police business' is also my business when it involves my bookstore."

Even through his sunglasses, Gracie could tell Officer Lowry was exasperated, nearly to the breaking point. He let out a grunt of frustration, then pointed a finger at her like a gun.

"Just don't make me sorry I helped you out," he said, in an ominous tone of voice. With that, he turned and stormed from the store.

"Helped!" she exclaimed to his departing figure. "Just exactly how do you think you've been of any *help?*" Gracie felt her body tremble, and she leaned against the nearest bookshelves. She had not expected a confrontation with Officer Lowry. If he had intended to intimidate her, he had succeeded, but that would not deter her from pursuing the matter.

CHAPTER EIGHTEEN

The rest of the day passed slowly with very little business coming in the door. Gracie went through her bills, scheduling online payments for each one based on their due dates and her income projections. She could pay them all on time—this month at least.

The last bill she opened was one she did not mind paying. It was from Wendell Owens for her ads in the *Glenville Falls Gazette*. The ads Wendell had suggested had helped bring in customers. Of that, she was certain. The *Gazette* was an institution in their small town. Wendell could always be counted on to be there, taking pictures and interviewing people, whenever anything of importance happened. Except for her break-in.

Gracie looked at the clock. It was nearly four. If she closed early, she thought, she would be able to deliver Wendell's check in person.

She pulled on her jacket, and Dickens appeared from some hiding place in the store.

"Sorry, baby," she said, stroking his back. "I'm just going out for a bit. I'll be back later to take you home."

As she turned the "Open" sign to "Closed" and locked her store, she realized the day had not warmed up much.

A gusty breeze stung her cheeks, and she wished she had worn a warmer coat. A cold, wet wind blew leaves across the street and sidewalks under a sky of gunmetal grey. Rain was coming, and Gracie wondered how long it would be before the first snow.

Pulling her jacket close around her, she bent into the wind and walked to the newspaper office on the green. She was glad to see lights on inside as she approached. It meant Wendell was there instead of out covering a story.

She opened the door to the store front, and was greeted with the smell of old newsprint and stale coffee. A large metal table stood against one side of the small room, and a high counter jutted out from the other. Behind the counter were Wendell's metal desk and three tall filing cabinets. The rest of the space was filled with stacks of newspapers of various heights and shades of yellow.

"Hi, Wendell," Gracie smiled and waved to the portly gentleman as she closed the door against the wind.

"Gracie," he said, standing. "What brings you here? Looking to put in another ad?"

"Not today," Gracie sniffed. The cold had made her nose run. She grabbed an old tissue from her jacket pocket, inspected it, and decided it was clean. In one movement, she wiped her nose with it and stuffed it back in her pocket. "I'm just here to pay my bill for the last ones."

"Personal delivery," Wendell said, crinkling his lively eyes. "The U.S. mail would have sufficed, but it's always nice to have a visitor. Coffee?" he asked, extending an arm toward a chair in front of his desk.

"No thanks," Gracie said, taking the seat. She looked at the glass pot sitting on a hotplate on top of one of the filing cabinets. It was about one-quarter full, and she wondered how many hours it had sat there. Even if she were a coffee drinker, she would have declined.

Wendell brushed his hands together and sat down at his desk. Gracie reached over and handed him her check. "Here it is," she said, trying to match her mood to Wendell's jovial personality. She scanned the room.

"Thanks," Wendell said, taking the check and placing it in his desk drawer. "You looking for something?" he said, with more curiosity in his voice than accusation. He didn't miss a thing.

Gracie felt her cheeks redden, but this time it was not from the cold.

"Well, I was just wondering, do you keep copies of all of your past editions?"

"Sure. I don't keep it up as well as I probably should, but I have all the past editions–somewhere." He glanced at some of the yellowing stacks.

Gracie gave another sidelong glance around the room.

"Where are they?"

"Uhh . . ." His eyes darted from pile to pile. "Is there something in particular you're looking for?"

"I don't know." Gracie said, looking sideways toward the ceiling. "Could I just go in and poke around at bit?"

"I have no objection," Wendell said with a chuckle, "if you want to take your life in your hands."

Gracie frowned. "That bad, is it?"

Wendell pulled his lips into a diagonal line and leaned back in his desk chair. "Well, keeping a morgue isn't my strong suit. I'm so busy just putting out the paper, I don't really have time to preserve it." He sat forward and leaned his elbows on the desk. "But, you know who is good at preserving things?"

Gracie shrugged.

"The library. They have most of the old editions on microfilm. You could check with them. I don't know how they have it indexed, but whatever they've got, I'm sure it's better than what I have here."

Gracie smiled and stood. "Thanks, Wendell. That's exactly what I'll do."

A sudden squawk made Gracie jump. "What was that?"

"My police scanner. Gotta keep up with what's going down," he said with a twinkle in his eye.

"I guess you do," Gracie said, zipping her jacket. She looked up and caught Wendell's eye. "Do you hear everything that happens where the police are involved?"

"Pretty much. I try not to miss anything that I should be reporting on."

"But you never heard anything about a week and a half ago about a store being broken into in town."

"Here? No. Nothing came across that I heard."

"That's what I thought."

"Do you know something I should know, Gracie McIntyre?" He looked at her over the top of his glasses.

"Not yet, but if I do, I'll be sure to let you know."

~

The library. Why didn't I think of that? Gracie chided herself as she crossed the green toward the old Sutter House next to the town hall. The large brick house was once the residence of one of the town's most prominent citizens. When the owner died, he left it and his personal library to the town. At first the library had a modest collection, but over the years it had grown. As the collection required, the building expanded to include what had once been outbuildings for carriage storage and a barn. All had been converted to a climate controlled maze of book shelves and reading rooms. Gracie knew that local history was kept on the main floor of the old barn. Entering the "Museum Annex" as it was called, Gracie took a look around. Journals, letters, and documents of early settlers were displayed in glass-topped cases that ran up the center of the room. Another case contained artifacts from the native tribes that once lived in the region: arrow heads, shards of pottery, hatchet heads, and even a stone mortar and pestle. The last case held pewter plates, flatware, jewelry, and even a lock of hair once possessed by a town founder.

Along the walls were four-foot tall bookcases with volumes of town and college history, including year-books from nearly every year since the college's founding in 1831. Hanging above the shelves were old photographs of the town and college, as well as of the waterfall that gave the town its name. Filling the rest of the space were wooden tables and chairs. A few people were seated in the reading room, bent over their books, but the room was nearly silent. Gracie tip-toed toward the desk at the back of the room. Sharona Antonello, Angela's mother, looked up from her computer terminal, her face breaking into a wide smile.

"Well, hello there, neighbor," Sharona said in a library-appropriate whisper. "Enjoying a little down time with the girls off on their field trip?"

"Hi, Sharona," Gracie said. "How's the library work going?"

"Very well, thanks. It's only part-time, but it keeps me busy and gives me some grown-up company." Even her laugh was quiet. "What brings you in today? Revolutionary War research?"

"No." Gracie shook her head. "That's strictly Spencer's area of study. My interest is in the town's more recent history, specifically about eighteen years ago. I understand you have local newspaper archives from back then?"

"We do, on microfilm. They're upstairs. Let me show you."

With Sharona leading the way, the two women went up a metal spiral staircase to a room filled with cabinets that looked to have been discarded when they went from the old card catalog system to computers.

"The *Gazette* archives are all in these drawers." Sharona said with a wave of her hand. "If you know the date you want, you can find it on the label." She pointed at one that said "Jan – Mar, 2009." "If you're looking for a specific name, though, you need to look at one of these indices," she said, indicating a desk with stacks of computer print outs in bright blue plastic binders. She pulled one out that was labeled "Glenville Falls Gazette—A-G." "Just flip through here. They're alphabetical, and will tell you when each name appears: date, edition, and page number. Once you find the correct film, you can read it over there."

Gracie looked where Sharona pointed and saw three microfilm readers on a shelf built into the back wall.

"There is a page of directions with each machine." Sharona ticked off the instructions like she'd been working there for years. "You can send any page you want to the printer for ten cents per page. When you're done, just leave the films in the basket on the desk and we'll put them away for you. And if you need any help with anything, let me know."

"Thanks," Gracie said with a wave. She put on her reading glasses and looked for the date she wanted. She found the right box without any trouble and went to one of the microfilm readers. Knowing she wanted to be home when Carrie got in, she set her cell phone to vibrate at 5:40. If she left then, she could be home by six, even with having to go back to the store for Dickens. She had a little over an hour.

In a few moments, she was scrolling toward the edition of the *Gazette* published just after the Mercer deaths. Then there it was. A huge headline on the front page:

Local Man Kills Wife, Self, in Alleged Murder/Suicide

Cheryl Mercer, 19, was found dead of knife wounds last Thursday evening in her home on Hastings Road. She was pronounced at the scene by medical examiner Samuel Davies who listed the cause of death as homicide.

Moments after the discovery, the victim's husband, David Mercer, was also found dead in the Pocomtuc River near the bottom of Glenville Falls. His cause of death is listed as an apparent suicide. A knife, thought to be the murder weapon used in Mrs. Mercer's slaying, was found near the body.

According to court records, Mrs. Mercer was granted a restraining order against her husband earlier in the day, alleging spousal abuse. . . .

The report went on to detail when Dave was served with the restraining order, how he had reacted to it, and interviews with people who knew the couple. Wendell even had a companion article in which he interviewed an expert on domestic violence from Glenville College. Gracie's name appeared in the news article, but she was not quoted.

She leaned back and took off her reading glasses. Emotions flooded back that she had tried for eighteen years to suppress. She had never found peace with the part she played in bringing about that night's events, and wondered if she ever would.

Leaving the front page, Gracie scanned through the rest of the paper to find the obituaries. She read Cheryl's first, a lump forming in her throat at the mention of being survived by her mother, Dorothy Walsh of Hyde Park, and an infant daughter. *Poor Kristen,* she thought, choking up. It was the same emotion that impelled her to hire the girl, why she shielded her from Officer Lowry, and the reason she felt a need to protect her from the peeping Tom, or whoever it was, who had frightened her.

Then she read Dave's obituary. It gave his full name, David Patrick Mercer, and listed his athletic feats during high school. *What an odd obituary under the circumstances,* Gracie thought. It also listed Kristen among his survivors along with his parents, Henry and Barbara Mercer, his paternal grandparents, and a younger brother Daniel, all of Billington.

Gracie tapped her finger on the desktop. She was not sure what she had hoped to find there, but whatever it was, it did not jump out at her. Then she flipped back to the front page, deciding to read the lead article more carefully. She felt a jolt when she read past the front page to where the article continued on page three:

> Richard Lowry, who was a friend of both victims, found the man's body.
> "Soon as I heard about the restraining order, I went looking for Dave," Lowry told the Gazette. "I knew he'd be upset, and I know he likes to go up to the falls when he's upset. I was several yards away when I saw him throw something into the water and then go over the falls. It was definitely suicide."

Gracie's first thought was how awful it must have been for him to see his friend die that way. Then she wondered how much of who Lowry was today was a result of that earlier trauma. I wonder what he was like back then. Was he ever just a good kid?

She remembered Hal saying Lowry had run with a tough crowd—well, tough by Glenville Falls' standards, at least. But that was before the murder/suicide.

She did a quick search on Lowry's name, and found him listed among police cadets shortly after Cheryl's death. Was this tragedy what made him want to become a cop? Even so, why was he being so deceptive now?

Gracie realized that she did not know enough about Officer Richard Lowry to guess what his motives might be, but hoped that Chief Johnson did—or at least soon would.

~

Gracie spent the rest of her time looking up other articles in which Officer Lowry was cited. There was a long list of newspapers to look up, most of which contained quotes for the press regarding various newsworthy crimes and incidents, but Gracie saw nothing she thought was worth noting. Everything followed the expected pattern of routine police work.

Then there was his wedding announcement, and three years later, his divorce.

Gracie's eyes were tired when her cell phone vibrated on the desk. She made a few quick notes about where she had left off with her research, gathered her belongings, and stopped back at Sharona's desk.

"I've got to run," Gracie said. "I have some pages I sent to the printer. Do I pick them up here?"

"Right," Sharona said, turning to collect Gracie's copies. "Six copies, sixty cents."

"Thanks," Gracie said, handing over a one-dollar bill.

"Did you find what you were looking for?" Sharona asked as she made change.

"I'm not really sure, but I know I'll be back."

"Here's a bookmark with our hours," Sharona whispered with a smile.

Gracie took the bookmark and tucked it inside her copies.

Packing up her papers took longer than Gracie planned, and with walking into the wind, when she got back to the bookstore, it was already five minutes to six.

"Dickens? Come here, fella. Time to go home."

She turned on the store lights hoping to see him coming, but no such luck.

"Here, kitty," she called in a high-pitched voice. "Come on, boy. Where are you?" She made kissing noises as she pulled out his carrier and opened the door. Still no sign of the orange tabby. She looked at the clock. Four minutes to six. "I don't have time for this, cat," she said, losing her patience. "Where are you?" She squeaked a rubber mouse. That used to bring him running, but not lately.

She checked his cat bed, under her desk, the tops of all the bookcases, the front window. No cat.

The clock said 5:58. Even if she left now, she would not be home by six. *Maybe Carrie will be a little later than she expected.* Gracie picked up the phone and called home. Spencer picked up.

"Is Carrie home yet?"

"No. Where are you? I called the store fifteen minutes ago, and there was no answer, but you still aren't home."

"I went out for a bit, and I just came back to get Dickens, but he's hiding somewhere, and won't come out. I wanted to get home before Carrie. I thought today, at least, I could be there to greet her when she got home and hear about her day."

"Wait a second. I think I hear her coming now."

Gracie heard Spencer put his hand over the phone and call out. She even thought she could hear Carrie's answer.

"Yep. It's her. Why don't you come home now?"

Gracie blew out a blast of air. "I will. As soon as I find that darned cat." Her tone was clipped, and she knew it. She was sorry to have been short with Spencer. It wasn't his fault, after all.

As soon as Gracie hung up, Dickens appeared.

"You did that on purpose, didn't you?" she accused the cat.

He sat down and looked at her, then started to wash his face.

"Heck with that. You're going into the carrier. Now." She grabbed the cat, put him in the carrier, and trudged home. Fat raindrops started to fall as she turned the corner from Commonwealth onto Elm. By the time she reached home, her jacket was soaked through. All she wanted was to take a hot shower and get into her pajamas, but she still had dinner to make, and a teenaged daughter to placate.

"Oh, darn!" she said as she let the cat out of the carrier. "I left those stupid papers back at the store."

"What papers?" Carrie asked, coming around the corner from the kitchen.

"Oh, just some . . . stuff I meant to bring home. Where's Dad?"

"Up writing." Carrie took a bite of an apple. "We should have gotten more cheese up in Vermont. What's for dinner?" Her face was blank and she wasn't making eye contact.

"I'm making a casserole. It won't take too long." Gracie knew dinner was at least forty-five minutes away.

"You know, Angela's mom makes stuff ahead of time, then all she needs to do is put it in the microwave when she gets home."

"I overslept this morning and didn't have time," Gracie said, feeling guiltier by the second. "I barely made it to the store on time. But this is a quick casserole. If you'll help me, we can have it ready before you know it."

"Don't rush on my account. I have an apple." Carrie took a bite, went upstairs to her room, and closed the door.

Gracie closed her eyes and let out a long breath. Walking into the kitchen, she pulled out a casserole dish and started dinner.

Before it was in the oven, Gracie had figured out her next step. It wasn't the library she needed to visit next. It was someplace far more revealing.

CHAPTER NINETEEN

The next morning, after leaving Dickens and the store in Kristen's hopefully capable hands, Gracie drove down the highway to Billington. It took her twenty-five minutes to reach the address from her file: the home of Dave Mercer's parents. At least it had been theirs eighteen years ago.

Gracie found a parking space on the opposite side of the street between a dented red pick-up truck and a blue, late-model hybrid. She looked around. It was in an established residential neighborhood with neat lawns and large trees. Yellow leaves rustled onto the grass with each new flurry of a breeze. Dave's house, like many surrounding it, was a late Victorian, with gingerbread decorating the peaked roof above a covered porch.

She had hoped for a rural mailbox with a name on it, but these houses were on narrow lots and had only small letter boxes next to their front doors. If there was a name on what had been the Mercer's home, she could not see it from the street.

A detached, single-car garage stood behind the house at the end of a straight driveway. Just behind it was a white fence marking the back line of the lot. From her vantage point, Gracie could see the remnants of a vegetable garden along the rear of the yard. Whoever lived there was active enough to keep a garden.

Gracie tried to imagine how old Dave's parents would be. Dave was nineteen when he died eighteen years before. He would have been thirty-seven now. Gracie raised one eyebrow. His parents could be as young as their mid-fifties to early sixties—not as old as she had expected.

She gripped the steering wheel, and tapped it with her index finger. She had come a long way but still knew nothing more than she had before. She had never met Dave; he wasn't present when she and Cheryl obtained the protective order. His photo was in the newspaper archives, but it hadn't told her much about the young man or his upbringing. Here was the house where he had lived, and perhaps where one or both of the parents who reared him could still be found . . . if they had not moved . . . and if they weren't both at work.

There was one way to find out.

She got out of the car and crossed the street. Scaling the three wooden steps to the porch, she examined the mailbox. It displayed only the house number.

Gracie searched for a doorbell, but there was no button beside the old oak door. Then she noticed a key protruding from the center of the wooden panel. She reached out and tried to turn it. It gave her some resistance, but when it budged, she felt a vibration in her fingers and heard a bell ringing on the inside. A small-sounding dog barked in response, but she could detect no sound of a human inside.

Gracie stepped back and was about to leave when she heard a deadbolt disengage. She turned to see the door open to reveal the face of an elderly woman. Warm air poured onto the chilly porch through the opening. At the woman's feet, a toy poodle barked and jumped like a circus performer.

"Oh shush, Bon-Bon. Go back in the kitchen. It's all right," the woman commanded, and the dog obeyed.

"Mrs. Mercer?" Gracie asked, hoping she wasn't disturbing the woman for no reason.

"Yes," she said. "Do I know you?" When she smiled, her face fell into a dozen folds. Her white hair was neatly coifed, and she wore a warm-looking, sapphire-blue suit. She peered at Gracie through thick, out-of-fashion glasses, and while her expression remained welcoming, Gracie had the feeling she was being given a serious once-over.

Gracie stood for a moment, her mouth open, uncertain what to say. Finally she found her voice. "Oh, uh, I . . . I am . . ." Should she pretend to be a solicitor? No. No props, nothing to sell. Should she ask for directions or say she had car trouble? Too late. She had already called the woman by name. There was nothing left for her but to be honest, and hope to find a diplomatic way of bringing up what was probably the most terrible memory in the woman's long life.

"My name is Grace McIntyre," she began. "I am . . . er . . . I used to be a lawyer. Does my name sound familiar?" Gracie smoothed back her hair with a quick swipe, and wished she had dressed a bit more professionally. Her sweater, slacks, and walking shoes did not quite give off the lawyerly look she needed to appear credible to this stranger.

"Used to be? What happened? You get disbarred?" The woman's expression turned from hospitable to suspicious.

"No, but I was, uh, somewhat involved in a case that I believe had an impact on your family some years ago."

Somewhat involved? Believe had an impact? Gracie chastised herself for being so mealy-mouthed.

The woman straightened a bit and her expression lost all hint of its former smile. "McIntyre, you say?"

Gracie nodded.

"I think I remember your name. What do you want?"

That was a good question. Why was she disturbing this poor woman? What did she have to offer her, and what could she hope to gain here?

"I'm sorry. I have just been thinking a lot lately about the incidents from all those years ago." She shook her head. "I didn't mean to disturb you. I probably shouldn't have come." Gracie raised a hand to her forehead and looked back toward her car. "I should probably go."

Gracie started toward the edge of the porch.

"Young lady," Mrs. Mercer barked in a school-teacher voice, "come back here."

Gracie turned and saw that the woman held the door open wide.

"Come in and tell me what you came to say."

Gracie followed the woman's command and entered the dark, warm house. She followed Mrs. Mercer through a doorway off of the entry hall into a small sitting room. The shades were drawn, and only one small lamp was lit. Heavy damask drapes ensured very little light came in, making it appear as though it were dusk despite the late-morning hour.

As Gracie's eyes adjusted to the dim light, she saw chintz furniture following the contours of two walls: a couch on one, two chairs against the other. A complementary carpet lay on the floor before them, giving the small room an air of faded gentility. Across from the sofa, a small table stood with an old-style television atop it. The rest of that wall was lined with bookshelves filled with books. The scent of vanilla from a bowl of potpourri next to the TV almost overpowered a different smell that Gracie could not quite place.

"Hello," an old-sounding voice greeted her from behind as she entered. Gracie turned, but saw no one.

"Hi," she said, a question in her voice.

"Oh, that's Tommy," Mrs. Mercer said, crossing to a cage in the corner of the room and picking up a clear bowl filled with carrot sticks. She pushed one through the thin bars. A parrot, its bright colors contrasting with the paleness of the room, moved from one perch to another inside the cage and grabbed the treat. "I've had this bird ever since my husband passed, so when I came here to live with my son, I told him I had to bring Tommy along. Someone to talk to, you know."

Gracie shook her head. "So you're not, uh, you're not David Mercer's mother?"

The woman chuckled, and the laugh lines once again appeared on her face. "No, dear. I am Davey's grandmother." Then the smile faded, replaced by a serious look in her eyes. "Is it Davey you came to talk about?"

Gracie looked down at her hands. "I guess so," she said, not wanting to make eye contact.

"Then sit down, and let me get you a cup of tea, and we can have a good chat."

Gracie opened her mouth to say something, but no words came to mind. She shut her mouth again, and sat at the end of the sofa. She suddenly felt very warm, and stripped off her jacket, laying it behind her on the couch.

Mrs. Mercer turned to a sideboard where china cups and saucers sat as if she had expected company. She removed a cozy from a matching teapot and poured a cup of tea.

"Pretty boy," the parrot squawked, followed by a whistle.

The woman's knobby hands were covered with transparent skin, but shook not even the slightest bit as she handed Gracie her tea.

"Thank you," Gracie said, looking down as she took the cup.

"Do you take sugar or lemon?"

"Black is fine." Gracie finally looked up, and saw compassion in the old woman's eyes. She felt emotion well up in her chest and swallowed hard.

Mrs. Mercer settled in a chair adjacent to the sofa, and picked up her own teacup. Gracie watched her take a sip, and then looked into her eyes. It was as if the older woman could see into her soul. Looking down at her own tea, Gracie took a sip. It was tepid at best, but she barely noticed. She was too focused on trying to figure out what she would say. Mrs. Mercer made no attempt to fill the silence caused by her guest's indecision, and the two women sat for some moments waiting for the awkwardness to pass.

The closeness of the room and the knot in her throat made it hard for Gracie to breathe. She forced herself to take a calming breath, and then another. When she finally spoke, even she was unprepared for her words.

"I have always felt responsible for what happened all those years ago." She felt the knot in her throat twist even tighter.

The woman looked surprised, but said nothing.

"I guess I felt, er, I *feel* that if I had not helped Cheryl get a protective order, that none of it would have happened. That they might both be alive today." Still the other woman said nothing, causing Gracie to feel even more flustered. She raised a hand to her forehead and went on. "I, I, I should have just helped her get out of town. I don't know why I didn't think of it back then, but I didn't. I just followed my routine for such cases. I

didn't even think such a horrible thing could happen."
She looked at Mrs. Mercer with tears in her eyes. "I am
very, *very* sorry."

The old woman put her tea cup on a side table, and
folded her hands in her lap. Looking at her hands, she
took a deep breath. "There is plenty of regret to go
around about those days, my dear," she said, not looking
up. "Perhaps it helps to know that you are not alone in
feeling responsible for those events." She raised her eyes
to Gracie's.

Gracie arched her eyebrows. "Really? I presumed
that you, your whole family, held me responsible. That
you hated me for my part in it."

Mrs. Mercer shook her head and looked over at her
parrot. "What you did needed to be done." Her voice was
emotionless.

Gracie felt a twitch pull at the corner of her mouth.
"It did?" Objectively, Gracie knew the woman was right,
but it had been a long time since Gracie could look at
those days objectively.

"Yes. My grandson was too young to be a proper
husband or father. That marriage was a bad idea from
the beginning. I don't understand how he could have
hit her like he did, but that poor girl needed someone
to help her get out of it. Someone on her side. You just
happened to be the one to do it."

"But if I hadn't, maybe . . ."

Mrs. Mercer shook her head and reached out to pat
Gracie's hand. "If lots of things had not happened as
they did. If only my poor son had not been so bone-
headed as to cut Davey off without a cent. . . ." The woman's hand slipped from Gracie's. "If they had taken that
young couple into their home as they should have, none
of it might have happened." She looked around, a far-
away expression on her face. "They could have helped

raise their grandchild here instead of letting those children fend for themselves." She stood and walked to the sideboard and poured more tea into her cup. Then she raised the teapot toward Gracie, offering her more.

Gracie shook her head. "No thanks."

"Or if my husband and I had made space for them in our little place on the other side of town," the woman continued as she crossed back to her seat, "they could have lived there. We could have made it work, but my husband didn't want to go against our son." She sighed as she sat. "I went along with their wishes, but I've had plenty of time to regret it since."

She took a sip of tea and held the cup in her lap before continuing. "It is the most horrible experience one can have in life to lose a child, or a grandchild, so young, before they even have a chance to find out what life has to offer. It is even worse when you lose them in such a violent way—and one that you believe to have been preventable." She closed the many folds of her eyelids and shook her head. "There is enough blame to go around, my dear. You need not take a share of it." The woman's voice sounded as old and fragile as she appeared.

Gracie blinked several times to fight back the tears.

Mrs. Mercer continued. "Not a day goes by that I do not wish I'd done something to keep things from happening as they did. And my son, although he would never admit it, feels the same way. He . . . none of us, has been the same since. We probably never will be." She took another sip of the cool tea.

The bird whistled in the corner. "Pretty boy, pretty boy." Mrs. Mercer did not appear to have heard him.

"But years pass, and what's done can't be undone," she said, brushing imaginary crumbs from her lap.

"What was it that Whittier said? 'For all sad words of tongue or pen, the saddest are these . . .'"

"It might have been." Gracie finished the quotation in a near whisper.

Mrs. Mercer shook her head. "We cannot change the past. We can only hope to learn from it."

Gracie pondered that for a moment. Had she learned from it? What lesson should she have gleaned from that experience? Or had she just run away from its lessons, as her father had once said, by leaving the law?

"I think my son learned some things," Mrs. Mercer said, her voice strong again. "I think all that happened is probably why he converted the garage several years ago as an apartment for Danny. He didn't want to make the same mistake twice."

"Danny? Their younger son?"

"Yes. He was three years younger than Davey, and he just adored him. Hero worship, you could say. He took it very hard when Davey left, or was kicked out, I should say. And I don't think he has yet forgiven his father for Davey's death. Many lives were ruined that day."

Gracie swallowed hard. Beyond them mourning their son, she had never given much thought to how this family had suffered. She realized she had held them partially to blame for raising a wife-beater and a killer. Her heartbreak had been reserved for Cheryl and Kristen, and to some degree herself. How selfish she had been to claim so much of the pain as hers alone.

Gracie followed Mrs. Mercer's teacup with her eyes as she placed it on the side table in front of what appeared to be a collection of family photographs.

"Do you have a photo of Dave?" she asked. "I never met him."

The older woman reached over and picked up a five by seven frame. "Here's one of happier days," she said, passing the photo to Gracie.

It was, in fact, a very happy picture. A tall, gangly young man dressed in the uniform of the high school's basketball team stood grinning at the camera, a basketball under one arm. A shorter boy, not in uniform, looked up at him, also smiling. Gracie looked into the eyes of the boy who had taken Cheryl's life and then his own. There was nothing there of the rage it must have taken to do what he did. On the contrary, his expression was one of joy, of hope, of anticipation. The boy next to him looked on with pride, even adoration. So much had been taken from both of these children. So much had been taken from the world.

"What happened after the deaths?" Gracie asked. "How did your family cope?"

"Not well." Mrs. Mercer stared off into the distance as if she could see the past. "My son was angry all the time for a while. He stayed away from home, threw himself into his work, not dealing with the family at all. I told him that they were grieving, too, but, of course, he told me that I just did not understand. He did not acknowledge that his father and I were also in pain—not just for Davey, but for him, his wife Barbara, for Danny, and for our great-grandchild, wherever she might be."

"How did the rest of the family get through it?"

"It was very sad." Mrs. Mercer drew her lips into a line. "It was more than poor Danny could take. He became quite ill, and was hospitalized for some time. Barbara became reclusive. She blamed herself as well, I think. She died while Danny was still in the hospital." She shook her head again. "None of us has ever been the same."

"What was her illness?" Gracie felt she might be pressing for too much information, but Mrs. Mercer did not flinch. She had opened the door on those memories. Perhaps the pain was no worse for examining them once exposed. The old woman patted Gracie's hand. "She took her own life—died of a broken heart." Mrs. Mercer looked away and shook her head again.

"And Danny?"

The woman cleared her throat. "Poor boy. They called it severe depression. He became a different boy—a different man. He never married, has no children. Like his father, all he has is his work—when he can hold onto a job." She took a breath. "And once in a while a game of cribbage with his old grandmother." She smiled and wagged her head as if she had said something funny. "Even today he and his father barely pass two words between them."

"How sad." Gracie had not really intended to say it out loud.

"It is. Now we're three people, all living in the same place, but not really living together. Each of us has our own world. I think it's the reason my son keeps Bon Bon. There can't be any other reason for it. That dog is a pest." She chuckled. "And it's why I insisted on bringing Tommy," she said standing and going over to the cage. "Pretty boy, Tommy. Pretty boy," she cooed to her pet. "He'll outlive me, of course. These birds live forever." She pushed another carrot stick into the cage, and her parrot did a little dance on his perch before reaching for it. "I didn't need any more loss in my life. I just hope someone will take good care of him after I'm gone."

Gracie stayed only a few minutes more before collecting her jacket. When she exited the house, she was surprised at how bright and warm the day was outside—more humid than before. She started her engine and navigated the streets of Billington toward the highway back to Glenville Falls, all the while thinking about their conversation. She felt suddenly exhausted.

Her mind turned to Kristen back at the bookstore. The Mercers were her family, every bit as much as the grandmother she had left in Boston. Should she mention this visit to Kristen, or would it only open the girl up to more sadness? This question deserved more thought before she took any action.

It might not be best for Kristen to get to know these people, but Gracie was not sorry she had made the trip. Perhaps, as Mrs. Mercer said, she was not responsible for what happened. She was not sure how she felt about that, but she did know one thing. After meeting Mrs. Mercer, in dealing with her sense of guilt, she at least felt less alone.

CHAPTER TWENTY

The long ride back to Glenville Falls gave Gracie time to think—not just about her meeting with Dave's grandmother, but about the entire puzzle swirling around her: the chalked message, the break-in, Officer Lowry, Ollie and his son Kenny, Hal, the person who might have been following Kristen—and possibly her, nearly being run down, and the reports of the peeping Tom and pedophile. Were they all connected?

She turned on the radio to her favorite classical station. It calmed her as the miles passed. After she wound her way out of Billington, the roads were less traveled. No street lights or stop signs curbed her progress homeward. She was in her own world on the two-lane highway, passing fields of dried corn stalks on either side, when she came around a curve. A tractor pulling a large wagonload of manure was pulling onto the road just ahead of her. She slammed on her brakes.

"Great," Gracie grumbled, looking at the clock on the car radio. It was twenty past twelve. She was going to be much later than she had intended getting back to the store. Kristen was alone, and it was only her sixth day working there. Could the girl handle everything all right without Gracie there? "She would have called if she had a problem, wouldn't she?" Gracie asked herself.

The rich, pungent smell of the heavy load ahead of her seeped into the car. Gracie wrinkled her nose, and closed the car's outside air vents. She watched the wagon tilting right and left as each of its wheels made it onto the pavement. Gracie hoped that once the farmer had pulled onto the highway, he would pull over to the side to allow cars to pass. Some farmers did; others didn't. As it was, she could not see around the load well enough to know whether the opposing lane was clear of traffic. The lines down the center were solid yellow. She had no choice for the moment but to creep along behind the odoriferous cargo.

Gracie gripped her steering wheel, and tapped it with her index fingers. The muscles in her jaw tightened. The classical music on the radio became an annoyance rather than a soothing presence, and she snapped it off. As she did, she glanced in her rear-view mirror. A black car came upon her fast—having to brake suddenly, as she had, coming around the curve.

"Okay, Mr. Farmer. Now you have a line of traffic behind you. Can't you pull over?"

The midday sun streamed into the car, turning it into a solar oven. Gracie blew a stream of air toward her forehead, trying to dislodge a few wisps of hair that clung to her moistened brow. She thought about opening a window, but considering what she was following, opted instead to put on the car's air conditioning.

She looked in her rear-view mirror again, to see if more cars had joined their little parade. Seeing none, she looked away, then back again. What was wrong with this picture? The driver behind her had lowered his sun visor so much that it hid his face. All she could see of him was a clean-shaven jaw line. But the sun is almost directly overhead. *Why would anyone use a sun visor at noon?*

The thought was fleeting, though, as the farmer pulled to the side of the road, and Gracie pressed on the accelerator to pass him. The dark sedan followed suit, but was soon several car lengths behind her as she sped along to make up for lost time.

Replaying the conversation with Mrs. Mercer in her head, she barely noticed the miles go by, to the point she nearly missed her turn off from the highway onto Old Billington Road leading toward the village of Glenville Falls. Making the turn at the top of a hill, she could see her town in the distance ahead of her, on past the meandering Pocomtuc River. From that vantage point she could trace the town's migration from the older buildings of the original mill settlement to the college town it became.

After cresting the hill, she was surrounded by thick woods with stone walls running through them delineating the boundaries of long-forgotten fields. Gracie noticed a white van behind her with its turn signal on. It was taking a left into one of the long driveways that led to hidden homes and hunting cabins in the woods. With the state wildlife sanctuary, that included the thirty-seven-foot water fall, so nearby, this was a popular place for hunters. Even those not winning the lottery for the special licenses that permitted hunting within the refuge, hoped to find game nearby that could not read boundary signs. Gracie hated driving this stretch of road during hunting season when the woods crawled with flashes of bright orange, and their peace was shattered by the blast of firearms.

The narrow road snaked along the side of a creek that eventually ran into the Pocomtuc River just below the falls. Following the serpentine path, Gracie slowed. Turning off the car's air conditioner, she opened her window. A gust of autumn air burst in, blowing back from the left, then circling around the car and pushing hair into her eyes. She smoothed her hair back and filled her lungs with the clean scents of woodland and stream before raising the window halfway.

Coming around a bend, she saw a yellow, fallow field, ringed by an ancient stone wall, on the other side of the stream. Behind it stood a tall slope, part of the wildlife refuge, composed of granite deposited by the glaciers and softened by eons of erosion, sediment deposits, and spotty forestation. The sun came out from behind a cloud and lit up the fall colors of the hill's birches. Gracie took her eyes from the road to scan the field hoping to see a pheasant. Sometimes in the spring a mother pheasant would stop traffic along there as a dozen chicks followed her across the road, all in a row. Gracie never tired of the sight.

Her heart felt a little lighter, having left some of its burden behind at Mrs. Mercer's. Despite all that had occurred over the past several weeks, a sense of optimism returned. Her problems felt manageable after all.

The road narrowed to just two lanes with no shoulder on either side. The stream had eroded the edge of the roadway, and with no oncoming traffic, Gracie steered over to her left and drove along the center of the road. As she took a particularly sharp angle, she slowed to only twenty miles per hour. A quick look into her rear view mirror surprised her. A black car was following her, only a few feet behind her rear bumper.

"Where did you come from?" she asked the mirror. She pulled over to the right and slowed. The rules of the road forbade passing in this narrow, meandering section, but Gracie still hoped the car would go by her.

She wanted to get back to the store, but without being pushed along by an impatient driver.

As she hoped, the driver moved out, but instead of passing her, it rode along just off her left rear fender, pinning her to the right side of the road. Gracie thought about the path ahead of her. It would not widen for at least another mile or two, and there was a single-lane bridge ahead where the stream split. There was no way they could cross it together. If she couldn't move her car toward the center of the road, she would have to yield at the bridge or slam into its concrete rail. If she stopped and the other car blocked the bridge, she would be trapped.

She slowed, willing the driver to move past her, but the other car matched her speed. *What's with this guy?*

Her mind began to race. She had to get ahead of this maniac before they went much farther. Pressing the accelerator, she looked at her speedometer. She was going thirty-six, but the black car stayed on her flank. This wasn't working. She tapped her brakes a couple of times, hoping to signal the car to back off. It seemed to take the hint. It fell in a couple of car lengths behind her, and Gracie took a deep breath. That was a relief.

Then the driver gunned his engine and raced up behind her. Gracie braced for impact, but the car slowed just in time. Her eyes kept darting between the curving roadway and the car in the mirror. She could not make out the driver—even to see whether it was a man or a woman.

"What do you want me to do?" she said, shouting into the mirror. She felt her heart beating in her chest, and her mouth was dry. Coming to a brief stretch of straighter road, Gracie pulled to the right and slowed, reaching out the open window to wave at the car to pass. The driver pulled up along beside her, but hung back in her blind spot. She slowed more, but the car again matched her speed. "Okay. I get it. You're annoyed. So pass me already," she said off her left shoulder. Still the car stayed in the left lane, keeping pace with her.

"Well, I'm not going to stop here in the middle of nowhere," she said, and pressed the accelerator to get ahead of the black car again. Instead of leaving it behind, she saw it speed up and continue to hang back off her rear fender. "And I'm not driving into the stream, either, if that's what you're thinking." She was yelling and leaning forward, looking ahead with a clenched jaw. Her hands cramped from holding on so tightly to the steering wheel. She searched the road ahead as far as its curves allowed. How far was it to that one-lane bridge?

She tried speeding up a bit more, but the car stayed with her. There was no way she was going to floor it; it would probably be useless anyway since the other car appeared determined to go whatever speed she did. Then, rounding a curve, there it was: the bridge was only about one hundred yards ahead. *How am I going to avoid being pushed into a bridge abutment?*

She pressed the brake, but not too much, hoping the other car would do likewise. She was in luck, the other car slowed down, too—still hanging off her rear fender. Her car was headed right for the barrier on the right side of the bridge, and it was getting closer by the second.

Car, don't fail me now, she thought as she came within twenty feet of the bridge, and jammed the gas pedal to the floor. Her car jumped out ahead of her pursuer, and cleared the bridge, leaving the other car swerving to navigate it without hitting the guard rails.

"Ha, ha, ha. I've got you now," Gracie crowed. But the other car was not done with her yet. It came up behind her at an alarming rate. A fork in the road was coming up, and she was too far to the right to take the route into town. She needed to shift left, but as soon as the thought crossed her mind, the other car was again at her left fender. She could go right at the Y, but that only led to more wilderness and the waterfall. She didn't want to be trapped up there with this maniac.

If this is the same guy I saw back in Billington, he sure picked a great place to corner me. There had to be a way to take the left fork ahead. After what happened at the bridge, she thought slowing down would not trick the other driver again. No. She had to go left, even if it meant getting hit. But if the front of his car hit the driver side of hers, she might spin around and not be able to get out of her car. She would be at his mercy.

"When a car swerves in front of you, it's the driver's natural instinct to swerve out of the way," her dad had told her when she was learning to drive.

"I hope you were right, Dad, because the Y is only a couple hundred yards ahead," Gracie said aloud as she inched her car over to the left a little bit at a time. The other driver showed no sign of noticing. As she approached the Y, she floored it again. She held her breath, and jerked the wheel to the left at the fork. Closing her eyes for a split second, she waited for the crash. Instead, a horn honked at her left shoulder. She jumped inside her skin and opened her eyes. She was on the right road, but the car had stayed with her—moving up far enough that she could see its hood in the corner of her eye, but still could not see the driver.

If we could only meet someone coming the other way, Gracie thought. Perhaps then he'd have to slow down and get behind me. Or, she thought with a grimace, we could all end up in a heap of twisted metal.

As they got closer to the village and the street straightened out, Gracie picked up more speed. But soon there would be houses along the road, then other cars, pedestrians, and children. She knew she could not keep up this speed for long. Then what?

As she approached the first house on the right, Gracie stepped lightly on the brake. If worse came to worst, she could pull into someone's driveway and honk the horn until she got help.

To her surprise, the other car slowed down and pulled behind her, letting a car length, then two separate them. Gracie slowed even more as she entered the village, the black car still following her.

"Okay," Gracie said, looking into the mirror, "let's see how you like this." She turned onto College Street, and took the back way toward the town hall. Stopping only for the two stop signs as she neared the green, she pulled into the parking lot behind the town hall nearest the police station entrance.

"Ha!" Gracie pounded the steering wheel, watching the black car cruise by the town hall and out of sight. Unbuckling her seat belt, she opened her door and stood. She had to steady herself against the car for a moment and take deep breaths to regain composure before going inside.

"I need to talk to Chief Johnson . . . immediately," Gracie said to the young woman staffing the desk.

"Do you have an appointment?" The officer did not even look up at Gracie.

"No, but I have a crime to report." That got her slightly more attention.

"What kind of crime?" Gracie felt the woman looking her up and down, possibly to see if she were injured.

"I was coming down Old Billington Road when a car . . ."

"Sorry, ma'am. Traffic offenses are not reportable. An officer has to observe it and write a ticket."

Gracie pulled herself up to her full five-foot-four-inch height. "This was more than a traffic offense," she said, hoping it sounded more professional than defensive. "A car just tried to run me off the road."

"Was there any impact with the other car, ma'am?" Was it Gracie's imagination, or was this woman speaking to her as if she were a child?

"No, but it was an intentional assault by motor vehicle," Gracie's voice was a little too high and too loud. "I'm telling you, the driver intended to do me harm."

The officer didn't even have the courtesy to look Gracie in the eye. "All right, ma'am." Pulling out a sheet of paper, she took down Gracie's name, address, phone number, and date of birth. Gracie could feel her adrenaline wearing off, and looked for a seat. She found a wooden chair in the waiting area and pulled it up to the desk.

"Do you have any injuries?" the officer said, pen poised over the paper. Gracie squirmed.

"As I said, I was able to avoid him." Realizing that response did not bolster her claim of assault, she hurriedly added, "He was in my blind spot, making me move over to the right, even at the one-lane bridge. I don't know how I got out of there without ending up in the stream or crashing into the bridge."

The officer put her pen down. "And there's no damage to the vehicle?"

Gracie looked at her hands. "No. When I veered away from the edge, he moved over, too."

The officer pursed her lips, then looked at Gracie. "Isn't it just possible, ma'am, that the car was just trying to pass you, and when they saw they couldn't get past, they pulled in behind you?"

"No. That is *not* possible. He continued to pursue me all the way into town. He was either trying to run me off the road or at the very least to intimidate me."

"Okay. Who was driving?"

She looked at the floor. "I don't know. I couldn't see the driver, but I am pretty sure it was a car that followed me all the way from Billington."

"Did you get the license plate?"

"It was definitely a Massachusetts plate. I was too busy trying to stay on the road to be able to record the plate number."

The officer supported her head with one fist. "Can you give me a description of the car?"

"Yes." Gracie nodded. "It was a black sedan."

"Make? Model? Year?"

"Uh, I'm not much of a car person. It looked kind of new-ish. Really, they all look alike, don't they?" Gracie flushed.

The officer sighed. "So you want us to put out a BOLO on a 'newish' black sedan with Massachusetts plates, driven by a man or a woman, that looks like every other car on the road"

Gracie rolled her eyes.

"Ma'am, you have given me absolutely nothing to go on. You know that, don't you?" The officer's clipped words told Gracie just how annoyed she was.

"Yes, I see that. I just drove right here to get away from him. The guy was still following me until I parked in the town hall lot. I don't know who he is, but I know that between this, the break-in at my store, being nearly run down, and . . . and . . . and . . ." Gracie had to swallow hard to retain control. After drawing a long breath, she shook her head. What had she expected coming in here? Of course they couldn't do anything without more to go on. Still, she needed help. "I wonder when I might be able to talk to Chief Johnson," she said to the officer. "He knows the background, and I have to talk to him about some other matters as well."

The officer looked skeptical. "Let me give him your message. He'll be in touch when he has time to meet with you."

Great, Gracie thought. *This officer will tell him I'm nuts.*

"Thanks," Gracie said, standing. "I look forward to hearing from him." With that she left the station.

"Enough of this," Gracie shouted, standing by her car. Checking the time in the town hall clock, she saw it was almost one o'clock. She drove back to the store, peeked inside the bookshop to make sure all was well, then ducked into Doyle's Hardware. There was something more she needed to do.

CHAPTER TWENTY-ONE

"I've decided to get that motion-activated lamp, Hal," Gracie said, pushing open the hardware store door with so much force it banged against the wall.

Hal looked up from paperwork, but not at Gracie. He watched the door as it swung shut, a look of concern on his face.

"Sorry about that," Gracie said, turning to make sure the window pane remained intact.

"Bad day, eh, Gracie?" Hal said, sliding his papers under the counter.

Gracie slumped her shoulders and rolled her eyes. "You have no idea."

"So, which post do you want for that lamp?"

"No post," she said, all business again. "I'm going to get the other kind you showed me and replace the light on our porch. It might not light up the whole yard, but it'll be enough for my purposes. And I'll figure out how to install it myself. It can't be that hard."

Hal shook his head. "Not hard at all," he said, "but you still might want to call . . ."

"Nope. I'm not waiting for an electrician. It's going in tonight. Is there anything else I'll need to make it work?"

"You got a Phillips screwdriver?"

Gracie clucked. "Of course, Hal. Doesn't everyone?"

"Well, you never know." Hal swept off his Red Sox cap and scratched his scalp. "What about electrical tape?"

Gracie pursed her lips. "Add it to the bill. How much do I owe you?" Gracie had her wallet out and was counting her money. After paying for the lamp and electrical tape, she tossed them in the back seat of her car and marched into the bookstore.

"Oh, I'm glad you're back," Kristen said as soon as Gracie was inside the door.

"What is it now?" Gracie snapped. Dickens, spooked, climbed a bookcase and glowered at her from above. "Sorry. It's been a tough day."

"Yeah, well," Kristen's hand shook as she held up two pink slips of paper. "You have some messages. A guy from L&S Security called wanting to know when they should come to install some stuff. Are we getting a security system?"

Did she say "we?"

"No." Gracie tried to sound less abrupt, but knew she failed. "I can't afford it right now. This store isn't making enough money for a fancy security system."

Kristen appeared flustered. "Oh, okay." She shuffled her notes. "Then there was a call from someone named 'Del' who said she'd call later. I asked for her number, but she said you already had it."

"I do." Gracie waved a dismissive hand at Kristen, and walked toward the back office to deposit her purse and jacket. Kristen followed several steps behind.

"And when you get a chance," she said, stopping a couple of feet from the doorway, "I wonder if I could talk to you a second?"

Gracie dropped her keys on her desk—right on top of the copies of newspaper clippings from the library about Cheryl's death. *Drat. I hadn't meant to leave these here where Kristen might see them,* she thought. She looked up at her clerk. From the girl's pale complexion and pained expression, Gracie surmised the damage was already done. "Did you read these?" she asked.

"I didn't mean to." Kristen looked down at her hands. "They were just there on the desk when I came in." She raised her eyes to Gracie's. "I don't know why you have them, like if you're checking up on me or something, but I guess I can't blame you. Is that why you want a security system?"

"No, it's not that . . ."

"I'm really sorry." Kristen searched for words. "I'd just never seen them before." Kristen looked so white that Gracie feared she might faint.

"Come in here," Gracie said, grabbing a folding chair and placing it next to hers. Kristen perched on its edge as Gracie sat beside her.

"I'm sorry if it was difficult for you to see these clippings," Gracie said, wanting to put her arm around the girl, but for some reason holding back.

"I just . . . never knew . . ." Tears welled in her eyes and she looked down.

Gracie felt the blood drain from her own face, and moved a box of tissues closer to Kristen. "You mean you didn't know that your mother . . . that your father . . ." How could she say it? How could she put voice to the horror that was Cheryl and Dave's deaths?

Kristen grabbed a tissue and dabbed her eyes. "Is that what really happened?" she said, looking at Gracie with pleading eyes. "Did my father really kill my mother like that?"

Gracie flinched. "It looks that way, dear."

Kristen looked down again, her lip quivering.

"What has your grandmother told you about them?" Gracie asked, tilting her head to find Kristen's eyes.

Kristen wiped tears from her cheeks and blew her nose. "She said they died in an accident when I was a baby, and that she didn't want to talk about them anymore." Kristen's voice wavered on the edge of breaking. "She never even showed me any pictures of them."

The poor girl. Gracie realized with Kristen growing up in Boston, no one else was apt to know what happened. It was probably a kindness for her grandmother to keep the awful story from her when she was young. But perhaps she should have prepared Kristen before letting her return to Glenville Falls. To find out this way *. . . and it's my fault she did.*

"Tell me what happened," Kristen said, clearing her throat. "I want to know the truth."

Gracie thought back eighteen years, then to the visit with Mrs. Mercer that morning. How could she describe it? Yet, she felt Kristen had a right to know.

"I met your mother when I was still practicing law," she began. "She was just nineteen, and you were still a baby."

Kristen leaned forward as Gracie continued to recount the tale Cheryl had shared with her of a high school romance and an unplanned pregnancy.

"So my parents didn't want me," she said, her voice flat, resigned, but pain apparent in her eyes.

"You were unexpected, but that doesn't mean you were unwanted," Gracie said, putting a hand on her shoulder. "But your parents were too young and ill-prepared for the responsibilities of marriage and raising a child. They did the best they could. They needed help, but didn't know where to find it."

Mrs. Mercer's regrets echoed in Gracie's head. *If only . . .*

"It all got to be too much for your father to handle, and he took it out on your mother."

Kristen swallowed. "How so?"

"There were times when he would yell at her, even strike her." She saw Kristen shudder, but continued the story. "Your mother came to me for legal advice, and I helped her get an order of protection. It was supposed to prevent him from ever hurting her again." Gracie realized a knot had formed in her own throat. "She packed you up to move to a friend's house for a few days, but later that night . . ." Gracie took a deep breath and forced herself to continue. "She went back to the house to pick up something she'd forgotten. He followed her there." Gracie cleared her throat. "And he killed her."

Kristen pressed her eyes closed and nodded. "Stabbed her," she choked out.

"They found the murder weapon with his body up at the falls the same night," Gracie said barely above a whisper.

"Just as the papers said." Kristen appeared to have tensed every muscle, fighting back the hurt.

"Your mother loved you dearly, Kristen," Gracie said, hoping it would comfort her. "She left you with her friend rather than expose you to danger. It might be why you're here today."

It took Kristen a moment to be able to speak again. "It was all my fault," she said, strangely calm. "If they hadn't had me, they never would have gotten married, and they would both be alive and happy."

Gracie rubbed her back. "No Kristen. It wasn't your fault. How could it be the fault of an innocent child? You cannot take the blame for what others did."

"But my father was an abuser and a murderer." Kristen shook her head. "No wonder Gram never trusted me." She grabbed more tissues.

"What do you mean?" Kristen had never said much about her life with her grandmother, but Gracie had sensed it wasn't a perfect relationship.

"It was like she was always waiting for me to explode or something." In her lap, Kristen twisted a tissue into knots. "I remember one time when I was about fourteen and my grandmother slapped me for using a bad word, and I just slapped her back, and she shouted at me, 'you're just like your father.'" As she recounted the scene, Kristen's voice became shrill in what Gracie surmised was a pretty good imitation of her grandmother's tone. "I asked her what she meant, but she wouldn't tell me." She glanced at the clippings. "Now I know."

Gracie stroked the girl's cheek. "I'm sorry," was all she could manage.

Kristen looked up at Gracie through reddened eyes. "So you knew all this, and you hired me anyway?"

Gracie knelt down and folded Kristen in a hug. "Of course I did," she said. *I hired her* because *of all this,* she thought. They held each other as Kristen dissolved into sobs. Over Kristen's shoulder, tears rolled down Gracie's cheeks.

Gracie stayed with Kristen until she had answered all her questions, and cried every last tear. When the girl finally composed herself, her eyes and nose were red, but she could smile again. Gracie suggested that she might want to leave work early.

"We haven't been very busy this afternoon." For that Gracie was grateful. There couldn't have been a better time for a slow shopping day.

"Thanks. I think I could use a little time to think," she said, picking up her jacket.

"Call me if you want to talk," Gracie called after her as she left. Kristen waved in response.

What a day, Gracie thought, watching Kristen go. Dickens walked by, rubbing against her ankle. "I'm completely wrung out, boy," she said, picking up her cat and caressing him against her chest. "What I need now is a rest-of-the-day that's drama free."

The cat leaned into her and purred, and she kissed his head.

CHAPTER TWENTY-TWO

After a good cup of tea, Gracie felt restored. She decided to make an effort to find the missing law dictionary. "I hope it wasn't taken during the break-in," she said aloud. It wasn't too late to file an insurance claim for it, but for that she'd need a police report—something she still didn't have. *Perhaps I should deal with that first.*

Back at her desk, Gracie called the police station. The woman who answered the phone sounded like the same one she had talked to about nearly being run off the road. She tried to lower her voice when she asked for Chief Johnson.

"Not available right now," was the response. Gracie decided not to leave a message.

As she hung up, her eyes rested on the day's mail, stacked on her desk. She pulled out her desk drawer to look for her letter opener. When she did, she found the diagram she had drawn when she was trying to figure out who might have broken into her store. *I'm so glad Kristen didn't see this,* she thought, studying it while drumming her fingers on her desk.

Pressing her lips together, she went to her trash can. She knew the crumpled estimate from the security company still had to be in there somewhere since she hadn't emptied the trash the night before. Her back started to ache as she bent over, so she pulled out the plastic liner and brought it to her desk to sort through the leftover crust of a sandwich, dried up apple core, and used tea bags. She held her breath as she searched. This wasn't exactly a bed of roses.

Within a few seconds she found the balled-up piece of paper. Then she closed up the bag to put it back in the container. As she was about to stuff it back in, she noticed a small, crumpled piece of yellow paper in the bottom of the trash can. She set the bag down and pulled out the scrap. It was torn from a legal pad. As Gracie smoothed it on her desk, she remembered what it was. The pencil rubbing still revealed the telephone number that Kristen had taken down, then taken with her, the first time she had been alone in the store.

Gracie inhaled deeply, then slowly let the breath out. After a moment's consideration, she opened her desk drawer and slipped the paper inside. She couldn't deal with it then. First, she needed to call the security company.

"L&S Security." A young man answered the phone on the first ring. That was probably a good sign.

"Hello, this is Grace McIntyre returning Chuck Salerno's call."

"Just a moment, please." Canned music came on the line and Gracie wondered if they used the same company for their on-hold service as the vet did. Sure enough, in a moment, the music was interrupted by an ad for their security systems. Gracie looked at the ceiling, wondering how much longer she would need to wait.

"Chuck Salerno here. How may I help you?"

"Hi, Chuck. This is Grace McIntyre from Gracie's Garret bookstore, and I . . . "

"Hello, Ms. McIntyre. I'm glad you got back to me because it looks like I might be able to squeeze in an install for you on Friday if you commit to it today."

"Friday's tomorrow." Gracie's eyebrows lowered.

"It sure is, but I know how eager you were to get some security around your place so when this opened up on our calendar, I decided I'd better give you a call and see if we could work something out."

Okay, I'll play this game, Gracie thought. "If I can't decide today, how long would I have to wait for an installation?"

"Oh, well that's hard to say. We like to get people in on a first-come, first-served basis, and it's only because I talked to you last week and you have such an urgent need for security that we might be able to make an exception in your case. Just a courtesy."

Gracie could practically smell the snake oil oozing out of him. "So probably Monday," she said, without inflection.

"Uh, well." Some of the bombast had blown out of him. "Prob'ly."

"Okay, let's get this straight, Chuck." Gracie was using her mother voice. "I can't afford anywhere near the system you guys priced out for me, but . . ."

"Oh, but that system will give you state-of-the-art protection, and you can't afford not to . . ."

"Don't interrupt me, Chuck." Her tone brooked no dissent.

Chuck fell silent, then, in a voice that could be described as timid he added, "Sorry, ma'am. You go ahead."

"Okay. As I said, I cannot afford what you priced out for me, but I do recognize my responsibility to provide for the safety of my employee, so I am only interested in your panic button." It was the least expensive option on the estimate. "That way, if I or my employees ever run into trouble in the store, we can get help right away. Isn't that the way it works?"

Chuck was silent, almost as if he were still uncertain whether he had permission to speak.

"Chuck?"

"Yes, ma'am. That's how it works. It runs through your phone line and notifies us if you need assistance." Chuck was off and running with his sales patter.

"It's called a wireless duress alarm. There's a base unit that acts as a speaker phone connected with our call center. You can also have one or more portable units that can be worn around the neck, at the belt, or on the wrist, and whenever you need assistance, just press the alarm and an operator will contact you to determine the kind of help you need and get it to you right away."

Gracie had to admit, he had the pitch down pat. "But you're in Billington. If I've got a robbery in progress, how soon would help get here?"

"As soon as we know the call is for a true emergency, we will immediately notify the local police. As you know, in a small town like yours, they can be there in no time at all. They respond fast to our calls because they know we don't forward false alarms."

Great, Gracie thought. *Glenville Falls' Finest. A lot of good they'll do me.*

Chuck continued in hard-sell mode. "There is no charge for installation, only a small monthly fee, with a three-month minimum sign-up. So can I set you up for installation tomorrow?"

Gracie felt like she was part of an infomercial. She placed her order, and set up six o'clock the next day for installation—after the store was closed.

~

The late afternoon crowd made up for the lull earlier in the day, and kept Gracie running. When six finally arrived, she thought about staying late to look for her law dictionary, but did not want to miss another dinner with Spencer and Carrie—especially because this time she had prepared something in advance.

After putting Dickens in his carrier, she turned out the store lights. She reveled in the realization that she was getting stronger from carrying Dickens to and from the store every day. They were making good time, and were almost to Elm Street before she remembered that she had driven to work that day.

"Oh, darn it. And I have a light to put up outside the house tonight, too," she complained to Dickens. It made no sense to leave her car and the new porch light parked in town all night, so she turned around to get the car. Driving home had taken her longer than if she had walked.

Coming in from the driveway, Gracie entered through the kitchen door. She was hit by the smell of beef, carrots, celery, potatoes, parsnips, rutabaga, onion, clove, and bay leaf from the Yankee Pot Roast she had put together in her slow cooker before leaving the house that morning. She closed her eyes and took in the aroma. *Oh, thank goodness I don't have to cook.*

Before she could set Dickens' carrier down, Carrie was in the kitchen.

"Hi, Mom, I need money for a fundraiser at school."

"Oh, really?" Gracie placed Dickens' pen on the floor and stacked the box holding the porch lamp on top of it.

"Yeah. We're supposed to sell wrapping paper, but I figured if you just gave me some money, I wouldn't have to sell anything." Carrie stood with a hand on one hip, almost daring Gracie to tell her "no."

"Could you run that by me again?" Gracie said, in a tone that did nothing to conceal her irritation.

Carrie forged ahead. "I just need some money so I won't have to do the dumb fundraiser at my school for the French Club trip. I don't want to sell wrapping paper. It's not worth my time to go door to door with that stuff when it's overpriced and nobody wants to buy it anyway." She said the last sentence very slowly as if her mother were mentally challenged. Gracie could almost hear the "duh," at the end of the sentence. Was this as bad as Gracie thought, or was it just that Carrie had chosen a bad day for such self-centeredness? Whatever the reason, Gracie let go with both barrels.

"Oh. So it's okay for your father to work sixteen-hour days, and for me to work at the bookstore, but it's not okay for *you* to work to get the money to support your activity at school?"

"I didn't say that. It's just I shouldn't have to . . ."

"And exactly who *should* have to pay for the French Club trip? All the taxpayers who won't be going on it? Or just your parents, because you should have everything you want without having to lift a finger for it."

Carrie decided to take a different tack. "Well, it's not safe for kids to sell stuff door to door anymore."

"It's not safe to visit our neighbors? Since when? It's safe enough when you want to do something at the Antonello's."

"But Angela's selling it, too, and . . ."

"And speaking of safety, was it our neighbors whose building was vandalized or was it my store? But I still work there every day."

"Yes, but it's different. You're an adult, and I'm just a kid, and . . . "

"It's interesting that you're 'just a kid' when it's something you don't want to do, but 'practically an adult' when it's something you do."

Carrie smiled at her mother's logic, and threw her hands in the air. "Hey, I don't make the rules." She giggled. She actually giggled. Did she not understand how angry Gracie was?

"Well, listen here, Missy."

Carrie's eyes flew open. She was getting the message. Gracie never used "Missy" unless she was royally ticked off.

"I am busting my rear end trying to make a go of the book store, and Dad is staying up late every night trying to get his book manuscript done, all so we can pay the bills around here. Just the bills."

Carrie looked away and rolled her eyes, but that didn't stop Gracie.

"Not the field trip expenses, not the souvenir money, not the money to replace what you should earn through fundraising, but just the money to keep you clothed and fed and with a roof over your head."

"Oh yeah," Carrie turned back to her mother and bared her teeth. "Well, it's not as if you're spending all your money on me. You're spending who knows how much to send Ben to college, and on the bookstore, and going out and buying things all the time. Like what's that thing?" She pointed to the box holding the porch light.

"It's a motion-activated light for the front porch. It's a security measure." Gracie could hear the defensiveness in her own voice.

"So the neighborhood isn't safe after all." Carrie pulled herself up, clearly proud of her parry. Gracie had done battle with lawyers who were less formidable.

"It is a purchase to benefit the entire family. I don't want you coming home from school after dark to a house with no lights on outside." Gracie blushed a little, knowing that was not the whole reason she had bought the lamp.

"It isn't dark when *I* get home, not that *you'd* know." The volume of their argument had Dickens yowling in his pen. Gracie bent over to let him out, and he dashed from the room.

"But it will be." Gracie spat out the words. "As it gets toward winter, you well know, it will be dark by four-thirty in the afternoon."

"And I get home at four-fifteen." Carrie crossed her arms and jutted out her chin.

"It's getting dark before then, and sometimes you might get home a little later than usual. And you won't have to remember to turn on the porch light for me or Dad for when we get home from work." Gracie glanced at the clock. It was nearly six thirty.

"And I suppose it's all *my* fault you get home late every night, too. You just had to open a bookstore to find some way to get away from me, right? After all, once Ben was gone, there was no reason for you to be home anymore." Carrie wiped fat tears from her cheeks and her lower lip quivered before she continued. "It's not like there is anyone here who's important enough for you to spend time with. The only time I have someone in the family to talk to is when I text with Ben, and he's always in a hurry to be someplace, too." Her tears fell freely now, and she reached for a napkin from the holder on the kitchen table.

There it was. Gracie finally understood. It wasn't that Carrie hated her or hated the bookstore; she hated the feeling of rejection that the bookstore represented. Gracie realized her mouth was standing open. Shutting it, she stepped over Dickens' carrier to give her daughter a hug. Carrie wrapped her arms around herself and turned away from her mother as she approached, but Gracie was not deterred. She opened her arms and engulfed her daughter in them, kissing the top of her head.

"There is no one in the world I love more than you, Carrie," Gracie said, her voice softening, tears filling her eyes. "I thought you understood that." Carrie squirmed within her mother's arms to wipe her eyes and blow her nose.

"Then why do you spend more time at the store than you do with me?" It came out as a whimper. "You don't even want me to come down to the store anymore. You have your books, and you have *my* cat, and there's no one in the house for me to come home to *at all*."

"Isn't Dad home some days when you get here?" Gracie loosened her hug and turned Carrie to look her in the face.

Carrie rolled her eyes. "He's up in his study with his music on. He doesn't even know I'm home."

"But he helps you with your homework, doesn't he?" Gracie was sure he did.

Carrie looked down. "I don't really ask him for help much anymore. He's so smart and doesn't understand why I have trouble with some stuff. He can't really explain it so I understand it . . . like you can."

Gracie bent her head, trying to catch Carrie's eye. "He's used to college students, not ninth graders," she said, pulling her daughter closer.

After a long hug, Gracie pulled out a kitchen chair and offered it to Carrie, then sat across from her. "To tell you the truth," Gracie said, looking at her hands clasped in front of her on the table, "I'm not having much fun at the store, either. I miss you, too, and I'm not at all sure I can make this store pay for itself. I've worked so hard, but I feel like I'm not getting anywhere."

Carrie reached across the table to take Gracie's hands. "Oh, it will work out, Mom. You always said that a new business takes time to turn a profit. You haven't been at it very long. I know you can make it work. I just wish you didn't have to spend so much time there."

"I do, too. I've always enjoyed spending my afternoons with you, having your friends over, helping you with your homework." Gracie looked across the room to a corner of wallpaper curling away from the seam. "I just don't know what to do about it." She looked back at Carrie whose expression was sympathetic. Gracie realized from the look on Carrie's face, *my daughter is comforting me as I complain about the very thing she resents me for.*

Gracie patted Carrie's hand. "Look, we're smart women. We can fix this."

"Can we? How?" There was a hopeful look in Carrie's eyes.

"I'm not sure yet," Gracie said, taking a gasp of air and laughing. "But I'm home now. We can spend tonight together, and maybe this weekend we can set aside some time to figure this out."

"Saturday. Let's talk about it then."

"Okay. Saturday when I get home from the store. It's a date."

They shook hands.

"And we can both be thinking about ideas on how to fix this until then." Gracie nodded her head, and Carrie mimicked the motion.

"At least now we each know how the other one is feeling," Gracie said, "so we can stop making assumptions that hurt our feelings and aren't true. And whatever happens, never, never again doubt that I love you and want to spend time with you. Got it?"

Carrie smiled. "Got it. And I love you, too." They hugged again, and Dickens returned to the kitchen.

"Now, I'm going to bake some corn muffins to go with that pot roast. That should take about twenty minutes. Why don't you go upstairs, wash your face, and tell Dad that it's safe to come out now." She winked at Carrie, who laughed.

"Okay. Be right back to set the table."

"Sounds great. Then maybe after dinner, I can help you with your homework." Gracie sat at the table, her smile fading as she watched her daughter leave the room. It took her several moments before she could work up the energy to bake the muffin mix. No matter what else was on her to-do list, spending time with Carrie was now at the very top.

After dinner, Carrie helped with the dishes without being asked. Then she and Gracie sat at the kitchen table together while Carrie did her homework. It wasn't that Carrie needed Gracie's help, but both of them enjoyed the company.

Carrie finished her math, French, English, and biology homework. Gracie used the time to make some final decisions about her holiday orders. Carrie only had a few pages left to read for history, and she would be done for the night.

"Do you want to go into the living room to do your reading?" Gracie said, shifting her weight on the kitchen chair.

"Okay," Carrie said, packing her other books in her backpack and picking up her history text.

Gracie brought the box containing the porch light into the living room and dug out the installation instructions. It didn't look too hard, but she decided to wait until Carrie was through with her homework before going to work on it.

Carrie sat in Spencer's reading chair and Gracie sat on the couch, tucking her feet under her. The room was quiet. The only sounds were Carrie turning pages, and the ticking of the grandfather clock in the hall. Spencer, who was working upstairs, must have been using his earbuds because Gracie couldn't hear his music.

Dickens joined her, sitting on her lap and kneading her stomach. He purred as Gracie stroked him. Once Dickens settled down on her lap, Gracie felt her eyelids get heavy, and shook herself awake. She needed to keep her mind occupied or she would fall asleep for certain, but she didn't want to disturb her sleeping cat.

There was a book she had been reading on the table at the other end of the sofa. It had been so long since she had had time to read, she could hardly remember what it was about. Picking up a legal pad on the near end table, she decided to jot down some notes.

Starting a to-do list, she numbered her tasks. "1. Spend time with Carrie." She looked over at her daughter and smiled. "2. Return Del's call." *Not now. Carrie will feel abandoned again.* "3. Send in holiday orders." All she needed to do on that was decide how much she could afford. She knew she wouldn't have to pay the invoices for ninety days, but didn't want to order more than she could reasonably expect to sell. That led to:

"4. Figure out how to improve sales." This was getting depressing. What else? "5. Do thorough search of store for missing book." It wasn't getting any better. But it did bring up number six. "6. Call Chief Johnson again, re: Lowry, break-in, and nearly being run down—twice!!"

She added two exclamation points—one for each incident. It was clear to her that neither one was an accident. Lowry had been there for the first. Was he also part of the second?

Gracie tapped the end of her pen on the pad, and Carrie looked up.

"Do you have to do that?"

"Sorry," Gracie said, and flipped the page over. Closing her eyes, she tried to envision the diagram she had drawn, and left in her desk drawer. Although most of it was clear in her mind's eye, there were some parts she couldn't remember. Perhaps it was time for a new approach.

Drawing two parallel lines down the page, she made three columns. *What were those three things Spencer said would be true of the vandal?* Gracie closed her eyes and tilted her head back. *Oh, yes.* She wrote at the top of the first column "something against me/store." Then she remembered "something to hide," and wrote it atop the middle column. *What was the third one?* It came to her and she wrote "something to lose" in the final column.

Gracie looked at it. This was more like it. Now she could start sorting the names.

Perhaps she should start by listing some names of potential suspects.

A few hours ago, Gracie might have been convinced that Kristen was to blame—that she held a grudge against Gracie for not saving her mother. Now it was clear that she had no such motivation. She was at the store both times Gracie was nearly run down by a black car—once in town, and once on the road back from Billington. And the girl who left work earlier that day wasn't the slightly secretive, potentially untrustworthy teen she had once appeared to be. *Why did I let Lowry make me suspect her?*

Hal had the key, but he didn't appear to have anything against her. He had helped her. If anything happened to the store, he would lose rent, and after all the work he had put into refurbishing the store for her, he wouldn't want to jeopardize it, would he?

Peggy from the flower shop was never too chatty. You couldn't even call her friendly. She had helped erase that awful sidewalk message, but hadn't she also advised Gracie to back off? Did she have something to hide?

Maybe someone had a grudge against Kristen, but she was new in town, and hadn't had time to make any enemies.

Who else? Maybe the Mercers? No. Mrs. Mercer made it clear they all blamed themselves, not her.

What about Ollie? Did he resent her being in his old storefront? Why would he? He had closed the furniture store before Gracie ever talked to Hal about opening the bookshop. Still, she really didn't know him, and couldn't guess at how he might feel about her being in his retail space. Maybe he minded Hal doing so much for her. Or maybe he just had something against Hal and thought attacking one of his tenants would hurt him, especially if he could get the store to close. She added Ollie to column one, for the moment anyway.

And Ollie's son Kenny. He was still in town, had worked for Hal, and would know where Hal kept his keys. She jotted "Kenny" under his father's name.

What about the delivery guy? He had been really angry when Gracie wouldn't make a copy of a map.

Didn't she hear him saying something about making her sorry when she saw him on the green? This was extreme revenge for such a slight offense, but some people are just unbalanced. She poised her pen over the paper, and realized she didn't even know his name. "Delivery Guy" went onto the list.

She had saved the biggest names for last: Officer Lowry and Chief Johnson. Lowry always seemed suspicious of Kristen. According to Hal, Lowry had grown up here. Wasn't he about the age Cheryl and Dave would have been? And he found Dave's body at the waterfall. But there was something more. He knew where Dave would go when he was upset. They were friends.

Gracie tapped the end of her pen on the pad again, and Carrie slammed her book closed. Gracie jumped at the sound, and Dickens picked up his head. *Might he blame me?*

"That didn't take too long." Gracie forced a smile, but her mind was still on her list. She flipped the pages back so her to-do list was on top. She didn't particularly want Carrie to see what else she had been working on.

"All done. You want help putting that lamp up?"

Gracie had nearly forgotten about the porch light. She looked at Dickens who had resumed his nap. "I am being held down by a cat at the moment," she said. "Besides, you should probably get ready for bed."

"It's not that late. I can help. Let me see the directions."

Truth be told, Gracie was happy for the help. She shifted her feet. Dickens glared at her and moved to the other end of the sofa.

"Okay. Let's get this baby installed. You find the flashlight, and I'll get the Phillips screwdriver."

They giggled together for the first time in weeks as they followed the directions and installed the lamp. Ten minutes later Gracie stood back to inspect their work.

"Okay, I'm going in to turn the light on. You go out to the sidewalk and see if you can trigger it."

Gracie went in and flipped the switch. When she returned to the porch the light came on.

"I think I triggered it," Gracie said to Carrie who was doing jumping jacks out in the street. "Let's stay still for a minute and then see if you can trigger it from there."

Gracie sat on a porch step, and Carrie on the curb. A minute later the light went out.

"Okay," Gracie called. "Now stand up and see what happens."

Carrie stood, but the lamp stayed dark.

"Move around a little."

"I am," Carrie said. Gracie didn't move her head to look, afraid any motion would ruin the experiment.

"Okay, then walk this way."

A moment later the light came to life. Gracie turned her head to see Carrie standing on their front lawn, about twenty feet from the front door.

"Looks good," Gracie called to her. "Now, how long should we set it to stay on? One, five, or ten minutes?"

Carrie rushed up onto the porch. "Five. It's a nice compromise."

"Okay. Five it is. That's enough time to get in from the driveway, and if it isn't, any motion will reactivate it." Gracie set the dial and high-fived her daughter before they went inside. They sat on the stairs until the light went out, five minutes later.

"It works!" Carrie high-fived her mom again.

"I told you. We're smart women. We can figure things out. But now it's time for bed."

As Carrie bounded up the stairs and prepared for bed, Gracie went back to her legal pad. She looked at her to-do list, and stuffed the legal pad into a canvas bag to take with her to the store the next day. It could wait until then.

Gracie grabbed her book and reading glasses and went upstairs to say good night to Carrie, then poked her head into Spencer's study. She found him laying stacks of file folders on the floor around his desk, like Continental soldiers. *What a filing system.*

"Don't let the cat in," he said, almost dropping some papers.

"Don't worry. I just wanted to let you know I was heading toward bed."

"I'll be in after a while," he assured Gracie.

She blew him a kiss and left him to his work.

After a relaxing shower, Gracie picked up her long neglected book and brought it to bed. She set her book aside after only one chapter. Between having trouble sleeping the night before, and an emotionally exhausting day, she was ready for sleep. She took off her reading glasses, laid them on her bedside table, and turned out the light. She relaxed into her pillow.

A moment later, she opened her eyes and glanced toward the window.

The porch light was on.

CHAPTER TWENTY-THREE

Gracie bolted out of bed and flew to the window. Peeking around the curtain she scanned the lawn. No one was out by the sidewalk, but the porch roof blocked her view of the area closest to the house. Someone could be on the porch and she would not know it. For a moment she wondered if they should take off the porch roof, then she shook her head at the notion. There had to be a better way of dealing with this.

She thought back. Had she locked the front door before coming upstairs? She had tried to remember to do so each night, but it was hard to develop new habits. She couldn't be certain. She stood in her pajamas in the dark, trying to decide what to do next. Should she alert Spencer?

She went to the top of the stairs. Although most of the door was obscured by the bend in the stairs and the upper floor, she could see the doorknob from there. It was locked. Tuning her ears to listen for even the slightest noise, inside or out, she heard nothing. Even Dickens was quiet. Then a sound caught her attention. Was it a car engine?

She ran back into the bedroom to look out a front window. A dark car was pulling away from the curb across the street. *Was it there when I looked out before?* She tried to recall, but couldn't be certain. The retreating tail lights told her almost nothing about the car and even less about the driver. Still, it was dark, and about the same size as the car that tried to run her down . . . and the one that almost ran her off the road. Who was it? And what did this guy have against her?

~

Gracie did not sleep well. It did not help that a little after midnight the sky erupted with a thunderstorm. Every time there was a flash of lightning, Gracie thought it was the porch light going on again. By the time the light coming through the window signified the start of a new day, a gloomy drizzle had settled over the town.

Cognizant of her to-do list, Gracie dragged herself out of bed. She let Spencer sleep in. He had no classes on Friday, so Gracie would help Carrie get off to school. She made her breakfast and even packed her a lunch.

"Will you be here when I get home?" Carrie asked her as she donned her rain gear.

"No, I can't. I'll be alone at the store today, so I have to stay there until closing. Then I'm expecting a security company to come by and install something. But I'll be home as soon as I can after that. Maybe seven or so, I'd guess. How about I bring a pizza."

Carrie looked disappointed, but not angry. *That's progress.*

"So work on some ideas for our meeting on Saturday. We're going to figure out some way to spend more time together."

Carrie shrugged and kissed her mother on the cheek before going out into the rain.

After Carrie left for the bus, Gracie fed Dickens and returned upstairs to get ready for work.

"Thanks for letting me sleep a little longer," Spencer said without moving from his side of the bed. "I was up until two working on that chapter."

"Did you get it done?" Gracie pulled a sweater over her head.

"Not quite," he said, propping himself up on an elbow, "but I know where I'm going with it. I should have it drafted by the end of the day." His eyes followed Gracie as she brushed her hair, collected her reading glasses, and slipped into her shoes.

"Great. I will probably be a little later getting home than usual this evening. I'm having a security company come in and install a panic button at the store."

"What's that involve?"

Gracie held her hands out to her sides and shook her head. "No idea. So I'll be there for however long it takes after the store closes. I'll come home as soon as I can." She bent over and kissed Spencer. As she straightened, she remembered the events of the previous evening. "Oh," she said, moving toward the bedroom door, "Carrie and I put in a motion-sensing light by the front door last night, so don't turn it off at the switch, okay? It ought to turn on whenever anyone comes up our walk at night."

"My, my, how industrious. I'm impressed." Gracie could see a hint of facetiousness in Spencer's expression.

"I decided I would rather have it and not need it than the other way around," she said.

Spencer nodded.

As she went downstairs, Gracie thought about going back to tell Spencer the light had already alerted her to what might have been an intruder. *No,* she told herself. *He'll say it was just a neighbor's cat. But cats don't drive dark cars.* "Everyone knows they prefer light blue," she said aloud with a chuckle.

Dickens resisted going in his carrier. He had no interest in being taken out into the rain. Gracie thought about leaving him home, but knew that Spencer would be holed up in his office all day. Besides, she liked having the cat at the bookstore.

"Come on, buddy," Gracie said. "You're coming with me." As if understanding, Dickens relented and went into his pen.

"Wrangling her shoulder bag, a cat carrier, and an umbrella was never easy, but fortunately for Gracie, the drizzle eased to little more than a mist as she walked to town. The sidewalks and street were splattered with fallen leaves, with only the hiss of an occasional passing car disturbing the quiet of morning.

When she turned the corner onto Commonwealth Avenue, Gracie looked down the block toward the triangle. Even there the rain had kept traffic down to nearly nothing. The green looked empty. Not even the Steaming Kettle had any customers coming or going. Gracie shivered. It was almost eerie to see her town look so deserted.

As she got closer to the bookshop something caught her eye. Was there something lying on the sidewalk in front of her store?

Gracie picked up her pace a bit, trying to cover the distance between her and the shop. As she got closer, it looked like a cardboard box, about the size of a shoe box, but wider.

Who would leave a box in front of my bay window? she wondered. Thoughts of the possible contents made her shiver. There was a reason airports and large cities did not tolerate unidentified parcels lying about. Where it was sitting, if it blew up, the whole front of her store would be blown off. When she was still a block away, she put her bag, umbrella, and Dickens' carrier down. "No sense risking us both," she said when he yowled.

She crept forward toward the box. She could tell that it was taped up tightly—at least at the top. She leaned over it to see if she could hear it ticking. *Do time bombs still tick?*

There was a note taped down on the outside of the box, but it was typed. She couldn't read it without her glasses, which were in her shoulder bag. She backed away from the package, and retrieved them.

Once again she approached the package with caution. *If it's a time bomb, they would have set it to go off during store hours, and I'm not due to open for another ten minutes,* she told herself. Then she second-guessed herself. *But what if they just wanted to send a message, like they did with the break-in? They might want it to go off before store hours.* She thought about calling the police. *Like they've been any help lately. Maybe the fire department would respond.*

By the time she finished her internal debate, she was once again hovering over the package. She put on her glasses, held her breath, and leaned over the note.

It was a mailing label addressed to Gracie's Garret, 128 Commonwealth Avenue, Glenville Falls, Massachusetts. There was a return address: a book distributor in New Jersey. *What the?* Then it dawned on her.

It must be the book order she had placed on Monday. Four books, special orders, now sitting in a puddle in front of her store. She stamped her foot, splashing water on her ankles.

"The delivery guy is supposed to bring my packages during store hours so they won't get stolen—or wet." Her voice was loud, but unheard over an approaching wall of rain coming from the south, moving towards where Dickens sat trapped in his carrier.

She tossed the box into the sheltered area by her front door and ran back to get Dickens and her other things. She didn't even bother to raise the umbrella, but ran as fast as she could toward the store. When she was about five feet away, she slowed. Could she be sure the package was books?

The rain caught up with her, and she darted into the doorway. In a few moments she, Dickens, and the package were all inside, leaving puddles on her hardwood floor. She closed the door and picked everything up again and took them to the back room. Placing Dickens' pen on the floor, she tossed the box into her trash can. One less puddle, she thought. Then she grabbed a roll of paper towels and went into the front of the store to mop up the water before it left a mark. Dickens yowled from his pen when he saw her go.

"I'll be back to let you out in a sec," Gracie called to him. The clock in the steeple of the town hall struck ten. It was time for the store to open.

She made quick work of cleaning the water off the floor, turned on the shop lights, and flipped the sign to "Open." Then she returned to the back room. A few swipes of the paper towels and the rest of the puddles were gone. Then she picked up Dickens' carrier and peered inside. She saw one very wet, very unhappy cat. She couldn't help but chuckle at Dickens' plaintive meow.

"It's only water, boy," she said, opening the door and reaching in to pull him out. She held her cat under one arm, wiping his feet and tail where he was wettest with a clean dusting cloth. Then she stroked his head until he started to purr. "If only all problems could be solved so easily."

Gracie heard the bell over the door ring. Dickens jumped from her arms to see who it was. As she rose to go to the front of the store, Gracie realized she hoped it would be Professor Chaudhry. It wasn't; instead it was a student looking for a book for one of her courses. The college bookstore was out of stock, but Gracie had four copies left. Despite Gracie's invitation to browse, the young woman completed her purchase and was gone.

Gracie knew from her month of experience as a shopkeeper that on a rainy day business was apt to be slow. Dickens had finished giving himself a bath and found a comfortable spot in one of the wingback chairs. As tempting as it would have been to sit with him, it would not check anything off of her to-do list. The first thing to do was to see if she could rescue the books from their soggy packaging.

She pulled the box from the trash can. As she did, the bottom of the box sagged. It was drenched. She pulled open the flaps.

Gracie was relieved to see that the books had been shrink-wrapped together. The plastic protected the books from the worst of the water damage, but she wouldn't know for sure if they were okay until she inspected each one.

She opened her desk drawer to look for her scissors. There sat the paper with the pencil rubbing of the number Kristen had written. She pulled it out and put it on top of her desk, then found her scissors. Opening the plastic, she laid the books, three paperbacks and one hardcover, on top of her desk. The paperbacks appeared undamaged, but enough moisture found its way in to leave the back of the dust jacket on the hardcover wet and rippled.

"Drat. What was that delivery guy thinking?" She pulled the dust jacket off to inspect the cover. A wet spot the size of her palm marred the cloth surface. "I wish I had my hair dryer here."

Gracie pulled the soggy packing slip out of the trash to see if the shipment was insured. She couldn't tell. She resolved to call the distributor later to see whether they would send her a replacement book, or if she had to absorb the loss herself. She couldn't face knowing it was her loss this early in the day, and made a mental note to file a complaint with the delivery company.

She needed a cup of tea. As the kettle heated up, she pulled her damp legal pad from her canvas bag and decided to get a start on the to-do list.

The first task was returning Del's call, but a quick look at the clock told her Del would be in court in Boston, and unable to talk. That would have to wait until lunch. After perusing the rest of the items, it was clear to her that the most important item was the last on the list: "Call Chief Johnson."

The desk clerk answered the non-emergency number on the first ring, but he was not much help. The chief wasn't in, and no one seemed to know when he might be back. Gracie sighed into the phone, and the officer offered to let her leave a voicemail message for the chief.

"Yes, thank you." Gracie heard a click on the line, then a brief message asking her to leave her name and number. After the beep, Gracie began. "This is Grace McIntyre. I wanted to check back with you about the matter we discussed on Monday regarding the break-in at my store at 128 Commonwealth Avenue. I also have some new information I would like to discuss with you. Please call me back." Gracie then recited her store phone number and hung up. She hoped the part about new information would tantalize the chief enough that he would return her call right away.

She checked it off her list. Just checking something off made her feel a little better. She poured her tea and inhaled the steam. Something about a hot cup of tea made even a wet October day feel more bearable.

Looking at the rest of the items left to do, the next highest priority was clear. It was time to do a thorough search of the store for her father's old law book. She had been putting it off, she realized, in part because she wanted to hold out the hope that it was still there somewhere, but now she needed to know whether it was truly gone, even if knowing wouldn't help her determine how it was lost.

I'm going to kill two birds with one stone. She grabbed a dusting cloth and the wheeled book cart so she could clean and organize the shelves as she searched.

Working quickly, she started at the front of the store, going book by book, shelf by shelf. When the bell above the door rang just after noon, she had completed nearly half of the store and had worked up a bit of a sweat, but there was still no sign of the lost book.

"Welcome," she said, smoothing back her hair and straightening her sweater.

"Yeah, we got an installation?"

Gracie looked at the dark-haired woman standing before her, wearing a blue uniform-style shirt and holding a cardboard box. Looking out the window, Gracie saw a white van with "L&S Security" painted in blue on the side along with a logo of a large padlock and the phrase, *"Keeping Your World Safe!"*

"You're not supposed to be here until after the store closes," Gracie said approaching the installer. She looked to be in her thirties. Above her shirt pocket was a patch that said "Darlene."

"You're my last install of the day and I don't want to have to come back later." The technician looked around. "Looks like you're closed already anyway."

Gracie couldn't argue with her. The store was dead.

"We got the base unit here," Darlene said nodding at the box under her arm. "Where do you want it?"

"Does it need to be plugged into the phone line?" Gracie said, turning her head from the front register to the door to the office.

"Yup, and a power outlet."

"I guess in the back room." Gracie could just imagine tripping over the power cord if she put it by the register.

"You sure? You want it where you'll be able to use the speaker phone if you need help. Aren't you more apt to need it by the register than in back?"

Gracie put her fingers to her lips. "Well, um . . ."

"I think you should put it out here. Let's take a look at your register. You've got that plugged in somewhere, right?"

"Yes, and there's a phone on the counter."

"I got a splitter. We can make it work there."

"What about the cord? Will it get in the way?"

The installer looked at Gracie with a condescending smile. "Don't worry. You're in good hands. I'll make it all nice and neat, and you'll never have a problem with it."

Such confidence. Gracie had to admire it, but hoped that Darlene was as good as she thought she was.

The woman ducked her head to look under the counter top, opened the cardboard box, and within a few minutes stood up again.

"All done," she said, pulling a couple of plastic bags from the box.

"Already?"

"Yeah. Let me show you how to use this."

The base unit just fit in the space between the register and the phone. Darlene gave Gracie a brief tutorial.
As she spoke, she pointed out which buttons did what,
and at the end of her spiel Darlene handed Gracie a
small plastic pouch.

"These here are your portable alert tags. You get two,
so if you have somebody working with you they can have
one, too." Darlene looked around the store. "It goes
around your neck, or you can put one on this wrist band.
We use these a lot for old folks living alone who might
want to have us call someone like if they fall or something." Darlene was speaking slowly and loudly, a habit
Gracie thought she might have developed while talking
to the elderly. "Sometimes they forget how to use a
phone, but they can still push a button. Trouble is, they
think sometimes it's only for if they're dying or something, so they don't use it."

"I hope I never need to use mine, either," Gracie
said, pulling out one of the call buttons and putting it
around her neck. She tucked it under her sweater to
keep it out of her way. Darlene looked at her sideways.

"Now, I just have to call in to our central station and
test the system, make sure it works," she said, punching
in a number.

"What if the phone is off the hook, or someone cuts
the phone lines? Will it still work?" Gracie asked as Darlene dialed in to the call center.

"You can get a special jack—an RJ31X. It will make
the call even if you're on the phone. But I can't do it. The
phone company has to put it in . . . Oh hello?" Darlene
turned her attention to testing the unit. Gracie even had
a chance to check her portable panic buttons. Everything worked as expected.

"Okay, that's it, then," Darlene said, dumping the
box that had held Gracie's unit in the trash. "You're all

set. Here's some stickers you can put in your window. Works to scare off the bad guys. Then there's some for your phones, too. Any questions?" she said, moving toward the door. "Okay. Have a nice day."

Without pausing, Darlene was out the door, in her truck, and pulling away from the curb. Gracie stood in her shop with her mouth open, watching the van pull away.

"Thank you," she said to the empty parking space in front of the store. The town clock struck the half hour and Gracie checked the wall clock. Half past twelve. If she were going to get hold of Del, she had better call soon.

Going into the back room, Gracie grabbed her cell phone and pressed Del's speed dial number. Just when Gracie had decided it would go to voicemail, Del answered.

"Hey, stranger. Long time, no talk." Del sounded relaxed.

"I know. It seems like you've been in Boston forever."

"Well, not much longer. We finished up about ten minutes ago, so I'll be coming home earlier than I expected. I should be there by dinner time . . . and I'm going to bring you a present."

"Oh good—hurry home." Gracie laughed, and realized it was for the first time that day.

"Yeah. I'll meet you at the store. I'm just going to do a little shopping while I'm here, then I'll head home. Barring bad traffic, I should get there about closing time. Then we can go over to the Kettle for a cup of coffee—or tea."

"Can't wait," Gracie said. Neither Carrie nor Spencer expected her to get home as soon as the store closed, and it would be a comfort to have a chance to sit and talk with her friend.

After hanging up with Del, Gracie dialed the police non-emergency number. She had called it enough to know it by heart.

"Glenville Falls Police." It was the same voice as had answered earlier in the day.

"Hello, this is Grace McIntyre calling for Chief Johnson again. Is he in?"

"He was, then he left."

Gracie rolled her eyes. "Is there a number where I can reach him?"

"Nope, but I'll tell him you called again."

This was not a satisfactory response, but Gracie figured it was the best she was going to get. It wasn't the desk clerk's fault that the chief didn't return his calls. She snapped her phone shut and put it in her pocket.

Sitting at her desk, she scanned her to-do list and put a check next to "return Del's call."

"Finish up holiday orders" was still on the list, as was "Figure out how to improve sales." They were linked. If she couldn't improve sales, how much could she afford for holiday orders? Conversely, if she didn't order a lot of new stock for the holidays, she might miss out on the improved sales that season promised.

And she still had to find that law book—if it was still in the store.

It took Gracie the rest of the afternoon to go through each shelf, pulling books out, rearranging them, and moving some books, which customers had misplaced, back to their proper location. By quarter past five, she still had not found the law dictionary. She even looked under the front counter and in the back office, knowing it wouldn't be in either place, before giving up.

"It's gone, Dickens. I know I didn't sell it. I know Kristen didn't sell it. I guess it grew legs and walked out of here." Dickens was focused on a fly that had made it into the store. It kept buzzing against a back window, hoping to find a way outside. Meanwhile Dickens stood on a box, watching its every move, then jumping up and pressing his paws against the last place it had landed. The fly was faster than the cat though, and always got away. It flew into the front of the store, and Dickens bounded after it.

"Go get 'im, Dickens," Gracie said, smiling as she put her cleaning materials away.

Five-thirty-five. Carrie would be home by now, and Gracie was still at the store. She felt a pang of guilt, exacerbated by the fact that there had hardly been any customers in the store all day. She could have been home and lost next to nothing.

But Del could arrive any time now, and Gracie wanted to have something more to tell her about the Officer Lowry situation, so went to her desk, picked up the phone and called the police station again. This time they put her through to the chief.

"Chief Johnson here." His voice was gruff. Before Gracie could say anything, he went on, "Ms. McIntyre, I know you've been calling here a lot, and I know that you really think you have a problem, but the kind of problem you have is not something I can help you with."

"What? Why not? I . . ."

"I've seen it before. Women getting a little older, maybe kids leaving home, and they feel the need of some attention. Most don't go as far as you did to stage a break-in, but since you did, I gotta warn you that if you do anything like that again, try to make a false police report, we're gonna have a run-in, you and me."

"False report? Chief, Lowry called *me* about the break-in—not the other way around. And what about the . . ."

"Now, I've talked to Officer Lowry and he told me the whole story. He doesn't think we should press any charges, and who knows, maybe you really think these things are happening the way you say, but I've got to warn you that if you call about any of this stuff again, you could get yourself into some serious trouble. I don't want to have to do it, but I will if you force the issue."

Gracie stood up at her desk and felt the rage rise within her. "Of course I am going to *force* the issue. I've had my store broken into, lost an expensive book by the way, been followed and nearly run down twice, and my employee has . . ."

"Okay, settle down now. I know you must think all these things are happening to you, but there's no easy way to say this. Everything you're telling me is in your imagination. You're making this up. You have a psychological problem, and you need some help. I know you're probably going through the change or something, but you really should see a doctor, not a police officer."

Gracie thought her head would explode. "Wait a second. You think that . . ."

"That's just a bit of friendly advice, now, and I hope you take it." Then the chief hung up. Hung up!

"Arghhhh." Gracie slammed the phone down, balled her fists, and clenched her teeth. "Now what am I supposed to do? I have some madman coming after me and the police think it's all in my head?" Gracie looked around the office for a safe way to vent her frustration. Finding no soft pillow to punch, she opted for yanking her security tag from her neck. "What good is a security system if the cops won't respond? I can't believe I am wasting good money on this thing." She threw it across the room.

Some of her fury vented, she sat, taking deep breaths. Then she looked at the legal pad on her desk. Well, if the police won't help me, I am going to have to do this by myself. Picking up her reading glasses, she flipped her tablet open to the page with three columns.

CHAPTER TWENTY-FOUR

Who has something against me or the store, who has something to hide, and who has something to lose?

She saw "Delivery Guy" on the list. "Nope," she said crossing him out. "He got whatever revenge he wanted by drowning my books out in the rain."

The others on the list were Kristen, Hal, Peggy, Ollie, Kenny, Lowry, and Johnson. Should she have listed anyone else?

She did a mental review of all of the things she had learned since the break-in. The high school once spotted someone they thought was a pedophile. Shortly thereafter, there was a shady character lurking around the college campus. Were they the same person?

A black sedan almost ran her over in town, and one nearly ran her off the road from Billington. Were they the same car and driver? She knew the one in town wasn't driven by Lowry. Was he in on it with someone else?

Lowry had a very keen interest in Kristen, both before and after the break-in. Could he have been the one spotted at the two schools? Was he looking around for Kristen? She wouldn't recognize him, but she looked enough like her mother that he might have guessed she was related. But what would he want with her?

Kristen had an aversion to talking to the police. Did she have something to hide? Some prior problem with the police? Something to lose—like her scholarship? What was the phone number Kristen had written down right before leaving work suddenly? Gracie picked up the rubbing and pinned it to her bulletin board.

Someone actually *had* broken into the bookstore, and possibly stolen a book that had sentimental value to Gracie. Why would they leave the store in a mess and start, supposedly, an investigation when the theft might otherwise have gone unnoticed for weeks?

Professor Chaudhry came and went, sometimes without Gracie knowing it, but did he have an agenda Gracie didn't know about?

Peggy from the flower shop told her to leave it alone. What did she know? DJ at the Steaming Kettle wouldn't talk to her about what he'd seen, but he and Peggy got along. Were they both in on something?

Ollie left town without much warning. Did he leave something behind at the store that he came back for? Or that he sent Kenny back for? Kenny would have known where to find Hal's keys. And Gracie could pull her key out of the bunch right away; it was the only new one. Could someone have borrowed it or made a copy without Hal knowing it? But that wouldn't explain trying to run her down, or the pedophile sightings.

Was Chief Johnson just defending his officer, or did he have something more at stake? If he knew his officer had broken the law, would he cover it up?

Lowry got in some trouble before becoming a police cadet. Did Johnson know that? Lowry and Dave Mercer were friends. Did they hang out with Kenny at Ollie's?

It was one of the addresses Cheryl gave as a place where Dave could be found.

Lowry lied about the break-in to his chief, making her look like a menopausal hysteric. If the break-in was legitimate, why would he cover it when he was off-duty? And why wouldn't he file a normal police report and follow up on the investigation? And Lowry was the one who told the police that Dave Mercer committed suicide. What if he lied then, too?

All the "what if's" ignited Gracie's imagination.

If Lowry lied, might that mean Dave didn't kill himself? What if Dave didn't kill Cheryl, either?

Cheryl had told Gracie that Dave was there. But did Cheryl actually see him, or did she just hear someone coming and assume it was Dave? If he didn't kill Cheryl, who did? And why? And if someone else killed her, why would Dave kill himself? If he didn't kill himself, how did he end up at the bottom of the falls with the murder weapon? Did Lowry witness it—or did he kill Dave? And Cheryl?

If Dave didn't kill Cheryl, someone got away with murder. But why would anyone involved with those deaths want to stir things up now? They would have to be crazy.

She closed her eyes and rubbed her temples. Images flashed through her mind. The farm house, the vandalized store, Mrs. Mercer's photos, the newspaper pictures. Something clicked in her head and her eyes popped open. Then she closed them again, trying to bring the images back into focus. *Of course.* Why hadn't she seen it before? Something against her or the store, something to hide, something to lose. It all made sense.

But now I have to plan my next move before he makes his.

Gracie looked at the clock. It was just after six. *Del should be here by now.* She took her cup of tea and the legal pad with her into the front of the store, locked up, turned out the lights, and flipped the sign to "Closed."

Choosing Professor Chaudhry's favorite reading nook toward the back of the store, Gracie sat down to wait for Del with her list. She wanted to make sure her hunch was right before taking the next step.

The waning daylight made the corner dark, so she turned on the floor lamp next to her chair. Dickens sat on her lap, kneading her thighs and purring.

"Owww. Don't pull threads in my slacks, boy," Gracie said, putting him on the floor and stroking his back. "Cat hair, I can deal with. Ruined clothes, I cannot afford." She made a mental note to trim his claws when they got home.

She pulled her hair behind her ear and looked at her list. Staring at the yellow pad, Gracie was hardly aware that her exhaustion was catching up with her. A moment later, she jerked herself awake and rubbed her eyes.

The scent of fresh, outside air had entered the shop. *Maybe Del's here.* But had she heard the bell? She stood and looked toward the front door. It was closed. *Of course it is. Del doesn't have a key to the new lock.*

Gracie rose and walked toward the counter, putting the legal pad and pen down. Surely no one was there. She checked her newly-installed security system. A glowing light told her it was functioning, but it gave her only a moment's relief. *Was that a footstep?*

"Is someone there?" she called.

There was no response. *Oh no—maybe the chief is right and at least this is my imagination working overtime.* She took a few steps away from the counter and a wave of uneasiness washed over her.

"I know someone is there. You might as well come out." Her breathing became shallow. "Is that you, Del?" She smiled a little as she thought how ridiculous she might feel if there were indeed no one there. The town clock chimed the quarter hour. Where was Del?

A floorboard creaked. She turned her head toward the back of the store. Whoever was there was still hidden.

I know it's you," Gracie said, now almost certain she was not alone. "Did you come to talk?" She hoped there would be no response. "Or are you just to trying to scare me again?"

"I'm not just tryin' to *scare* you." A low growl replied.

In spite of herself, Gracie jumped at the sound. Taking a deep breath, she answered, "True. You had me quite frightened, but that was before I figured out who you were, and why you were doing what you were doing."

"You have *no idea,* lady," the voice barked and Gracie froze.

"I think I do." Gracie swallowed to keep the fear out of her voice. She reached for her panic button, cursing when she remembered throwing it across the office. Then she remembered the cell phone in her pocket. As she pulled it out, a book flew toward her, hitting her hand, sending the phone toward the front window—the battery coming loose. Gracie looked toward the source of the flying book, but didn't see anyone.

Switching into attorney mode, Gracie sought to take control of the situation. "I know you're not really here to hurt me. You just want me and my bookstore to go away. It isn't easy going through what you've experienced. I'm sure Kristen arriving stirred things up. She looks a lot like her mother, doesn't she?"

"Shut up!" the voice erupted and a figure in dark clothing moved between bookshelves, blending into the shadows.

Gracie drew in her breath and pressed her lips together. She could make out broad-shoulders, but couldn't see his face. She felt exposed, clearly visible against the light coming through the front window as she inched toward the counter. Did she dare make a move toward the panic button? Her eyes darted back and forth, looking for a way to defend herself. In a test of strength, even with her newly-developed muscles, she knew she would be at a disadvantage.

The gruff voice came again. "You just don't know how to take a hint, but you've caused about all the trouble you're gonna. If you won't leave on your own, I'm gonna get rid of you *and* her. I want you both *gone*." As he spoke, his voice became louder. "You, you can't do this. You can't bring her back like this. She's dead. She has to stay dead," he shouted.

Gracie cleared her throat, not sure whether she should speak. She thought about making a break for the door, but with two locks to unlock, she doubted she could get out before he reached her. She didn't know if the man was armed, or if a sudden movement might make him do something crazy. She moved behind the counter and put her hand on it to steady herself. "I'm sorry if my store being here has upset you." She edged toward the alarm, reaching behind her. It was too far away.

"Sorry ain't gonna cut it. If I can't *scare* you out, I'll *take* you out." He moved toward her and she realized that she had trapped herself behind the counter. He could cut off her escape simply by following her there. He saw it, too, and moved closer. That was when Gracie saw the knife in his hand.

"You're the reason. You're responsible for Dave dying," he yelled. "If it weren't for you . . . I heard you admit it."

Gracie heard a catch in his voice. "Look, we can talk this out." She spoke in soothing tones. "You don't want to hurt anyone. Let me turn on a light. I can make you a cup of tea and we can . . ."

"Damn it, lady. Will you STOP!" He blocked the end of the counter and thrust the knife toward Gracie. Eyes only on the weapon, she backed up a step, groping for the alarm button.

"Even if you killed me, it wouldn't stop this memory from haunting you. It would only give you one more thing to regret." She cringed a bit, hoping it would placate him, not enrage him further. She had her answer almost immediately.

The man pulled himself up to his full height, shifted the knife in his hand, and brought it up over his head. With a roar, he lunged toward Gracie. She backed into the cash register, pushing it off of the counter. It crashed to the floor, coins spilling out and running along the boards.

Turning she bashed the alarm button. Kicking backwards as she tried to climb up and over the counter. The man's hands grabbed her upper arm and pulled her back to face him. What was wrong with the alarm? No comforting voice came over the speaker phone to tell her help was on the way.

Her attacker pushed Gracie backwards against the counter. She extended an arm against his chin, using all her new-found strength. It worked. He stepped back, only to lunge forward again and press one arm across her chest. He leaned over her, pinning her shoulders. His body weight overpowered her efforts to push him back. She smelled body odor and stale cigarettes, and wondered if this was the last scent she would ever know.

She kicked her feet, trying to raise a knee, but couldn't find the target. Feeling around for a weapon, she pulled on the alarm box, but Darlene had stapled down the wires so tightly, it wouldn't budge. She reached for the scissors that should be hanging from the cup hooks, but Darlene had moved them, too. Looking into her attacker's eyes, Gracie saw anguish, then watched as he raised the knife blade, aiming it at her chest. Terrified, she closed her eyes and turned away trying to move, but unable to break free.

There was a thud as the man's yowl of pain filled the bookstore. When Gracie opened her eyes she saw the knife embedded in the countertop not two inches from her shoulder. The man stood up and backed away from her, writhing and yelling.

"Get it off me. Get it off me!" He turned and Gracie saw Dickens had jumped from the top of the bookshelves and latched on with all four claws in her attacker's back, raking the writhing figure. The man's gyrations increased until Dickens let go and dashed up another bookcase, hissing from above.

The attacker tried to follow, but lost his footing and fell to the floor, pummeled by books. Gracie climbed over the counter, but could not open the door. The fallen register was wedged against it. Gracie nudged it with her foot, but the heavy machine wouldn't budge.

The man slumped down onto the floor, and Gracie thought she heard a sob. Yes, he was crying. Stepping over the register, Gracie tried to pull the knife from the countertop, but couldn't budge it. Then he spoke.

"Dave liked the falls," he whimpered, staring at the floor, looking into the past. "He always said the sound of the water was soothing, washing his troubles away. If he was ever upset about anything, we all knew, that was where we could find him."

Gracie watched as he turned to focus on her.

"Your brother didn't kill Cheryl, did he, DJ?" Gracie asked, struggling to keep her voice from wavering. Danny Mercer shook his head and looked at his hands.

"I was just sixteen. Dave was my hero, you know. My big brother. He understood me. Nobody else understood me. Nobody." DJ shook his head and looked away. "He had friends. People liked him. And he was smart. He was all the things I wanted to be."

Gracie couldn't help but be touched by his agony, still so raw after all these years.

"And then that lying bimbo wrecked his life. He was a really good guy. She told him she was pregnant, and he married her. But my parents said he shouldn't." His voice was choked with grief and anger. "They disowned him. Said I couldn't see him anymore. That he was dead to us." He turned his face toward Gracie. "Why did they do that?"

Gracie flinched. It was the same question Mrs. Mercer still asked. "I don't know," she said.

"We could only see each other here. It was Ollie's then. He left us a key to the back door under a brick in the alley. It's still there."

Gracie's eyes went to the ceiling. Two new locks on the front door, and one old lock, complete with a hidden key, for the back. No wonder there were no signs of forced entry. Danny had used the key for the break-in.

"I know Dave hit her," DJ continued, "but she made him miserable. It wasn't his fault. It was all hers. He hated when she made him do that. If only she and that kid were gone, out of the picture, everything could go back to how it was."

Gracie didn't dare speak.

"I had to kill her," Danny said without emotion. "Once she was gone, everything was supposed to be okay. But when I went up to the falls to tell Dave, he got mad. He said I had done something really bad, that he didn't want her dead. He said she and that baby were his family now and he had to fix things. He had to take care of the baby. How could he say that to me? Didn't he know how hard it was to go and kill her like that?"

Gracie thought back to the crime scene—the reason she'd quit the practice of law—and shuddered.

"But I didn't get the kid. She wasn't there. Maybe if I'd a gotten her, too, Dave wouldn't have been so upset."

Gracie swallowed a lump in her throat and took a calming breath. "So what happened to Dave?" she asked, hoping to take DJ's mind away from wanting to kill Kristen.

"He took the knife away from me and threw it in the water. I tried to grab it back from him so I could, you know . . . but as I reached for it, Dave lost his balance. I grabbed for him, but there was nothing I could do." He looked at Gracie with a face filled with pain. "You can see that, can't you? It wasn't my fault."

Gracie nodded. "Yes, I can see that. It was an accident, nothing more." DJ had killed Cheryl to bring his brother back into the family. Instead, he lost his brother, his mother, and his sanity. He had paid a heavy price, despite never being convicted of the one crime of which he was truly guilty: killing Cheryl.

"Won't you let me call someone, DJ? Is there someone you'd like to have come over?"

"You can't. I cut your phone line." Danny looked down at his hands. That explained the alarm system being down.

"My cell phone might work," Gracie said, looking toward the front window without turning her back on

DJ. She picked it up and replaced the battery. She pressed the power button. "It looks okay."

"Okay, you can call Rich."

"Do you have his number?"

"Yeah." He recited digits that sounded familiar.

Gracie thought about tossing him the phone and making a break for the door, but wasn't sure that was her best move. He was calm now, and she didn't want that to change—especially since the knife was still in the counter, and DJ was strong. If he wanted it, he could probably pull it out.

Gracie punched in the numbers and handed Danny the phone.

"Hey, Rich. I'm at the bookstore. Come and get me."

At that moment, she saw the beam of a flashlight bounce around the inside of the store. It came from the front window. She turned to see Office Lowry at the door, focusing the light on the toppled register. Gracie wasn't sure whose side he would be on until she saw Del right behind him.

"May I let them in?" Gracie asked Danny.

He threw a hand forward in a "go ahead" gesture. Gracie stooped and, with some effort, pulled the register away from the door, then unlocked it and let Lowry and Del in. She pointed to DJ who was still on the floor.

"I saw the register on the floor when I came by," Del whispered after embracing Gracie, "and called 911. Are you all right?" Then Del saw DJ still sitting in a heap on the floor. Gracie pointed to the knife sticking out of her countertop.

"I'm okay now, but it was a little scary there for a bit."

"Okay, man. You called and I'm here," Lowry said to DJ.

"You're Rich?" Gracie asked the officer.

"Yeah, Richard Lowry."

Gracie realized that, for the first time, Office Lowry was not wearing his sunglasses. He did not waste a moment on Gracie, however. His focus was all on Danny.

"Dude, what did you do now?"

Gracie looked toward the door and saw Peggy standing there, shaking her head, compassion filling her eyes.

"I know. I know I shouldn't of. You told me to leave her alone." DJ had his head in his hands and was shaking back and forth.

"I don't know if I can get you out of this one, man." Then in a stage whisper too loud for Gracie to miss, Lowry asked him, "How much did you tell her?"

"Everything." Danny's once-broad shoulders were hunched around his neck.

"Oh, man," Lowry said, leaning against the counter. "You've ruined everything."

CHAPTER TWENTY-FIVE

Del, Spencer, and Gracie reopened the store together the following Tuesday morning. The store had been closed all day Saturday while the police processed it as a crime scene, and Gracie was just as glad to have an extra day to recover.

As she unlocked the two locks on the front door, she scolded herself. "I can't believe I didn't ask Hal to put an additional lock on the back door, too."

Del said, "Well, maybe if you locked your house every once in a while, you would've thought of it." Gracie grimaced.

"It was the front door that was open after the break-in," Spencer said, carrying Dickens' carrier into the shop. "Don't beat yourself up over it."

Gracie wasn't sure how she would feel about being back in the store after all that had happened there. The gouge in the counter left from where the knife was embedded was the first thing to catch her eye. She doubted even Hal could make it look as good as new.

After letting Dickens out of his carrier, she took it to the back room. Stepping out the back door, she turned over all the loose bricks collected in the alley, making sure there were no more hidden keys. The police had the one that DJ had used, but she could not rest until she was sure no one else could get in. *Hal will install a new back door lock before close of business today,* she thought as she went inside, closed the door, and locked it.

She had already called the phone company to come to repair her line and install an RJ31X jack, although she hoped she would never need it again. They were supposed to arrive between noon and five.

After she put some water on to boil, the bell over the front door rang, and Gracie saw Lois Heller enter. "I know it's before store hours, Grace," she said. "I just wanted to let you know the Village Business Association is glad everything worked out all right here."

"Thank you, Lois," Gracie said, a little surprised by her attempt at generosity.

"Yes, well, at least now you shouldn't be bringing us any more of that sort of . . . problem, will you?"

"I sincerely hope not."

Lois looked at the gouged counter top and sniffed as she exited.

"Hey, at least she *tried* to be nice," Del said with a chuckle.

Gracie grimaced as she went back to prepare the tea. As she filled her tray she looked at the bulletin board above her desk. There was the phone number Kristen had written down. Gracie looked at it sideways, then pulled out her phone. Checking numbers dialed, she scrolled back several calls. Sure enough, there it was. The same number. It was the number DJ had asked her to dial to get Rich Lowry. Kristen said Lowry had come to the store the first time Gracie left her alone there. He said he wanted to warn her to leave town. Then he gave her his cell number to call if she needed help. All it did was scare the poor kid.

As she brought out the tea tray, the bell rang again at the door, and Wendell Owens arrived.

"I have your special edition of the *Gazette* here," he said as he entered. "We ran a special Tuesday edition, dedicated only to the Danny Mercer story. It's selling out fast, and I wanted to make sure you all got some copies."

"Thanks very much," Gracie said. "I have some refreshments. Everybody take a seat."

Spencer and Wendell pulled two folding chairs into the back reading nook and they sat as Wendell passed a copy of the paper to each of them.

They all leafed through the edition, looking at Wendell's photos of the falls, Cheryl, Dave, DJ in handcuffs, and more. The *Springfield Republican*, the *Boston Herald*, and the *Boston Globe* had already reported on the case, but Wendell's coverage was far more comprehensive.

Danny Mercer had confessed to everything, including the murder of Cheryl Mercer. He also admitted to the break-in and damage to the books, the sidewalk chalking, following Kristen and Gracie, trying to run Gracie down in his car—twice, and even trying to break into her house before being scared off when the porch light went on.

"So much for it all being in my imagination."

In addition to murder, DJ was charged with a host of other crimes, including attempted murder, breaking and entering, burglary, assault with a deadly weapon, stalking, and malicious mischief. There were no charges against him for Dave's death, at least. Instead of granting bail, the court ordered him to undergo a mental health evaluation. His lawyer was talking about an insanity defense.

"Never let it be said," Spencer said in his lecture voice, "that my wife will be deterred by anyone telling her she is wrong when she knows she is right." He nodded his head for emphasis.

Gracie looked at him sideways, and he grinned back, a look of pride in his eyes.

"Well, I *was* right, you know," Gracie said under her breath.

Deciding that too much notoriety wasn't good for business, Gracie had declined all requests for interviews, but spoke to Wendell on background. She was glad to see, as she leafed through the *Gazette,* that he'd discovered more details than she had known. She was especially glad to learn more about Rich Lowry's connection to it all.

"According to my sources, he told the cops he heard about Cheryl's murder on his father's police scanner," Wendell summarized for them. "Then he went up to the falls to find Dave, but when he got there, he heard Danny and him yelling. Then he saw Dave stumble over the falls, and smash into the rocks below. He couldn't believe it at first, but then he saw Danny sitting there, rocking and muttering that he wanted to die. He figured the only thing he could do for Dave at that point was to look after his little brother. So he took him down here to Ollie's, then called it in. He told everybody it was a suicide, and the authorities just rubber stamped it. Jumping from the top of the falls on the day he killed his wife—nobody questioned it."

"I remember that," Del said. "There was Cheryl's funeral and Dave's all happening at the same time as Danny's breakdown. Everyone thought it was his brother's death that sent him over the edge."

Gracie cringed.

"Oh, sorry. Poor choice of words. Explains a lot, though, doesn't it?"

"Yes it does," Gracie said. "From what Mrs. Mercer told me, Danny's never been the same. He was hospitalized for some time, and then his mother killed herself while he was there. He still lives in a garage apartment at his family home in Billington. I guess he never returned to what we'd consider normal." Gracie turned her head and shrugged. "Maybe he never really was."

"Fortunately for him, we don't have the death penalty in Massachusetts," Wendell said.

"Well, he won't have to worry about employment anymore," Spencer said. "He'll be making license plates for the rest of his life."

Wendell sighed. "Seems one day last month he told Lowry he saw Cheryl here in the bookstore. Lowry told him it couldn't be, but he was so sure that Lowry came over to investigate. You said he showed an unusual interest in your employee?"

"Yeah. She looks a lot like her mother. I can see why DJ didn't like that. I think Lowry wanted me to fire her. Now I know why."

"Anyway, that's when Lowry decided to start looking after you two, so to speak, while still trying to keep Danny out of trouble—trying to keep the break-in from being reported and all that. He even tried to get into Gracie's files to get the name and number of Kristen's grandmother in the hopes that he could enlist her help in getting Kristen to go home."

"Peggy told me yesterday that she also knew Danny was going off the rails," Gracie interjected. "She knew his family, and tried to help him hold it together."

"But it got too big for everyone," Wendell continued. "Lowry couldn't make it work anymore, and it all collapsed on him." Wendell blew out a mouthful of air.

"Too bad he didn't just arrest the guy and save everyone a lot of trouble. No one would ever have found out about the rest of it."

"What will happen to Lowry?" Spencer asked, taking off his glasses and cleaning them.

"He's already been suspended from the force," Del said. "At the very least, he'll lose his job. They can't have a sworn officer whom everyone knows to be deceitful. But they're investigating him for possible charges. If he knew DJ killed Cheryl, he could be charged as an accessory after the fact. And there's no statute of limitations for accessory to murder."

"What kind of penalty would that carry?" Spencer asked.

"Twenty-five years," Del said, wiggling her eyebrows.

Wendell cleared his throat. "Until they sort that out, he'll probably work for his father's company."

"What company's that?" Gracie asked.

"Lowry and Sons Security," Wendell said with a chuckle.

"Wait a minute," Gracie said. "Lowry and Sons? You mean L&S Security?"

"Yeah, that's it," Wendell said, a twinkle in his eye.

"That's my security company." The other three laughed.

"My bet," Del said with a chuckle, "is that the cops will have a lot of cases where Lowry testified that'll get new trials now that this is out. And I might have one or two myself that're worth dredging up. It's going to be one huge headache for Chief Johnson and the D.A., I can tell you that much."

"Don't even mention Chief Johnson to me." Gracie's look pierced Del's jovial façade. "If you hadn't been the one to call 911, Del, they probably wouldn't have even come over here."

"Well, he didn't know about Lowry then. I'm sure he's embarrassed about how he acted," Spencer said in his calming voice.

"Not so you'd notice. He hasn't exactly apologized to me."

"He can't," Wendell said. "He's afraid you might sue him. If I were you, I would, too."

"I'll think about it." Gracie looked at Del who clicked her tongue.

"A lawyer who's reluctant to haul somebody into court? It's a good thing you got out of the profession when you did."

"He'll get his," said Wendell. "The Selectmen have called a special meeting to discuss whether to fire him. Their meetings are often dull, but this one promises to be a doozy."

The bell rang above the door, and Kristen entered.

"Welcome back," Gracie called to her.

"Thanks," Kristen said as she started toward the back room.

"How's she doing?" Del asked in a whisper.

Gracie shrugged her shoulders. "We'll see. I'm glad she came in today. I have a bit of a surprise for her." Gracie pulled out her cell phone and dialed a number.

"Oh, what are you up to?" Del said, accusation in her voice.

Gracie winked. Wait a sec, she mouthed, holding up an index finger. "She's coming," she said in a whisper into the phone.

"Wait a sec, Kristen." Gracie hung up before the girl could take off her jacket, "I wonder if you could go over to the Kettle and pick up some muffins for me. I called Kelly with the order. I have a feeling that we're going to be a little busier than usual around here today, and I thought it might be nice to have some food on hand."

"Okay," Kristen said, reversing direction.

"And there's no rush. Take your time."

After Kristen left, Gracie leaned forward, using a conspiratorial tone. "I invited Kristen's great-grandmother, Mrs. Mercer, to come by the Kettle this morning. She was so eager to have a chance to see Kristen, so I told her I would send her over for muffins. Kelly will let her know when she arrives."

"Oh, you didn't. Are you sure that's a good idea?" Del's eyes sparkled.

"Well, she's pretty old and doesn't get out much, but she said she would find a way to be there—maybe even bring her son, Kristen's grandfather. I'm hoping she'll say something to Kristen—maybe make a connection. I think they could be really good for each other." Gracie held her hands out in front of her. "I've put them together. The rest is up to them."

"Sounds like I ought to go be a fly on that wall," Wendell said, rising from his chair, tipping his non-existent hat, and taking his leave. As he went out the door, Professor Chaudhry entered.

"Professor," Gracie said, standing. "Welcome back. I haven't seen you in a while, and there's something I've wanted to ask you."

"And there is something I want to tell you, my dear," the professor said, a mischievous glint in his eye.

"Oh?" Gracie wondered if he had come to admit to taking the book. Despite all his other confessions, Danny Mercer claimed to know nothing about the missing dictionary. "You go first."

"Well, dear lady, I come with good news. You have a treasure you did not know you had."

"Really?" Gracie tried to imagine what he was referring to, but came up empty.

"Yes," he said, his face opening up into a broad, creased grin. "And it is right here."

He crossed to the chair where Del sat, and asked her to stand. When she did, the professor tilted the chair back. Underneath was the law dictionary.

"My book," Gracie cried out, partly in surprise, partly in relief. "What's it doing under there?"

"Well, I couldn't allow it to stay on the shelf, once I discovered what it was."

"You're right. I didn't really want to sell it. My dad had it in his law office, and his dad before him, I think."

"And perhaps another generation or two before that," the professor said. "It is an original Black's Law Dictionary, 1891 edition—the first ever."

"It is? I knew it was old, but . . ."

"I surmised as much. When I did a little research, I discovered that your book should never be put on the shelf with a price of four hundred dollars on it."

"Oh," Gracie said waving her hands in front of her. "I just put that price on so that it wouldn't sell. I'm so glad to know where it is. I thought I'd lost it. Thank you, professor."

"Don't thank me yet, dear lady, until you know the rest of what I discovered."

"There's more?"

"Yes."

Spencer piped up. "If it's a first edition, it's probably worth more than you've got it priced for. Am I right, Chaudhry?"

"Quite right. It is a first edition, in its original binding, and in exquisite condition. That makes this extremely rare—and extremely valuable."

Gracie's mouth hung open. "Valuable?"

"Extremely," the professor assured her. "Maybe not as much as a first edition of *The Catcher in the Rye,* but a treasure nonetheless." He quoted her the price he thought appropriate for the book, and Gracie had to grab a chair to support herself. "As it happens, I make used and rare books a bit of a hobby. Some of the others in the store are also worth more than the prices you have chosen for them. And some, I fear, are worth less. It would be my pleasure to advise you on their value, if I am not overstepping."

"Overstepping? No. Obviously, I need the help." Gracie thought about a request from someone at the college for an out-of-print book. "Does your expertise extend to more recent books that are out of print?"

"It is part and parcel of the process. I would be happy to assist you with that, as well."

"Wonderful. I already have an order where I could use your help."

"I am at your disposal." The professor hesitated before adding, "And you might think about developing a website to sell your books beyond the Glenville Falls market. I could help you with that as well. We must keep up with the times, you know." The professor wagged his head, his eyes shimmering with joy. He patted his brief case. "I have some templates designed on my laptop that I would love to show you," he said, pulling out his computer. He raised his eyebrows so high, Gracie did not have the heart to disappoint him.

"Go for it," she said

"I'll set it up over here," he said, moving to a reading nook near the front counter. "It has a convenient power supply."

"I'll be over in a minute," Gracie said.

"I have a present for you, too," Del said. "I brought it back with me from Boston, but with all that has been going on, I haven't had a chance to give it to you yet."

"Oh, yeah. What is it?" Gracie clapped her hands together.

Del pulled out a cloth bag. "I went over to Quincy Market while I was there—it's not far from the court-house, you know—and I found all these great Halloween decorations for your window. Once I'm through putting them up, no one will be able to resist coming in. And I have some great ideas for Thanksgiving and Christmas displays." Del pulled several large spiders, at least one bat, and a black cat from the bag. "I don't suppose you'd let me dye Dickens black for the occasion, would you?"

"Absolutely not." Gracie hoped Del was kidding, but there was something in Del's expression that made her wonder.

"Sorry to break up the party, but I have an office to get to." Del put the decorations back in the bag. Pushing herself out of her chair and moving toward the front of the store, she tucked the bag behind the counter, and reached out to give Gracie a hug. "I'll see you later."

Gracie followed her to the door. "Thanks, Del. I don't know what I'd do without you."

"Are you going to be okay here?"

"Oh yes. I look forward to working with Professor Chaudhry, but I have something even better to look forward to."

"What?"

"Today, and every school day hereafter, Carrie and her friends will hold a homework help club here in the store. Kids will come here after school and the older ones will help the younger ones with their homework. It's not daycare. Only serious students are invited. But it will bring kids and their parents into the store. Best of all, Carrie and I will spend our afternoons together again." Gracie realized she had butterflies just thinking about it. "I can't wait." She crossed her arms and hugged herself.

"Nice to see you smile again," Del said as she waved good-bye, and walked to her car to drive one block to her office.

Spencer joined her at the counter. "I have a present for you, too," he said, opening his brief case.

"Why did you get me a present?"

"Actually, I bought it a while ago, but this is the perfect time to give it to you." He pulled out a paper bag with something inside that made Gracie think of an old record album.

She reached inside and pulled out the yellow sign Spencer had suggested she get when they went to Vermont: "Premises Protected by an Attack Cat."

"It's perfect," she said, propping the sign in the window.

"And so are you." Spencer smiled and leaned in for a kiss. "But I have to get up to the college. My classes won't teach themselves, you know."

Gracie stopped him at the door. "Thank you for never doubting me," she said, putting her arms around his neck.

"I never could," Spencer whispered, pulling her close and kissing her again. "You're the sanest person I know. You'd have to be to put up with me."

Gracie laughed, and blinked back a tear. She didn't want to let him go, but knew she must. But only after one more kiss.

As she watched him walk toward College Hill, Gracie sighed with contentment. Her family was safe, her bookstore had survived, and she had plans for making it thrive. No one was hurt despite a very troubled man wishing others ill. Kristen was safe, and since she had not yet come back with the muffins, she was probably having a wonderful chat with her great-grandmother.

Dickens wound around her ankles. Gracie picked him up and held him in front of her face. "Ugh. You're getting heavy, buddy." She cradled him and scratched his neck while he purred. "But you saved my life, and that makes up for a lot of cat hairs and snagged sweaters over the years." She kissed the top of his head. "Now," she said watching as a group of shoppers crossed the street heading toward her store, "I wonder what other adventures lie ahead for us."

Acknowledgements

Writing and publishing a book is an amazing journey, and like any journey worth making, it is best done in good company. I was fortunate enough to be in the best of company. So many people helped bring the story of Gracie and her world to life that I must take more than a few moments to be sure they know how grateful I am to them.

Huge thanks go out to the members of the Bethlehem Writers Group, LLC, both past and present. BWG has been my critique group for the past many years. Members know that the worst thing a critique group can do is to hold back lest they hurt a writer's feelings. We need to hear what they think—not what they think we want to hear. Not afraid to offer criticism that might sting, the organization's regular members, have provided innumerable bits of wisdom and encouragement—and just enough scolding—to keep me on the right track.

Special thanks go out to BWG's Long Form Critique Group whose members reviewed the entire manuscript to help make the story and characters what I hoped they could be: Courtney Annicchiarico (who helped with character voice), A. E. Decker (who has an exceptional eye for detail), Marianne Donley (who has read everything, and knew just how to tweak it), Ralph Hieb (who gave pointers on action scenes), Jerry McFadden (who gave thoughtful critiques, despite its genre), Emily Murphy (a terrific editor who consoled me after Carrie and Gracie argued), Sally Paradysz (a New England native, whose belief in me, for whatever reason, never wavered), Jo Ann Schaffer (who made me rework the opening—and then rework it again), Paul Weidknecht (whose talent amazes us all—even if he didn't like the cat), and Will Wright (who let me know where to take out the parts a reader might skip). Thank you all. It's a pleasure to write with you.

Marianne H. Donley and Diane Sismour deserve special recognition for their enthusiasm, dedication, and energy—freely offered, and much needed as my journey toward publication progressed.

Sally Paradysz and Jo Ann Schaffer, founding members of the Bethlehem Writers Group, have given me much more than their valuable editorial input. As we each travel life's path, our friendship makes the hard times better—and the good times great. Together, they have offered me some of my harshest critiques ("It's DEATH, Carol!") and most loyal support, without either of which this book would not be what it is. I look forward to each of our future journeys—perhaps discussed, like Gracie, over a cup of tea.

Paul Barros, a manager for Barnes & Noble, first suggested starting what became the Bethlehem Writers Group, and taught me the ins and outs of book selling. His tutelage lends whatever verisimilitude Gracie's bookstore has.

Members of Sisters in Crime, and especially its Guppy Chapter which is unfailingly supportive of its members, have been a source of much assistance. I wish to extend thanks especially to those members who offered critiques of all or part of this manuscript at various stages of its development: Sharon Nelson, Doug Elerath, Ann Gooding, Marilynn Larew, Mary Ann Stewart, Janice Sultenfuss, and June Shaw.

Valerie Horowitz has offered not only the benefit of her knowledge and advice as a writer, editor, and publisher, but has become a valued friend, as well.

New England newspaper editor Caitlyn Kelleher taught me just about everything I know about the newspaper business, from chasing a story to writing headlines. She helped me understand the unique importance of a small-town, weekly newspaper, and gives me hope that the medium will endure.

Many thanks to Lee Lofland for his continual efforts to help writers avoid errors when writing about police procedure. Any errors in my description of the workings of a small-town police department are entirely mine.

But all of this help could never have been enough without the support of my family. We are a clan full of writers. Among those who write fiction are my brother Will, who was why I took myself seriously enough as a writer to attempt this book, and my treasured daughter Emily, who, during the entire journey, has been a true writing partner. Her husband Adam has always been a strong supporter of both of our efforts. I thank him for that and for loaning me his wife when I needed her. (I'm also pretty grateful for those two wonderful grand-children, Grachea and Edward.) My beloved son, Geoff, not only writes, but is an accomplished actor, whose artistic talents inspire me to be more creative. His quickness and imagination has amazed me since he was a young boy, and amazes me still. And my husband, Bruce, while not a writer of fiction, is a college professor, legal scholar, and the author of several judicial biographies and other nonfiction. I couldn't have done any of this without his love and support. And no, he is not Spencer. Well—maybe a bit around the edges.

About the Author

Carol L. Wright is a former book editor, domestic relations attorney, and adjunct professor. She is the author of articles and one book on law-related subjects. Now focused on fiction, she has several short stories in literary journals and award-winning anthologies. *Death in Glenville Falls* is her first novel.

She is a founding member of the Bethlehem Writers Group, LLC (http://bethlehemwritersgroup.com), is a life member of both Sisters in Crime and the Jane Austen Society of North America, and a member of SinC Guppies, PennWriters, and the Greater Lehigh Valley Writers Group.

Raised in Massachusetts, she is married to her college sweetheart. They now live in the Lehigh Valley of Pennsylvania with their rescue dog, Mr. Darcy, and a clowder of cats—including one named Dickens.

You can follow her Facebook page: (https://www.facebook.com/Carol-L-Wright-Author-190854476717/) or learn more on her website: (http://carollwright.com).

Made in the USA
Middletown, DE
29 August 2017